DARKLEIGH

by

Lee Pennell

Lee Pennell

Published by New Generation Publishing in 2025

Copyright © Lee Pennell 2025

First Edition

The author asserts the moral right under the Copyright, Designs and Patents Act 1988 to be identified as the author of this work.

All Rights reserved. No part of this publication may be reproduced, stored in a retrieval system or transmitted, in any form or by any means without the prior consent of the author, nor be otherwise circulated in any form of binding or cover other than that which it is published and without a similar condition being imposed on the subsequent purchaser.

ISBN: 978-1-83563-880-4

www.newgeneration-publishing.com
New Generation Publishing

Chapter One

"He can't do that!" Mrs Latham wailed.

"As you very well know, he can. Mr Edwards is the rector, and I am his lowly curate, allowed only the crumbs from under his table." John Latham's bitterness was all consuming.

Dinner at the rectory in Knight's Darkleigh was rarely a cheerful occasion but, thought Sophie, this was even worse than usual. The cause of the misery: a letter from the rector. Other than saying that Mr Edwards was threatening to reduce his stipend, her father had not revealed the reason for this. Sophie had no doubt he would eventually tell them, and in the meantime, there was no point in speculating about it. She just hoped that this miserable meal would be over sooner rather than later.

She glanced at her mother. Unlike the philosophical Sophie, Mrs Latham was unable to stop herself imagining all the disasters that could be looming over them.

For the past five years, the Reverend Septimus Edwards, had employed her husband as his curate while he resided in Oxfordshire. *Perhaps*, thought Mrs Latham, *he has decided to move here and evict us from this pleasant home.* She saw a homeless, abandoned future before them and entirely forgot the constant stream of complaints about Knight's Darkleigh with which she bored her family and infuriated her neighbours. From being a remote, uncultured – even heathenish – parish in the cold, stony Cotswolds, it was transformed into a charming pastoral valley filled with all the timeless joys of quiet country life. The rectory, a modern house built only the year before they came, was no longer poorly designed and shoddily built, draughty and too small; now it was light, airy, convenient, and a gentleman's residence.

Misery swept through Mrs Latham. Life had been so unfair to her; when she married John Latham nearly thirty years ago, he had been an ambitious young curate, handsome, well-connected, and with a bright future before him. There had been the prospect of his own living, maybe even two or three if he found the right patrons. She had every reason to be pleased with her matrimonial prize. Now, thirty long years later, he was still only a curate and with no prospects at all. Annie Latham's despondency grew to be almost as deep as her husband's.

Sophie saw the familiar drooping of her mother's mouth and with a sinking heart recognised it as the signal that her mother was going to succumb to a migraine. This would mean that during the next twenty-four hours at least, Sophie would have to be her mother's handmaid, constantly at attention to administer to her demands, culminating in the most tiresome one of all: sitting quietly in a darkened room in case the sufferer needed her when she awoke. The migraine would be particularly severe if whatever it was that was so upsetting her father meant that her mother was to be in any way inconvenienced. Sophie felt a moment of resentment; why couldn't Lucy for once be the nurse?

Unconscious of the dismal atmosphere around her, Lucy sat wrapped in her dream of the handsome George coming home. The magnificent victory at Waterloo had taken place three months before and yesterday she had heard that

George should be home by the end of the summer. Sophie's good nature reasserted itself. In her present idiotic state, Lucy would be hopeless as a handmaid. At the best of times, Lucy was apt to drift into a dreamworld of her own and the ordinary realities of life were left far behind. At twenty-four years old, Lucy was two years older than Sophie, but often Sophie felt much the older of the two. Soon the gallant George Harries would return to take on the role of protecting Lucy from any unpleasantness.

Sophie's thoughts turned from George Harries to her brother Robert, also one of the soldiers in Wellington's army. She did so hope that Robert would come home soon; it had been four years since she last saw him and that had been only a fleeting visit. Indeed, from the age of twelve, Robert's visits to his home had all been brief. Sophie could not blame him, though. Mrs and Mrs Latham had not created between them a home of light-heartedness and laughter, which were two of Robert's outstanding characteristics. And with these attributes, he had never experienced difficulties in being invited by friends to their more congenial homes.

Sophie felt a clutch of fear that she would never be able to escape from her parents' unhappy home, a fear substantiated by the warning sign of her mother putting her hand to her forehead. Fortunately, Mr Latham also saw it and gave a hasty cough to gain attention.

"The letter from Mr Edwards," he said and then stopped. The silence lasted long enough for even Lucy to feel some curiosity about the Rector's letter. Mr Latham roused himself to continue:

"It's in response to a letter of mine which I sent to him over a month ago." Again, he lapsed into silence and then said in tones of outrage: "To be more accurate, it barely addresses itself to my letter at all. That was dealt with in a post scriptum of two lines, I quote: 'I do not consider the time is suitable for you to seek preferment and cannot recommend it.'"

Silence again as Mr Latham brooded over his disappointment. Without his rector's recommendation, he had no hope of obtaining his own living. Mrs Latham thought, *So, we are to remain here in this dreary place for ever, ignored by the few gentries, and patronised by the increasingly prosperous yeoman and tenant farmers.* Her head throbbed.

Lucy was indifferent to what happened to her parents. She would soon be married to George and would be living half a mile away in a snug farmhouse in Middle Darkleigh. Perhaps, she would prefer her parents to be farther away. The hamlet of Middle Darkleigh was in her father's parish and a respite from his sermons would be welcome. She supposed that she would have missed Sophie.

Sophie felt some relief that they were to stay in Knight's Darkleigh; she had unhappy memories of some years living in Birmingham, but she would have liked to have moved if it would have meant her parents would be more contented with their lives.

Mr Latham sighed wearily. "The main subject of Mr Edwards' letter is a complaint against Mr Jarvis Harries. He wants me to define the boundary between the Glebe lands and Manor Farm as he believes Mr Harries has taken some Glebe land into his own. He wants me to remonstrate with Mr Harries and supervise the restoration of the boundary to its proper line. He says if I do not do this, he will have to reconsider my stipend as he cannot afford the drain on his resources if the Glebe lands are reduced."

"He cannot do that," wailed Mrs Latham again.

"You must not quarrel with George's father," said Lucy, who had gone pale with alarm. "He might forbid our marriage!"

"At present there is merely an understanding between the families, that's all," snapped Mr Latham.

Lucy dissolved into tears: "That's only because you wouldn't allow us to be betrothed before George went off to that horrid war."

"I am not convinced that my daughter, the daughter of a gentleman, should marry a mere farmer's son."

Lucy sniffed. George was an officer in a regiment far superior to that which Robert adorned.

"How much land is involved?" asked Sophie, determined to be practical.

"Nearly ten acres," replied Mr Latham.

"I don't understand," moaned Mrs Latham. "How can there be a dispute over so much land?"

"Which land is it?" persevered Sophie.

"The strip of woodland beside the lane leading to Millington."

Sophie visualised it. The track to Millington led off westward, halfway along the road between Knight's and Middle Darkleigh. The woodlands were on the northern side towards Middle Darkleigh and on the face of it, more likely to be part of Jarvis Harries' land. The Glebe lands stretched southwards back to Knight's Darkleigh and the ancient road was a natural boundary. She said as much to her father.

"I know," he groaned. "I have had correspondence on this matter before with Mr Edwards and have pointed these facts out to him most forcefully. Unfortunately, he's convinced that he's somewhere seen a map showing the Glebe as including the wood and he's certain that Harries has altered current maps to exclude it."

"Mr Harries wouldn't do a thing like that. He's a most responsible man, besides being a churchwarden. It's a shocking thing to suggest," said Mrs Latham.

Unlike her husband, Mrs Latham was reconciled to Lucy marrying George Harries. Lucy was quite an exceptionally pretty girl, but without a dowry and living in a rural backwater, she could not expect to make a glittering marriage. Although George was from yeoman stock and not gentry, the Harries' were a family of considerable prosperity. George's grandfather might have been unlettered, but Jarvis had received some education and George himself had attended a respectable school in Cheltenham. And whereas Robert had had to make do with an unfashionable line regiment with a commission purchased by his uncle, George's family had been able to buy him a cornetcy in the cavalry.

Mrs Latham agreed with Lucy that Mr Latham must not antagonise Mr Harries. But Mr Latham also must not antagonise Mr Edwards as for sure, they could not afford a reduction in their pitiful income. She herself had no fortune. Her father had been a prosperous attorney in a Suffolk market town, but shortly before he died, he had made some disastrous investments. Mr Latham was the second son of the squire of a neighbouring village, but the estate was entailed to his elder brother and his inheritance from his mother had been small and soon spent. Mr Latham received only half of the income which the rector obtained from the Glebe, and their resentment at the rector's parsimony was one of the few matters on which Mr and Mrs Latham were united.

"Why is the rector making such a fuss over a piece of scrubby woodland?" asked Lucy, petulantly.

"I think it must be in anticipation of the enclosure of the common land," said Mr Latham. "I believe the more land you own in the parish, the more of the common land will be awarded to you. It probably will be a good few years before the necessary Act of Enclosure goes through Parliament, but no doubt the rector is looking ahead to that time. He must, of course, do his utmost to look after the Church's interests."

Seeing his family's scepticism at the suggestion that the rector was acting with high-minded altruism in the matter, Mr Latham added that as they had finished their meal, he would say a prayer of thanks. *It should be a prayer of thankfulness that this horrible meal is over*, thought Sophie, as she obediently put her hands together and closed her eyes.

As they moved out of the dining parlour and into the hall, Mrs Latham announced that she was going to lie down as she had one of her headaches coming on. Sophie looked wistfully out of the open doors at the golden sunshine of a late afternoon in August. She would dearly have liked to sit under the beech tree and finish reading the enthralling novel lent to her by Mrs Firth, but dutifully she asked, "Would you like me to assist you, Mama?"

"Just to draw the curtains. The sun is so bright, so glaring."

Lucy went up the stairs before them and vanished into the bedroom she and Sophie shared. Sophie followed her mother into her bedroom and carefully undressed her and wrapped her in a loose comfortable robe. This was accompanied by sighs and moans and cries of "Do be careful," from Mrs Latham.

Mrs Latham sat down at her dressing table and let Sophie gently brush her hair. An onlooker, seeing the two reflections in the looking glass would have been struck by their resemblance despite the uncomfortable contrast between youth and age. Aware of this, Mrs Latham closed her eyes. Both had urchin features with high cheekbones, grey eyes and light brown hair that curled attractively. Sophie was thinner than Mrs Latham had been at twenty-two and she had been prettier than Sophie. She took comfort from this thought. But the onlooker would have surmised that Mrs Latham, having been born with a discontented nature, would never have had the open sunny look that made Sophie so appealing.

"I hope this lovely weather continues so the harvest is good," said Sophie, searching for a neutral topic so as not to exacerbate her mother's woes.

"The sun hurts my eyes," Mrs Latham said fretfully, "and the curtains are so thin and shabby, they let most of the light in. But we can't afford to buy new ones so there is nothing to be done even though my poor health suffers dreadfully. And what are we going to do if Mr Edwards does what he threatens and reduces your father's stipend?" She started to cry.

"Come, Mama, don't upset yourself. It was just a silly threat. By all accounts, father is the best curate he's ever had here. Do you remember, the last one allowed pigs to be kept in the church? And it would seem he was never sober. Mr

Edwards would be foolish to make life so difficult for father that he would be forced to leave."

"Perhaps it would be for the best if your father did decide to move, with or without Mr Edwards' blessing. If only he could get one of the new churches in Cheltenham. I'm sure my health would improve if we lived there. I hear it is elegant and refined, and much more suited to me than this dreary little valley."

"Do you recall Mrs Harries mentioning a new draper's shop in Cirencester?" asked Sophie, beginning to feel some desperation that she never would lift her mother's spirits, and the migraine would go on for days. "Perhaps he's so anxious for custom that you could get new curtains very reasonably priced."

Mrs Latham allowed herself to be tucked up in bed, but she sat up looking at the faded bed hangings and even more faded curtains.

"I think I will lie down and hope to get a little sleep."

After a few minutes she said, "Perhaps a light blue material with a small flower pattern, do you think?"

"That sounds very pretty."

As her mother seemed to have settled quite happily, Sophie dared to ask, "Will you need me for the next hour? I promised father I would call to see how Mrs Briggs is."

"Perhaps a light pink with a blue flower would be better. No, no, you go and see old Mrs Briggs. I'll have to manage on my own, as usual. But don't be too long."

Sophie escaped. She went across the small landing into her bedroom where Lucy was seated at the dressing table viewing her reflection with wholehearted admiration. She could not fault the dark curls, the lovely peach complexion and the huge brown eyes which looked dreamily back at her.

She was shorter than Sophie, more rounded and infinitely more feminine. Whereas Sophie was universally friendly, Lucy was only interested in being regarded as the prettiest girl in the room, an ambition she usually achieved. It did not, of course, make her popular with other females.

So self-absorbed was she that she barely realised that Sophie had come into the bedroom, collected her bonnet and her book and had silently vanished. Sophie ran down the stairs, paused at the door to the dining parlour from where she could hear her father's rumbling snores, grinned and went out into the garden to the chairs on the front lawn which were shaded by the large beech tree. There she finished the last chapter of *Eveline* and sat for a while, reluctant to leave Miss Burney's world.

She tied the ribbons of her bonnet under her chin, picked up the book and went down the steep stone steps to the lane below. Gently sloping down to the little River Dark, the lane went past the decrepit outbuildings and barns of Glebe Farm on one side and a row of four small cottages on the other. The river crossed the lane in a shallow ford and beyond this, the land started to rise again. There were two houses beyond the ford. One, a small cottage occupied by the shepherd, the other a house of some size. This, the Chantry House, was tucked into the side of the valley, rambling, very old and decayed. It had been empty for over a year.

The Briggs' cottage was the last of the row and nearest the stream. In winter, it was cold and damp and prone to flooding but on this August evening, with late roses rambling over the doorway, the sun on the mellow stone and with ducks drifting on the ford, it was a picture of idyllic rural life. Mrs Briggs was sitting outside her front door, her hands busy shelling peas, her eyes, milky with cataracts, sightlessly staring at the haybarn opposite.

Sophie felt a twinge of guilt. She had not told her mother the entire truth. It was true that she was going to see Mrs Briggs, but it was to be a few brief words on her way up the valley to Middle Darkleigh to return the book to Mrs Firth. She was all too aware that if her mother had known this, she would never have been allowed to leave the sickroom. So, she had used subterfuge and consequently felt some pangs of conscience, but not too sharply.

Mrs Briggs spoke in a soft monotone of the problems with Farmer Glover's ducks coming into her kitchen, of the rapacity of the wood pigeons attacking Briggs' cauliflowers, of the assaults by butterflies on his cabbages, and the depredations made by the fox on the chickens. Sophie felt that the Battle of Waterloo must have been a haven of peace compared with the relentless warfare waged by the Briggs' against the natural world.

Polly Brown appeared from the cottage at the other end of the row while Mrs Briggs was inveighing against the fox, a pretty vixen which Sophie had seen playing with her cubs in the grassy banks above them.

Mrs Briggs stopped mid-sentence, her mouth shutting like a vice. Polly saw it and laughed.

"One day Oi'll creep up on 'ee."

"That 'ee won't. Oi can smell 'ee a mile off."

"Like my perfume, do 'ee?"

"Yer knows well 'tis the smell of sin."

"I must go," said Sophie hurriedly. "I'm on my way to Middle Darkleigh."

"Oi'll come with 'ee," said Polly. "Oi be going to see Mr Harries."

"Ee shouldn't allow 'er to go with 'ee, Miss Sophie."

"Oi don't see as 'ow 'er can stop me. Oi've got as much right to go up the valley path as Miss Sophie."

Mrs Briggs muttered under her breath as the two girls used the stepping stones to cross the ford. Polly was a year or two younger than Sophie, a large moon-faced girl whose over-developed charms she all too generously shared. She was immensely good-natured and Sophie, although more aware of her propensities than her parents would have felt right for a young lady, could not help but like her.

They took a path that branched off the lane and ran between the river and the high stone walls of the Chantry garden. Polly explained that she had heard (Sophie often wondered how Polly always heard the news first) new people were coming to the Chantry and she wanted Mr Harries to give her a recommendation. Sophie knew that for some unspoken, but all too obvious reason associated with the cowman, Polly had been turned off by Mrs Harries. And now Polly was blithely asking Mr Harries for a recommendation. Sophie could only admire her impudence but guessed that Polly would get her recommendation and felt some slight pity for the unsuspecting newcomers who would inevitably soon learn about her over-willing nature.

Polly waved gaily to Mr Briggs at work in his garden on the other side of the stream and even though he was seventy and rheumaticky, he acknowledged the wave with a nod and a sly shift of his eyes. Belatedly seeing Sophie, he hastily looked down at his cabbages, apparently transfixed by their dark green leaves. Sophie couldn't help giggling, which she changed into a cough and asked Polly whether she knew anything about the new people.

"No. Just that they come from London way."

"It will be nice to have people at the Chantry again."

Polly wholeheartedly agreed. "Ol' Mr Bannerman was a right miserable so-and-so. 'Ee shouted and shook 'is stick at me when Oi picked blackberries in his wood. They was going to waste, the mean old beggar. Serve him right for yelling and dancing at me, as 'e took ill and died soon after."

"The new people, are they tenants or are they buying it from Mr Bannerman's nephew?"

"Tenants. 'E can't find anyone wanting to buy such a tumbledown old house, miles from anywhere. Oi don't blame 'em. Oi would like to live in Gloucester or Cheltenham or somewhere exciting. Even Cirencester would be better than this."

Polly looked back with scorn at Knight's Darkleigh. High above them, the church clinging to the side of the hill was etched by the evening sun. The valley was in shadow, cool and faintly damp. The river ran under overhanging trees, clear and swift, tumbling over stones chattering its way to its undistinguished meeting with the River Churn in Cirencester as an open drain.

They walked by the river following the curving arc of the valley. Its steep wooded sides broadened out and meadows took over from trees as the scattered houses of Middle Darkleigh came into view. They parted company: Polly to carry on by the river until she reached Manor Farm and Sophie to climb the eastern side of the valley to the small, neat house occupied by Mrs Firth.

She was panting a little by the time she reached the wrought iron gate set into the garden wall. She turned to look down on Middle Darkleigh and saw Polly, a small, brightly coloured figure, walking away towards the farm. She looked across the valley, the sun dazzling her eyes, and over the fields to the woods in the far distance. It was a lovely open view and as always, gave her an uplifting sense of freedom—of escape from the confines of her dull world.

Caroline Firth was sitting in her little garden when Sophie arrived and was delighted to see her. She was just beginning to admit to herself that she was becoming bored with her rural retreat and Sophie, although some ten years her junior, was the only person in the valley with whom she felt any affinity. She was a very handsome woman and dressed with an understated elegance which baffled her country neighbours. They dimly felt the clothes must be expensive but as their manifestation of dressing smartly was to overload with frills and furbelows, Mrs Firth's simple clothes were not particularly admired.

She had allowed it to be known that she was the widow of a respectable man who had been in trade in one of the great northern cities, but she had been left in somewhat straitened circumstances. In the early summer, she had taken a year's tenancy on the house in order to adjust to the change in her life and lived very quietly. She did not mix in society and anyway the local gentry were disinclined to acquaint themselves with people in trade and far less with the widow of one who had been unsuccessful.

Mrs Latham had called, and the visit had been dutifully returned. However, as Mrs Firth had not felt she had retired to this remote valley to become a sympathetic ear to Mrs Latham's endless complaining, the association had not prospered. She had been introduced to Lucy and Sophie and on impulse had invited them for tea. Since then, Sophie had been a frequent visitor, and they had rapidly become firm friends. Mrs Firth had all the latest books sent down from London and was generous in lending them to Sophie for whom they opened worlds previously unimaginable to her. Mrs Latham was barely literate and Lucy not much better and any intellectual curiosity her father might once have had had been deadened by disappointment, an indolent nature and constant domestic disharmony.

Caroline Firth was aware of the limitations of Sophie's home and enjoyed widening her horizons. She did, however, occasionally worry that she could be making Sophie dissatisfied with her life without any prospect of changing it. So far as Sophie was concerned, knowing Mrs Firth was the most pleasant thing that had happened to her life, and she dreaded the inevitable time when she would leave. She had her suspicions that Mrs Firth's circumstances had been far more exalted than was admitted but did not feel that she had any right to pry into her past.

"I saw you walking along the stream with young Polly," said Caroline. "She looked like a huge, overblown peony in that dress."

"It's an amazing colour, isn't it? She's on her way to see Mr Harries for a reference as she's hoping to obtain work at the Chantry. New people are coming as tenants."

As Sophie expected, Caroline laughed at Polly's bravado. Seeing Sophie's smile, she said in mock admonishment, "As a well brought up young lady, you shouldn't know about such people as Polly."

"That is a little difficult when one lives next door to her," retorted Sophie. "But I hasten to add that no-one but you has any idea that I'm aware of her failings."

"How very wise. And here comes Mathilda with some tea."

Mathilda and her husband Fred looked after Caroline as if she was a fragile piece of porcelain or, thought Sophie, as someone recovering from a serious illness. Sophie had been regarded with misgivings but had unknowingly passed a test of approval by always returning the books in immaculate condition and by never staying too long.

As they drank their tea, Sophie recounted Mr Latham's problem with the rector's glebe.

"Who's the patron of the living?" asked Caroline.

"Trinity College, Oxford," said Sophie. "They also own some of the land Mr Harries farms."

"Then are they not the people to ask for an opinion?"

"Of course they are. How very clever of you to think of it."

"Living here, high above everyone, gives one a lordly, detached view of life. Very good for one's mind."

"I can't believe the unexciting goings-on of Middle Darkleigh can be very stimulating."

"No, they are not at all. Watching Mrs Harries and her daughters sent out on an expedition to Cirencester is a pinnacle of excitement."

"I think they would agree with you. Mind you, so would I. It's ages since we went into Cirencester, but I hope my mother might want to go in soon, so I'd have that to look forward to."

"How is your mother?" asked Caroline, courteously.

"She's retired to bed with a migraine," Sophie said with a sigh. "So I must go back in case she needs me."

Sophie departed shortly after with another book tucked under her arm. She decided to walk back to Knight's Darkleigh along the road and look at the disputed woodland. This confirmed her belief that it must be part of Jarvis Harries' land.

She returned home to a fractious Mrs Latham, angry at being left for so long. The bright sunlight of her visit to Caroline Firth disappeared.

Chapter Two

Mrs Latham's headache lasted all the next day, and Sophie dutifully attended upon her. The weather turned cold and grey with drizzling showers and the week slipped by with nothing to break its predictable routine. Church on Sunday followed the pattern of all Mr Latham's services; the congregation was small and confined to the Harries family, Caroline Firth, and one or two cottagers. The sermon, as always, was very dull.

Mr Latham had grasped at the suggestion (Sophie did not admit whose it was) that Trinity College should be asked to adjudicate on the question of the woodland and he had accordingly written to the rector. He warned Jarvis Harries after church of the rector's claim and Mr Harries had immediately determined that he also should write to Trinity to put forth his case. This was entirely satisfactory to Mr Latham, who rejoiced that he should not become any further embroiled in the unseemly dispute. His spirits rose sufficiently for him grudgingly to agree to his wife and daughters taking the carriage into Cirencester the following Friday.

With an expedition to Cirencester to be looked forward to and with the arrival of two servants on Monday to open up the Chantry, it seemed, thought Sophie, that things were happening in Knight's Darkleigh, as if it were waking from a long sleep.

Polly, with a warm reference from Mr Harries, had immediately been taken on to help with the task of making the Chantry habitable and she kept the village informed of all that was being done. She also reported that Mr and Mrs Freeman and their son were expected within a week and Polly hoped that they would prove a little more cheerful than the housekeeper and butler whom she described as being as dismal as Darkleigh in December.

The weather improved during the week, and Friday morning was warm and sunny with a pleasant light wind when the rectory ladies set out for Cirencester. Mrs Latham's mission was for curtain material and Lucy's for a new bonnet in preparation for George's return. She was very much her father's favourite and had managed to cajole him into giving her the money for the bonnet.

Consequently, it was an unusually cheerful party that was conveyed in the ancient, creaking carriage down the valley to Cirencester. After a successful morning, they treated themselves to lunch at The King's Head. Lucy was glowing with pleasure, giving her hat box frequent happy glances. Mrs Latham felt she had bargained cleverly with the new draper, a pleasant man who seemed to know his trade. She was as satisfied with her material as her nature allowed her to be and with the promise that the curtains would be made up and delivered within a fortnight. The draper's elder son had been unable to take his eyes off Lucy, who enjoyed the effect she was having on him, and stood with her eyes demurely lowered. Sophie struck up a friendship with the younger son who, at the age of twelve, was oblivious of Lucy's beauty but delighted to tell Sophie all the circumstances (including a fire described in dramatic terms) which had resulted in their leaving Gloucester and setting up shop in Cirencester. Sophie imparted all this to her mother and Lucy, who were not particularly interested in anything other than their purchases, and added, "They hope that the slump in the wool trade is over with the war ended, and Cirencester will become prosperous again. I hope they are right."

Realising her audience was less than attentive, she gave up conversation and looked out of the window onto the Market Place. Its lunchtime somnolence was broken by the clattering of horses' hooves and coach wheels.

"The Oxford coach is arriving," she noted.

"How I wish I could go to Oxford for a visit. Or even better, London," said Lucy.

"I went to London as a girl," mused Mrs Latham. "I would, I am sure, have enjoyed it more if the people I was staying with, very respectable acquaintances of my father, had been more sensible of what was required of them as hosts to a delicate young girl but they…" She was interrupted by Lucy, who anyway had not been listening but watching the hustle and bustle outside.

"Mama, Sophie – it's Robert! Robert is outside!"

Sophie, unable to stop herself, ran out of the parlour and into the street calling, "Robert, Robert!"

He was with another man, and both turned at her cry. Robert opened his arms, and she ran into them. She cried and laughed, and it was only when she drew back that she realised that he was holding her with only one hand. His left arm, the sleeve neatly pinned up, had been severed just below the elbow.

"Robert, your arm. Why didn't we hear that you had been injured? Oh, poor Robert," and she burst into tears.

"Good heavens, Sophie, it's not the end of the world! I am alive, after all."

"I'm sorry, I don't know why – but here are Mama and Lucy."

"Sophie," complained Mrs Latham. "You shouldn't rush out in such a vulgar way. Robert, why didn't you let us know you were going to return so soon?"

"I didn't know myself until last week, when it was too late. Aren't you going to welcome me home, Mama?"

Sophie watched with exasperation and bewilderment as Mrs Latham unenthusiastically raised her face for his salutation. She did not know the reason behind the near hostility between mother and son, just that it had been there for as long as she could remember. Time and absence had not diminished it, and to make matters worse, her mother was looking with revulsion, not pity, at the empty sleeve.

Lucy greeted him with more warmth than her mother, but it was apparent that her interest was more taken up with Robert's companion, an interest that was being returned with as conspicuous an enthusiasm. Robert shrugged. His family never changed.

"Mama," he said, "may I introduce you to Major James Howard? Major, my mother and my sisters, Lucy and Sophie."

Major Howard was a striking looking man with dark hair, a rather swarthy complexion and quite remarkable blue eyes.

"Your servant, Ma'am. Miss Latham, Miss Sophie." The Major bowed.

"Mama, I've invited Major Howard to stay. I was sure you would have no objection."

Unable to say anything else, Mrs Latham said they would be delighted. But under the Major's charming smile of thanks, she visibly thawed, and Lucy raised her big brown eyes and smiled shyly at him. The Major gave every sign of a man dazzled by her beauty and Lucy lowered her eyes, well satisfied.

"Have you heard anything of George Harries coming home, Robert?" asked Sophie with some malice.

There was a slight pause and Robert replied, "By coincidence, we were with him yesterday in Oxford. I believe he had some business to attend to, so will not arrive until tomorrow."

At this, the image of George as the ardent suitor dimmed a little, and Mrs Latham, observing Major Howard's enchantment, began to wonder whether her husband was perhaps right: Lucy could do better than George Harries. Robert would have to tell them more about his friend.

Sophie, seeing the Major smiling at her sister, felt envy at Lucy's ability to attract.

Robert recalled with amusement the scene at the unsavoury inn late the previous evening, when George, unpleasantly drunk, had lurched off after a garish whore and had not been seen again. Robert did not like his prospective brother-in-law well enough to bother to look for him in the morning to get him on the mail coach, so had shrugged his shoulders and left George to his own devices. He, himself, had not been that sober and his recollection was more than a little hazy as to how Major Howard, whom he had met for the first time that evening in George's company, had come to be invited to stay at the rectory.

An hour or so later, Robert and Major Howard, riding hired horses, turned off the highway and rode down the bumpy lane that ambled its way up the valley of the River Dark. In the fields the barley stood golden as it waited for harvest and the buzzing of flies irritating the horses was the only sound to invade the silence on a peaceful day.

It's the first time I've been to this part of the country," said the Major, breaking the silence. "It is very attractive."

"Yes. But I grew up in Suffolk and still think of that as 'my' country."

Thinking this was a good an opening as any, Robert asked, "Which is your part of the country?"

"Hampshire, near Lymington, between the forest and the sea. The best of both worlds, in my opinion. But it has been a long time since I've been back. My parents died when I was young and I was shunted around various relatives, none of whom could stand me for very long: I was rather wild. Eventually, I went into the army, the thought being that I might be tamed a bit. Or be killed. I'm not sure but one or two of them would have preferred the latter. Still, I survived, perhaps to spite them all!"

"What will you do now? I assume you have sold out?"

"Yes. Peace-time soldiering is not for me. As to what I will do, I'm not sure. I've sufficient to live on for the time being but, alas, my tastes are more expensive than my income."

"I sympathise. Lord alone knows what I will do. This," Robert looked with loathing at his stump, "does not help matters."

Major Howard glanced at his bleak face and changed the subject.

"George Harries tells me the hunting is good round here."

"It's tolerable, I suppose, perhaps not even that."

"George's ability to appreciate hunting country being on a par with his horsemanship?"

Robert laughed: "I was so envious of George going into the Hussars whereas I had to make do with an obscure line regiment. It seemed so damnably unfair when he was such a poor horseman. And he was superior and condescending with it, the pompous fool." A sudden thought struck him. "I say, he isn't a particular friend of yours, is he?"

"No, we were merely in the same regiment. That's the only connection. It would perhaps have been better for him to have lowered his sights and joined a less fashionable one. He was the butt of a number of rather cruel jokes. He was given the nickname of 'The Yokel'."

"It suits him. For all his airs, he remains just that. He's hoping to marry Lucy, you know."

"Oh no, surely she can do better than George?"

"No dowry."

"But she is very lovely."

They rode on in companionable silence through the straggling village of Laine and were watched with some curiosity by cottagers as they trotted by. After Laine, the valley narrowed and steepened, and the track cut into its side so they could look down on the little river winding its way through the green meadows of the valley.

"There's the Rectory," said Robert, as the house came into view above the trees. The farm and the cottages could be seen below it.

"The church is immediately behind the house and it's so small it is entirely obscured by it. I'm not sure how much respect was shown when the house was built."

"The house of the rector of greater importance than the House of God?"

"Something like that. The previous house was lower, nearer the cottages you can see on the right. They're by the stream and get pretty damp in winter."

"It is a very picturesque scene. Is this all of Knight's Darkleigh?"

"Yes. Not the great metropolis, is it? Middle Darkleigh, where George Harries' family lives, is half a mile further up the valley. Beyond that is Prior's Darkleigh and then Darkleigh St Mary. And that is all there is to the Dark Valley. A backwater where nothing happens."

They turned into the rectory drive and approached the house, a high unadorned building, built of the silver-grey local stone.

"It's a little austere for my taste," said Robert. And then he added with a grin, "I've now complained about the valley, the village and the house. I'd better stop, or I might be tempted to describe my family in similar terms."

"No family could be as dreadful as mine," said James Howard with great certainty as Mr Latham and his wife and daughters appeared at the front door.

Sophie lay in bed that night, unable to sleep. She knew she was like an overexcited child, but it had been a most exciting day. She would have liked to have talked over the dinner party with Lucy, but Lucy, basking in Major Howard's admiration, was not interested in mulling over what had been said, except insofar as the comments had related to her. So, Sophie had soon given up and tried unsuccessfully to settle to sleep.

It was a hot, sultry night and Lucy's steady breathing began to irritate and increased her restlessness. She pushed the covers off and sat up. This merely confirmed that she was wide awake, that she was not going to get to sleep and that she might as well give herself some fresh air and sit outside for a while. She had done this before when domestic strife or general monotony had made life too stifling. It was the first time she had done it because life had become too exciting.

She went softly down the stairs and, to her surprise, found the front door unlocked. She cautiously opened the door and went out and squeaked with surprise as she saw Robert leaning against the wall beside the door.

"Sophie! What on earth are you doing?" he whispered.

"I couldn't sleep," she whispered back. "It was so hot that I thought I'd get some air. What about you?"

"Much the same. Come on, let's go down the garden so we can talk without whispering."

As they walked across the lawn, she glanced at his face. The moonlight emphasised its plains and angles, making it remote, gaunt and unfamiliar. He was, she thought with something close to fear, a stranger. The only member of her family with whom she felt any true affinity had gone away and left her far behind. In the years since she had last seen him, her life had been one of small happenings and deadening routine, whereas his had been one of uncertainty, action, responsibility and pain. If she didn't know anything of what he had been through, then the fine strand of affection linking them would break. But she couldn't yet find the courage to ask outright.

They sat in deep shadow underneath the beech tree and watched the near full moon sailing through gauze clouds in a silver blue sky. An owl hooted and was answered shrilly by its mate. Then silence. Over the roofs of the cottage, they could see the Chantry with its old stones glistening in the moonlight.

Robert asked idly about the inhabitants of the cottages and of Mr Bannerman, and Sophie explained the imminent arrival of the new tenants.

"Do you remember," she asked, "you persuaded me that if the French invaded England, I must learn to reconnoitre without being observed? You challenged me to go across the Chantry garden without being seen and then into the woods above it to find a message."

Robert's face relaxed into a reminiscent grin and at last he seemed more the brother she had known. "And you managed it, much to my surprise. And I do remember your being punished, poor Sophie, for ruining your dress from crawling through the bushes and of course for the dreadful crime of being childish and a tomboy!"

"I think it must have been the last time I did something that was outrageous and – and fun! The relief and triumph of getting through the garden and into the wood were wonderful."

"Is life so very dull?"

"Most of the time. We do so little and see so few people. I quite enjoy teaching the children their numbers and letters, though I'm not very good at it. But since Mrs Firth has been here, things really have been much, much better."

"Ah, the mysterious Mrs Firth."

"She's not. She just wants to live quietly, that's all." Then going into the attack, she said, "Major Howard was interested in her."

"So you noticed that as well?"

"It's the only time he stopped gawping at Lucy."

"Jealousy, jealousy!"

"Nonsense. You say Mrs Firth is mysterious. What about Major Howard? Why is he here? You aren't old comrades in arms, are you? Anyway, you never used to invite friends home, let alone bare acquaintances."

"You know, I'd forgotten you could be quite sharp at times. You're right. He is not an old friend. To be precise, I met him for the first time last night in Oxford. Unfortunately, I had rather too much to drink, and I can't remember inviting him to stay, but I must have done, as he's here."

"How strange. But then, I suppose you must have imposed yourself on your friends in much the same way."

"No I did not!" said Robert, indignantly. "They were friends, and I was always warmly invited."

"And they were always richer and grander than you."

"That wasn't difficult. Actually, I believe he was intending to stay with George, but I will say, with all due modesty, that if it were a choice between my company and George's, I think I would win hands down, every time. Even if I were in a paltry foot regiment and not the cavalry."

"What was it like? Was it terrible?"

He didn't answer for a while and then said, "It was hell on earth. We were the centre and all day we were bombarded by wave after wave of French attacks. It was awful: the mud, the noise, the screams of injured and dying men and horses, the confusion, the whole dreadful carnage. I'll never forget the arrival of Blucher's detachments. We were almost finished and then they came swirling in. It was tremendous. We were able to hold until Wellington mounted the counter-attack with the cavalry."

"You fought for hours in the mud and then the cavalry came charging in at the last moment and got all the credit?"

"Well, not quite that bad."

"I don't like the thought of George being regarded as a dashing hero and you just a foot-slogger."

"Nor do I. George loves it, though. By a bit of bad luck, we landed up in the same field hospital and I haven't been able to avoid him since. I believe he was thrown from his horse in the first charge and knocked unconscious. My arm must have been blown off at the same time."

"Does it hurt?"

"At times. What's worse, though, is the itching I get in my third finger."

"Whatever do you mean?"

"My body still seems to believe that I've got a complete arm. A sort of ghost arm and hand which you can't scratch when it itches."

"It sounds awful. Poor Robert."

"Now don't start crying again."

"I promise this will be the last time."

"Have a handkerchief. Come on, we must go to bed. You're shivering."

He put his arm around her shoulder, and they walked back to the house. Major Howard, as wakeful as they, watched from his bedroom window, high above.

Chapter Three

Despite her night excursion in the garden, Sophie was up long before her parents and Lucy, so joined Robert and Major Howard for breakfast.

They may not be old friends, she thought, as she sat down, but there was no doubt about the easy rapport between them. An earnest discussion was going on about the merits of different rivers for fishing, and although it was briefly interrupted by her appearance, she was soon forgotten which amused her rather than annoyed her. After all, it was something she was quite used to in her family.

Major Howard was the first to remember his manners. "We must apologise, Miss Sophie, for neglecting you."

"Oh, Sophie's used to it," said Robert, with a brotherly lack of tact and Sophie, who a moment before had been content to be ignored, now felt mortified that her attractions were evidently well below those of a trout. Major Howard's bright blue eyes which missed little, saw the hurt cloud Sophie's expressive face.

"I've never had any sisters," he said quickly, "but I have a cousin who would have boxed my ears if I'd suggested she should expect to be overlooked in favour of a fish!"

"Oh." Robert digested this and then said with his engaging grin, "Sorry, Sophie. I didn't mean to be rude. In a way, it was a compliment. I mean, you don't fuss for attention."

The unspoken words "like Lucy" hung in the air.

"Tell me, Miss Sophie," said Major Howard, firmly changing the subject, "where does the lane that goes across the ford lead to? I went up it a short way this morning, but it seemed to peter out."

"It leads to the high road about half a mile away. Mr Bannerman, the old owner of the Chantry, didn't like people using it, so he put up a fence to stop people from crossing. Eventually he sold most of the land to Mr Harries – George's father – who hasn't done anything to clear it, either."

Robert was interested. "So, Jarvis Harries must now own a fair amount of land, apart from what he rents from Trinity."

"Father says he is a very successful farmer, bringing in a lot of improvements. But then he can afford to experiment, not like poor old Farmer Glover in Glebe Farm." Sophie laughed. "Polly says that when George inherits, he'll want to be Squire Harries of Knight's Darkleigh."

"Is Polly still here?" asked Robert, remembering some very enjoyable times with her in the Chantry woods.

He was unaware that his companion recognised the implications of his reminiscent smile. The Major was a little surprised on seeing Sophie's pink face, to discover that she was perhaps not the innocent little country mouse he had first taken her for.

"I met a young girl from one of the cottages on my way back from my walk. She could only be described as a buxom wench," Major Howard said with a straight face. "Would that have been Polly?"

Robert laughed and Sophie was unable to stop herself giggling.

"That's our Poll," said Robert.

"She seemed a remarkably friendly girl," continued the Major, smoothly.

"To a fault," said Robert, still laughing. "I'm amazed you got away."

"She explained to me that she was in a hurry as her new employers arrive today. Otherwise, she implied, things might be different."

Sophie firmly called a halt to this conversation by asking them if either of them would like some tea. Slightly abashed, they hastily changed the subject back to sport. This time, it was shooting and the merits of rival gunmakers and, realising this could go on indefinitely, Sophie excused herself. As she went upstairs, she thought that Robert seemed surprisingly knowledgeable about the sporting arts and surmised that he had used his visits to his wealthy friends to good advantage.

The shooting discussion was interrupted shortly after her departure by Mr Latham's arrival. The evening before had been a more convivial one than the Lathams were used to, and Mr Latham had succumbed to drinking rather more port than was good for him. Consequently, he was suffering from a severe headache and feeling even more sorry for himself than usual.

Although there was none of the outright hostility that lay between Robert and his mother, the relationship between father and son was an uneasy one with too little filial respect and paternal pride to warm it.

Mr Latham watched Major Howard cut some bread and spread it with butter and then handed it to Robert. This small service, done in a matter-of-fact way, brought forcefully home to Mr Latham the problem of Robert's future employment.

It could not be said that Mr Latham would have preferred his son to be killed rather than maimed, but the former would have presented less demands on his chronic indolence. Robert's death would have been mourned for a decent period and then he would have become a distant memory, only occasionally recollected and then without much sense of loss.

The reality of a disabled Robert, unable even to spread himself a piece of bread with butter, was more than Mr Latham could cope with and he resorted to querulous complaining. But in a catalogue of woes at the iniquities of life, Robert's injury inevitably came up and Major Howard decided it would be tactful of him to withdraw so father and son could talk. He had espied Lucy standing by the front door, tying the ribbons of her bonnet. She was holding a small basket and seemed to be preparing to set out for a walk. The Major thought this was an excellent idea.

Lucy had been in the process of dressing, always a lengthy affair, when Sophie came up from the dining room to collect her bonnet. Even to Lucy's incurious gaze, Sophie seemed exceptionally bright and happy.

"What's the matter? Where are you going?" Lucy asked.

"Nothing at all is the matter. It's a lovely sunny morning and I'm going to pick blackberries." Only her family would think there was something the matter if one was happy, Sophie thought.

Lucy also was thinking. An idea was growing in her mind.

"Where are the best ones?"

"Along the Millington Lane."

"So far?" Lucy frowned. Her idea didn't entail traipsing miles across country. "Aren't there any nearer?"

"On the common land behind the church. But I want a little more exercise than just going there."

Sophie left, collected a basket from the kitchen and from there, walked briskly across the churchyard and the common land beyond. She had an inkling of the reason behind Lucy's unusual interest in blackberries but forgot all about it until she returned the same way an hour later. When she saw Lucy and Major Howard standing close together, she remembered her suspicions all too well. She stopped. Major Howard was disentangling a bramble from the sleeve of Lucy's dress but that done, his hand remained on her arm, and he looked down at her upturned face.

Sophie turned and swiftly walked away to take the road back to the rectory. She was quite unable to bring the emotions which possessed her under control. To her deep shame, the dominant one was envy; no man had ever looked at her as James Howard had looked at Lucy. Even though it rose from the sin of lust and should be abhorrent to all that she had been taught, yet Lucy had never looked so entrancing, glowing under that hungry look.

Sophie caught herself when she began to wonder what had happened after she left, and embarrassment at the way her thoughts were tending washed over her in a huge, hot wave. She stooped down, pretending to take a stone from her shoe while she waited for her crimson cheeks to cool down.

As she straightened up, she could see a carriage pulled by four horses coming up the road from Laine. It was covered with dust, but this did not disguise its opulence. As it turned down the lane towards the ford, Sophie glimpsed the profiles of two of the occupants: one, a thin, tired looking lady; in complete contrast, the other was a big corpulent man, highly coloured with a face dominated by a large, fleshy nose.

The new tenants of the Chantry had arrived.

* * *

The next morning saw James Howard standing in front of the tiny looking glass that hung above the shabby little chest of drawers, the only furniture other than the bed, which the Lathams provided for the convenience of their infrequent guests. The room was a reasonable size, but its decoration was as poor as its furnishings. However, as a self-invited guest, he could not complain of the lack of comfort.

He finished tying his cravat and was pleased with its neatness and then went over to the window. His bedroom was on the second floor and the view entirely compensated for the deficiencies within. He looked down the valley and over the cottages of Laine to the great tower of the church in Cirencester – and beyond that, far in the distance, he could see the rounded slopes of the Marlborough Downs.

For the first time for many years, he was voluntarily going to a church service and was eagerly looking forward to it; not for religious reasons as he was indifferent to religion, but to see one member of the congregation. And he wanted to see the yokel's face when he saw him walking in with Lucy on his arm.

Lucy was lovely and silly and beneath her conventional upbringing, she had the same instincts as the luscious Polly. He could have seduced her with ease yesterday morning and was almost amazed at his gentlemanly restraint. The likely consequence that he would have ended up saddled with her one way or another had been the most compelling reason for his holding off. Lucy had been put out by his sudden retreat. Kissing her hand and looking ardently into her eyes had led her to expect, and to want, more. He smiled as he remembered her little pout of disappointment.

He looked down on the lawn. Sophie was there, sitting in her favourite place under the beech tree. A nice child, he thought, dismissing her. Robert came into view, walking across the lawn to Sophie and as he watched the two talking and Sophie's face breaking into laughter, he felt envious of their easy companionship. Maybe, he mused, the ability to be companionable was a much-underrated gift, as for sure not everyone had it. A rapid overview of his acquaintances narrowed them down to about six. And one of them had been the mysterious lady, Mrs Firth, the reason why he had come to this valley and thus had imposed himself on the Lathams.

George Harries' family was to have had that pleasure, but the meeting in Oxford had changed that plan, a change he did not in the slightest regret. From all accounts, the Harries' house would have been more comfortable and the food far better, but companionable Robert and pretty Lucy were unlooked-for bonuses compared with Yokel George.

He turned away from the window, put on his coat and ran lightly down the uncarpeted stairs. Lucy must have been waiting for him as she emerged from her room just as he reached the first landing. She looked prettier than ever in her new dusky-pink bonnet and simple white dress with a sash the same colour as the bonnet. He gave her a look of whole-hearted admiration which she acknowledged with a gleam of her brown eyes. She walked down the stairs before him, smiling in satisfaction with the results of her exhaustive toilette.

James had not realised that the rectory party would be the first to arrive in church and that seated as they were, immediately behind the rectory pew at the front of the nave, he would be frustrated from seeing most of the congregation.

The church was very old and very small, an unpretentious building prettily situated on the steep side of the little valley, in harmony with its surroundings. The interior was bare of ornamentation: the Norman arch to the chancel was undecorated, the windows plain glass, the font and pulpit purely functional. The walls were lime-washed but dirty and specked with mildew and even on a warm September morning, the church smelt of damp and neglect. James' initial reaction, as he sat in the uncomfortable narrow pew, was that the church reflected the drab poverty in which most of the inhabitants of this valley must be condemned to eke out their lives. In front of him were the bonnets of the three rectory ladies: Mrs Latham's grey one in need of refurbishment, Lucy's smart new one which was perhaps a little fussy and elaborate for the church, and Sophie's simple straw, which he decided was the most appropriate.

Having inspected as much of the church as he could without turning his head, and having considered the bonnets in front of him, he sat back and waited for the service to begin, idly listening to the rustles and whispers as people came in.

"A full house," breathed Robert. "The Harries family in strength, the new people, what's their name – Freeman? – from the Chantry, Farmer Glover and his family – that must be a first – and I think it must be Mrs Firth behind them."

James involuntarily looked behind him and did indeed see Caroline Firth near the back of the church. She was staring at him with incredulity and as their eyes met, he gave what he hoped she would recognise as a reassuring nod and then turned back. He was now impatient for the service to be over and done with so he could speak to her. He was impressed with the way Robert seemed to have eyes at the back of his head, since he could have sworn that Robert had looked politely ahead throughout. It must be a technique acquired by sons of the cloth to help them overcome the tedium of all the services they had to attend.

The service certainly was tedious. Mr Latham, unable to resist the temptation of making the most of a fair-sized congregation, preached at interminable length, constantly repeating himself and losing the thread of his argument. There was an almost audible sigh of relief when the service eventually ground to a close and they were released into the bright sunshine.

Robert and James politely waited for the Latham ladies to precede them and were therefore privileged to see George Harries push his way ahead of his family to greet Lucy. George was handsome with a thatch of fair hair and round blue eyes, but with his large hands and feet and his ruddy complexion, there was, despite his fashionable clothes, a distinct air of the rustic about him.

Lucy was in a quandary. She knew very well that George was a good catch for her. He would make her an amiable and malleable husband but as he looked down at her with his pale blue eyes which were perhaps a little too close together in his large face, she was unable to stop herself comparing them with Major Howard's deeper, more vivid blue ones and George's plump lips with Major Howard's thin, well-shaped ones. She blushed and dropped her eyes, for once involuntarily, and those watchers who were sentimentally inclined were charmed by the picture she and George presented.

James sighed and consigned Lucy to history. Robert heard the sigh and gave him a wicked grin which James returned with a mock salute of surrender. Last to leave the church, they stood at the church entrance surveying the chattering groups. Symbolically, Lucy stood beside George with his mother and sisters. Mr Harries was with Mr and Mrs Latham being introduced to a tired looking Mrs Freeman and important looking Mr Freeman. Hovering behind Mrs Freeman was a young boy of about eighteen. He was slim and dark with huge, timid brown eyes and he gave an impression of deer-like grace and shyness.

Sophie was standing with Caroline Firth, who nodded and smiled at James Howard when she caught him looking across to her from the church porch.

"Well, James," she said as he and Robert approached. "This is a surprise. What are you doing here?"

"I'm delighted to see you, Caroline," he kissed her hand. "But I could ask the same of you?"

She smiled but did not answer. Instead, she gave her hand to Robert, saying, "You must be my dear Sophie's brother. I am so pleased to meet you."

From the moment he had seen her from the church porch, standing coolly elegant, detached from the other people, Robert knew he had fallen in love. As if from a great distance, he could hear his voice replying to her greeting and was relieved that it sounded coherent, however, he flushed as he realised that she was having some difficulty withdrawing her hand from his clasp. Sophie and James looked on with bright-eyed interest. Then Sophie turned accusingly to James.

"Why did you not say you knew Mrs Firth?"

She felt that for reasons of his own, her family had been used by Major Howard and this angered her. The Lathams might be poor and shabby and unimportant, but he had imposed himself upon them to contrive this meeting with Mrs Firth. She felt even her friendship with Mrs Firth had been tainted.

"I truly wasn't aware that you were referring to my cousin." To his surprise, the contrite note in his voice was not entirely assumed.

"You're cousins?" Sophie exclaimed, looking from one to the other.

"Unfortunately for me, yes," Caroline laughed.

"It was always worse for me. You were held up as the paragon of all the virtues, above the follies committed by mortals like me," James retorted. Caroline flinched and he regretted that, unintentionally, he had hit a raw nerve. Really, first Sophie, and now Caroline was making him feel guilty. Country life was having an alarming effect on his character, he thought to himself.

"Have you recently seen the witch?" he asked.

"James, you shouldn't call our grandmother a witch."

"So far as I'm concerned, she is. Maybe," he lowered his voice and looked with exaggerated fear at the rooks cawing in the trees, "those rooks are her familiars, reporting back to her."

"I doubt if they would fly as far as Bath," Caroline said.

"Then you are out of touch," James laughed as if at some private joke. "She quarrelled with everyone in Bath and no doubt is now doing the same with everyone in Cheltenham."

"Cheltenham!" Caroline went quite white. "She can't be. You must be teasing me."

"On my word, Cheltenham has had the pleasure of her company for the last month."

Caroline looked appalled. Robert felt a desperate need to comfort her and was furious with James for being the cause of her distress. All he could do was to remain a silent onlooker. Sophie said anxiously: "Are you all right? Would you like to sit down?"

Caroline shook her head. "I'm sorry, I'm just being stupid. I don't know why. But perhaps James will walk back with me to Middle Darkleigh so that we can talk family without boring you and your brother. In the meantime, should we not be sociable with our neighbours?"

"Why?" asked James.

"Because one should."

"Everyone is happy. If you were to join, say, Miss Latham and George Harries, you would be decidedly de trop."

Sophie looked down, colour flooding her cheeks. She was scandalised at the way Major Howard could one day be making ardent love to Lucy and the next, observing her on the arm of another man with seeming complete indifference.

"It does look as if George is going to become one of the family," said Robert, gloomily.

"Maybe it will be more Miss Latham becoming part of the Harries family," said Caroline.

"That's true," Robert brightened.

"Don't deprive him of an intimate relationship with George's sisters," said James as loud laughter burst forth from the two large, noisy girls.

"Oh Lord, I hadn't thought of that," Robert said with horror, and grinned as the others laughed at him.

Lucy saw the four standing together, talking easily. She glanced round at the large, cheerful Harries family enclosing her, trapping her in their comfortable self-satisfied provincialism. A shudder went through her as Miss Anne Harries shrieked with even more than her usual vigour. A faint but noticeable odour emanated from George, flushed and perspiring in his smart but a little too tight jacket. She looked across at Major Howard who met her beseeching look with one of stony indifference and then turned his back on her. Lucy felt as if she had been hit and it was with a great effort that she stopped herself from crying out. Then angry pride came to her rescue, and she looked up into George's face. There she beheld his look of besotted admiration, and it was almost enough to blot out the humiliation of the Major's snub. She started to flirt more openly with George, hoping the Major would see and be jealous.

"Who is Major Howard?" asked Miss Mary Harries.

"In my regiment," replied George.

"We know that," said Mary, impatiently.

"Not too sure who he is. Don't know him awfully well. No money but seems to know the right people. Strange, that." George pondered the puzzling fact that he, by all accounts more comfortably placed that James Howard, had found the right people elusive.

He saw James move off with Mrs Firth, who he supposed was handsome for her age, if you liked them thin, and then saw Robert and Sophie approach. To his relief, they were beckoned by Mrs Latham and walked by. George found physical abnormalities disturbing and Robert's stump held a horrid fascination for him. He was uneasy with Sophie; if it had been credible, he would have said that she held him in some contempt. As that was out of the question, he had to assume that it was the envy of her sister's good fortune in being singled out by him that made her so off-hand with him. He watched Robert and Sophie being introduced to Mr and Mrs Freeman and the handsome lad who must be their son and therefore, fortunately, he did not see the look on Lucy's face as she watched Major Howard and Mrs Firth disappearing up the church path to the road.

Jarvis Harries, released from making conversation with the Freemans, joined his family. He smiled at pretty Lucy. He was pleased with George's choice. She might not have a dowry, but her family was genteel and well-connected, and he had no doubt that she would help the Harries rise up the social scale. He himself had married the only child of a farmer whose land had been on the outskirts of the then small town of Cheltenham. Now, with the ever-expanding development of the town into a fashionable spa, the uncouth farmer's unsophisticated daughter had become a considerable heiress. His Bertha had remained, under her silks and satins, a peasant, and his boisterous daughters should learn from Lucy's gentility. Mr Harries was aware that a succession of governesses had failed to curb their high spirits but as he had no wish for them to be turned into simpering misses, he thought all they needed was a little gloss, which Lucy would provide.

Jarvis Harries was proud of his achievements; he was the son of a small tenant farmer, and he had, by a judicious marriage, by hard work, by shrewdness, by yet more hard work, increased his acreage, improved his land by experimenting with the new ideas in agriculture and he had prospered. His son had been a hero at Waterloo, and his daughters were handsome and vivacious and with comfortable dowries, would be assured of a place in society. In his conversation with the Lathams and the Freemans, he had been treated as an equal, his opinion as churchwarden sought and respected.

He looked across the little churchyard with its decaying graves and down to the river which flowed through his land. His own, his very own land. He was pleased with his lot. There was the dispute with the rector, Mr Edwards, but he had no doubt that he would win that argument. He was amused by Mr Latham's dilemma and a little contemptuous of the way he was so frightened of displeasing either of the principals. Mr Harries smiled down at Lucy Latham and admired her bonnet.

As she joined her mother, Sophie could see that Mrs Latham was being gracious to their new neighbours. Mr Freeman's deep, rich tones rolled over his listeners, and his large gooseberry-like eyes transfixed them. Mrs Freeman said little, just smiled timidly and seemed only to be partly aware of the conversation. Most of her attention was upon her son. Sophie thought she had never seen a more beautiful boy than Richard Freeman. He remained detached from the circle but did enter into a stilted conversation with her when she asked some questions about their journey.

When the Harries' and Lucy joined them, his fawn-like shyness became more pronounced. Lucy was disconcerted by him: the boy's delicately handsome features were not the sort of foil she wanted. His looks were too close to being a rival to her own. She positioned herself as far from him as possible in the group. Robert appeared to be listening politely to Miss Anne Harries, who was chattering about having some sort of celebration to welcome home the military heroes, but his thoughts were entirely taken up with the image of Caroline Firth. Even less than Sophie did he believe that she was the impoverished widow of some tradesman but for the moment, he was happy to be in ignorance of her real circumstances and just dreamed of when he would next see her.

At the mention of a soiree, a shadow crossed Mr Freeman's face, and he gave a sigh and a sad shake of his head.

"My friends," he said, mournfully, "I am distressed to hear talk of parties, of music for dancing, of such worldly pleasures. And this on the Lord's day, the sacred Sabbath. I realise young people can be forgetful of propriety, of the need to be ever vigilant to prevent a lapse of moral standards and the inevitable sinking into the pit of wickedness and sin. Do not, I beg of you, talk of riotous parties in my presence."

After this, it was not surprising that the company was too stunned to talk of anything at all. Even Miss Anne was bereft of speech, something, as Sophie said later, one would never have thought could happen.

With another heavy sigh, Mr Freeman flowed on: "Have you heard of the Spiritual Barometer?"

Silence.

"I feared not. Then with Mr Latham's leave, in next Sunday's service I will explain and demonstrate to you, my friends, the Spiritual Barometer."

Mr Latham was nonplussed. He had vaguely heard about the Evangelical Movement but had taken no interest in it and thus now, out of the blue, confronted with a zealous adherent, he was completely at a loss. He felt a justifiable resentment that his service was being annexed by Mr Freeman, but there was the compensation that he would escape the wearisome task of composing a sermon for next Sunday. He did not take kindly to the inference that as leader of his little flock, he was not showing sufficient moral guidance.

"I, er, it's most kind of you to, er, do so," he managed to say.

"Not at all, not at all. It's my duty. God, in his infinite wisdom has chosen this unworthy vessel to uphold His moral teaching. Now, my friends, we must depart. It's been a most welcome, a most auspicious meeting of like minds and spirits. I am filled with joy."

Whereupon Mr Freeman bowed and doffed his hat with a flourish and with the inexorability of a large boulder rolling down a slope, he marched off, his wife and son insignificant pebbles drawn behind him.

A crushed party watched them go. Lucy touched George's sleeve to gain his attention. He whispered a few words to her, she nodded, and then he drew Mr Latham aside. Lucy had made her decision. She was to marry George and get away from the rectory before her family were sucked into the vortex of Mr Freeman's moral crusade. Sophie guessed what was happening and could not blame Lucy for making good her escape. She herself had been oppressed and frightened by Mr Freeman's fervour and could not believe it was a force for good.

* * *

James Howard and Caroline Firth walked away from the church in silence. When they reached the road, she broke it.

"Well, what are you doing here?"

"Looking for you."

"Oh. Why?"

"It was in the faint hope that you would intercede for me with Grandmama. But, as you know even less than I did of her whereabouts, I have to conclude that there is no communication between you."

"None. When Henry died, she assumed that I would live with her as a superior companion. I refused, she took offence, and that was that."

"So, it was just coincidence that you both came to Gloucestershire?"

"Yes. But I suppose it was time she moved from Bath. Three years is the most she spends in one place. Tunbridge Wells and Harrogate have had the pleasure of her company, so Cheltenham would be a likely choice. And no doubt, Cheltenham is less expensive than Bath, so she'd have the added satisfaction of saving money."

"But why have you come here?"

"By chance. Lady Rivers was enthusing over the charms of this part of the country, so when I was deciding to look for somewhere to live for a while, it seemed as good a place as any."

So that he didn't pursue further the reason behind her decision to bury herself in the country, she added, "You know that Benedict Rivers has inherited his uncle's estate near here?"

"No. Where?"

"At Millington. The lane we've just passed on the left leads to it, about five miles away in the next valley."

James was pleased. A friendship, somewhat surprising in view of their very different characters, had grown up between himself and Benedict while at school and had continued afterwards on the rare occasions when their paths had crossed. James had gone into the army and Benedict, after taking a degree at Oxford, had been called to the Bar.

"Have you seen him?"

"No. I heard that he had come down to Millington only a few weeks ago. His uncle was apparently a recluse, and the estate had become badly neglected. I understand that the old man lived in squalor in one room, refusing to spend any money, although he was a very rich man."

"Lucky Benedict. I'll go over to see him as soon as possible."

"In fact, why not transfer yourself to Benedict's hospitality before you wear out your welcome at the rectory?"

"Yes." James gave a wolfish smile. "I was relying on you helping me with Grandmama, but as you've let me down, I must have time to think of another approach. I'll persuade Robert to ride over to Millington with me tomorrow."

Caroline glanced at him. As always, she was troubled by his frank admission that self-interest was the motivation for his actions. But considering his upbringing, it was not surprising he was so self-centred. Lady Theodora Howard, their grandmother, had opposed her son's marriage to a pretty nonentity and had disinherited him. James was seven when his parents had died of a fever. After a year or so of his being passed round various relatives, his grandmother had suddenly taken a fancy to him, and he went to live with her. She was determined to mould him into a complaint tool, but as he was as strong-willed as she, they clashed disastrously. Her methods of disciplining him rapidly deteriorated into beatings of increasing savagery, interspersed with periods of mental torture. Nothing she could do to him, however, could break his spirit, but merely fuelled his recklessness.

The childhood friendship between James and Caroline had been severed by James being dispatched to the army and Caroline, at seventeen, being forced into marriage with a dissolute man, thirty years her senior. James had embraced army life with enthusiasm; Caroline had been released from an unhappy marriage the year before.

She brought herself back to the present. They had reached the steep descent into Middle Darkleigh; a handsome farmhouse could be seen through the newly planted trees with glimpses of lawns sloping down to a small lake.

"The Harries' house," said Caroline. "They have recently extended it and made a number of improvements. George and Lucy will live over there." She pointed to a smaller farmhouse on rising ground opposing them.

"It will be a charming love nest, I've no doubt," said James sardonically.

"Have you tried to flirt with Lucy?"

"I don't try. I either do or I don't."

"How conceited you are. But Lucy can look after herself. Just leave Sophie alone. She's different."

"A challenge. You put me on my mettle."

Caroline stopped, "Then there is no need to go any further. Goodbye, James."

"Oh, don't be silly, Caroline. Just don't interfere with the way I run my life, and I won't interfere with yours. I'll merely watch with interest Robert's obvious infatuation. He's a bit young for you, but that won't worry you, will it?"

Caroline turned and half-walked, half-ran, to get away from him. James swore and ran after her, catching her arm.

"Caroline, calm down. I'm sorry, I truly didn't mean to distress you. Is that the reason why you're hiding yourself away in this backwater?"

She didn't reply and they walked on as she struggled to regain her self-possession. They arrived at her little house.

"You used to be braver," he said, gently. "I never thought I would see the day when Caroline Stanley ran away from anything."

She looked at him and said sadly, "Maybe not Caroline Stanley. But Caroline Firth is a very different creature."

"Aren't you going to invite me in? Even if you're angry with me, it would be far too cruel a punishment to deprive me of Mathilda's cakes."

"Yes, come in. Mathilda will be pleased to see you. I really don't know why."

"A woman of great perspicacity. And you can tell me how Caroline, Countess of Firth, has been entertaining herself in her retreat."

* * *

Polly Brown stood at the table of the kitchen in the Chantry. It was a large room, low ceilinged, dark and gloomy as it was built into the side of the hill and little light filtered through the small window. She was serving Sunday dinner to the cook/housekeeper, Mrs Bryant, the butler, Mr Crane and Mr Freeman's valet, Simkins. It did not please Polly to be waiting on her fellow servants, particularly as they showed no gratitude and were uniformly silent and morose.

Polly had worked hard all week under the direction of Mrs Bryant and Mr Crane, but other than a string of orders, there had been no conversation. They did not talk between themselves and meals, eaten in a forbidding silence, were preceded by a long prayer and concluded by an even longer one. Polly was sorely tempted to leave, despite the good wages.

She sat down and quickly ate her own food. One bonus for working in the Chantry was that Mrs Bryant was a good cook. The meal finally over, Mr Crane droned his thanks to The Almighty who, thought Polly, must be as bored by it as she was. After clearing the dishes, she could escape for an hour.

The previous day, this precious hour had been occupied by an enjoyable reunion with Robert Latham in a pretty clearing in the woods above the house. It had helped to restore some self-esteem in Robert and for Polly, well, as she explained to him, he always was her favourite young gentleman. She was tempted to repeat the experience and to this end, slipped out of the Chantry garden and stood in the lane, a false picture of rural innocence, where she knew she could be seen from the rectory garden. Today, however, no-one was seated under the beech tree so there could be no casual movement by Robert away from the group and into the woods with her.

Disappointed, Polly couldn't decide what to do. She didn't want to return to the Chantry; Mrs Briggs was sitting outside her cottage but, unusually, Polly had no heart for a set-to with the old lady. She was tired. Rarely had she been worked so hard, but it was the atmosphere in the Chantry which oppressed her. Whatever her other faults, Polly was hardworking, and she regarded the normal banter and jokes with the other servants as part of the reward. The silent, withdrawn domestics employed by the Freemans chilled her. The first day, she had chatted away in her usual fashion, but this had provoked disapproving looks and, in the prayer after dinner, a diatribe against levity and gossiping.

She had hoped that things would improve when the master and mistress arrived, but Simkins proved as unapproachable as the other two. As for the Freemans themselves, Polly felt a sort of pity for anxious, wishy-washy Mrs Freeman and something close to fear of Mr Freeman. The previous evening, as she was clearing the dining room, Mr Freeman had returned and in his syrupy voice, had questioned her minutely on her family. Although he had smiled at her as he interrogated her, she found his large, cold eyes unnerving. She escaped from the dining room, determined in future to avoid Mr Freeman at all costs.

But Richard Freeman was another matter. Like Sophie, Polly had never seen a more handsome boy and she could not get enough of looking at him. With her mouth hanging open, she would feast on his beauty. He was something so exotic, so different from anyone else she had seen, that her usual sensual impulses were not aroused; just to look at him was enough.

Aimlessly, Polly took the path by the river to Middle Darkleigh and soon cheered up as she ambled along daydreaming about Richard Freeman. She was therefore surprised and delighted when she came upon him sitting motionless on a fallen tree trunk. He was looking intently into the stream and thus unaware of her presence until, greatly daring, she gave a little cough. He looked up, startled, but then smiled and, putting his finger to his lips, pointed down at the stream. In a muddy pool, lay an eel about five feet long. Polly let out a squawk and backed away.

"Ee, Mr Richard, you'd best come away from that nasty thing."

"It won't hurt."

"Oi'm not so sure about that."

"Come and look at it properly. Come on."

"If ee don't mind, Oi'll stay here."

He laughed. "Then I shall bring it to you."

He jumped off his tree trunk and snapped off a twiggy branch and with a quick scoop, lifted up the eel and held it above the stream. It writhed and Polly screamed again and ran some yards away, watching in horror, her hands to her mouth, as it wriggled and rippled.

This increased Richard's laughter. "You really are scared, aren't you, you stupid girl."

With a larger, convulsive move, the eel disentangled itself from the branch and slip back into the water and out of sight.

Polly sat down abruptly. She was ashamed of her fear. But the picture of the creature being out of its element, dangling and twisting in the branches, and held aloft by the beautiful, laughing boy, had upset her and she didn't know why.

"There, it's gone," he said and threw the branch away. He added, scornfully, "I thought country girls weren't frightened of things like that."

"Oi've never seen one of them things before."

"It's an eel. It's harmless. Come and look at it again."

Polly approached cautiously and peered into the stream. The eel lay barely discernible, browny-yellow in its dark mud pool. She stooped down, curiosity at last overcoming her fear.

"Do you see it?" asked Richard, standing behind her. Then he shoved her large, round bottom with his foot and toppled her into the stream. Shocked and angry, dripping with wet mud, she crawled back onto the bank. She sobbed and coughed and spluttered and cursed him. But he was running away, up into the woods and his high-pitched laughter echoed across the valley.

Polly shook out her dress, dirty now beyond even her minimal standards of cleanliness, and trailed back towards the Chantry. Her usual cheerful face was ugly with fury. She would get her own back on him, that she would, even if she died for it.

Chapter Four

Mr Latham's scruples, sharpened by thoughts of Mr Freeman's strictures on the observance of the Sabbath, had prevented him from allowing George to apply for Lucy's hand on the Sunday afternoon. George was therefore to attend upon him at 11 o'clock the following morning. Robert had no desire to become involved in the inevitable subsequent celebrations and seized upon Major Howard's suggestion that they should ride over to Millington Hall to call upon Benedict Rivers.

Sophie listened enviously as they made the arrangement over breakfast. It was so much easier for men to escape. Their desertion, temporary for the moment, would soon be permanent. Major Howard had made the contact he wanted with his cousin and his stay at Knight's Darkleigh must therefore be drawing to a close. Robert would disappear somewhere, sometime as it would be impossible for him to stay with his parents in a state of ever-increasing tension and animosity. In a few weeks, Lucy would be married and gone; Miss Lucy Latham would be transformed into Mrs George Harries, a different person in a different family with a new life. And she, Sophie, would be left. She sighed.

"Why the despondency, Miss Sophie?" asked James Howard.

"It's envy, though I shouldn't say it."

"What of? Surely not of Lucy marrying George?" asked Robert incredulously.

"No, oh no. But of course, I'm sure they'll be very happy," Sophie added hastily.

"Of course," echoed James gravely. "Then who are you envying? Surely not Robert and me – two war-weary soldiers with no money and no prospects? You should pity us, not envy us."

"Our only skill, that of avoiding being killed, no longer of much importance," contributed Robert, mournfully.

"True," James sighed deeply. "So, what can we do?"

"Marry heiresses?" suggested Robert.

"Perhaps the only thing left for us. Unfortunately, finding heiresses takes time and patience."

"And what if they're not very attractive?" asked Robert.

"Ah, the larger the fortune, the more beautiful they are."

"No father in his right mind would allow the likes of you two near his daughters," said Sophie.

"You are too harsh," said James. "Look at us: two upstanding young men back from vanquishing the tyrant, both of good character, with no vices…"

"Or virtues, either!" interjected Sophie.

"Sophie, how can you say such a thing?" asked Robert.

"It is a challenge, though. What are our virtues?" asked James.

There was a pause.

"A good seat on a horse," offered Robert.

"That's a skill, not a virtue," said Sophie.

"All right, define what you think are virtues," said Robert.

"Honesty, kindness, dutifulness, patience…"

"They seem a bit dull," said James. "Perhaps the vices do suit me better."

"But the Seven Deadly Sins all need money to be supported. So, we're back where we started," said Robert. "Ah well, as Sophie has been no help at all in organising our future, shall we make a start before we get involved with George coming and everything?"

"George isn't seeing father for another hour," pointed out Sophie.

"He might be early – you never know. Love's winged feet, or something."

"Then we had better go, as the last thing our hacks have is winged feet."

Sophie watched and waved goodbye to them as they rode down the drive. She was going to miss them dreadfully when they left for ever.

* * *

George duly presented himself to Mr Latham; Mrs Latham cried a little and Lucy cried a little and even Sophie, affected against her will by the sentimental occasion, felt a slight prickling in her eyes.

George and Lucy were a handsome couple, each the physical foil for the other, thus feeding the vanity which was the mainspring of their natures. Sophie, watching them smile at each other, thought how pleased they were with themselves and wondered whether this was something peculiar to George and Lucy or general to all couples who became betrothed.

George departed soon after on a lovely, highly-strung horse which jibbed and pulled under his heavy hands. When he could look down on Middle Darkleigh, he paused, just as James Howard and Caroline Firth had done the day before.

Below lay Manor Farmhouse, above it, Hill Farm which was to be his and Lucy's and the scattering of neat, well-kept cottages. All exuded prosperity and one day all would be his. He would start to call the farmhouse 'the Manor' and he thought it would not be long before everyone else, except perhaps a few backward cottagers, did likewise.

The Harries' of the Manor, Middle Darkleigh. He liked the sound of that, and he smiled as he clattered down the steep slope to the ford. Then he thought, *I like the idea of George Harries of the Manor even more*. Well, when Anne and Mary were married and he and Lucy had some children, it would seem sensible for his parents to go into the smaller house. Life stretched ahead and looked good for George.

He was so absorbed in his dreams (by the time he reached the ford, he had added another wing to the Manor) that he didn't become immediately aware of Richard Freeman, who was lounging gracefully against the rail of the tiny footbridge.

The nervy horse refused to go into the water and Richard laughed. George glared at him, but the boy looked back at him with guileless, smiling eyes.

"He's a beautiful horse, sir," said Richard and George's annoyance dissolved under the lad's admiration. He gave a gracious nod.

"Just trying him out. M'father gave him to me as a welcome home present."

"You were at Waterloo?" Richard's voice was filled with respect.

"Oh yes. Hussars, you know. Horse shot under me in the first charge." George had satisfactorily buried the humiliation of an ignominious fall from his horse long before they were under enemy fire and now firmly believed this more heroic version of events.

"I wish I could go into the army," said Richard wistfully, "but my father says I must go into the church."

"Not quite the same," agreed George.

He nodded farewell and persuaded his reluctant horse to start walking through the ford. When he was level with the boy, he looked down at his upturned face and, unable to resist the engaging smile, smiled back. George was not used to such wholehearted hero-worship and was charmed by it. He hoped he would meet up with the boy again. His men had been surly under his unpredictable command; exasperated with the way he vacillated when decisive action was needed but was reckless of danger to them when he should have exercised caution. He did not have the common touch and was either condescendingly hearty or, more usually, unpleasantly arrogant in his dealing with his inferiors. His equals and superiors in the regiment had tended to avoid him but George, armour-plated in his self-satisfaction, was entirely unaware of his unpopularity.

Richard watched George ride away. He gave a little crow of laughter, leapt over a wall and into the meadow and ran along the stream back towards Knight's Darkleigh.

* * *

In the parlour of Manor farmhouse, a vigorous discussion was in full swing. Miss Anne Harries, never one to let a good idea of hers go to waste, had persuaded her parents that despite Mr Freeman's strictures, a small gathering of friends to celebrate George and Lucy's betrothal and to welcome the heroes home, could not be regarded in any way as a function of wicked depravity. Her mother also took the point that if the Harries' pre-empted the Lathams in celebrating these momentous events, they would undoubtedly score in the social stakes. The discussion was on the tricky problem of who was to be invited.

George, arriving with a beaming face, was loudly congratulated and enthusiastically hugged by his mother and sisters. Mr Harries called for wine to toast his health and future happiness and there was great noise and laughter, and it was all rather different from the restrained and lachrymose scene he had endured at the rectory. Delighted as he was, having won Lucy's hand, he could not help but think that he was doing her a considerable favour in introducing her to his really rather splendid family.

Mary called them to order. "So far, we have ourselves, the Lathams, the Cantrells, the Agars, the Harpers and Mrs Brigstock. Now, do we or do we not invite Major Howard and Mrs Firth?"

"He's not a particular friend of mine," said George.

"But we can't not invite Mrs Firth, she being his cousin," said Mrs Harries.

"Don't see why not," said George. "Seems a pleasant enough lady."

"And Major Howard seems a pleasant enough man," retorted Mary.

"It would seem," said Mr Harries, who had been listening with amusement, "that the ladies would like to invite Major Howard, but not Mrs Firth, and George would like Mrs Firth to come, but not Major Howard."

There was a moment's silence and then Anne and Mary burst forth into good-humoured laughter. George smiled sheepishly and it was agreed that both would be invited.

"What about Mr and Mrs Freeman?" asked George.

"They won't want to come, not after what he said," said Mrs Harries.

"I can't imagine them enjoying it," agreed Anne.

"Worse, they would make sure we didn't either," said Mary.

"It seems a bit hard on the young lad," mused George. "Besides, may not be the done thing. I mean, not to invite them when they are new to the district."

"I suppose we should invite them, then," said Mrs Harries, who found etiquette difficult to grasp and was ever anxious not to commit some terrible social solecism.

"I suppose we can ask them, and hope they don't come," said Anne, and Mary put the Freemans on her list and counted up.

"That will be thirty-two in all," she declared.

After further discussion, it was agreed that if they sent out invitation cards that day, the party could take place on the coming Saturday, the short notice excusable in view of the spontaneous nature of the occasion.

* * *

On their way to Millington, Robert regaled James with a description of Mr Freeman's diatribe on the wickedness of parties and all forms of entertainment and added, "And next Sunday we are going to be told all about the Spiritual Barometer. I can't wait to hear it. I think the man is an out and out humbug. You wait until you meet him."

"I've trespassed long enough already on your parents' hospitality. I really shouldn't do so much longer, though I confess Mr Freeman sounds irresistible."

"He is. But so far as my parents are concerned, please don't worry. Your being here keeps us all civilised." Robert's face was bleak as he thought of his parents.

After a little while, he said, "I had the stupidity and tactlessness when I was about eight to say to my mother than I preferred my aunt Emily's company to hers. I had always spent quite a bit of time with my aunt and uncle; they were childless, and it seemed that my aunt would never produce, so I was regarded as the prospective heir to Sibley, and my aunt and uncle were close to adopting me. My mother was jealous of my affection for my aunt but accepted it because of the inheritance.

"Then to everyone's surprise, my aunt produced Harry. My mother seemed to believe this was a personal insult and quarrelled with Aunt Emily and I was refused permission to go to Sibley when I was invited. The quarrel became more and more acrimonious and inevitably drew in my father and uncle, and it was decided that it would be preferable for my father to resign as curate of Sibley and move to another parish a few miles away.

"I said loud and long that I didn't want to move from Sibley and from my uncle and aunt and in the middle of an angry exchange with my mother, said the unforgivable words. And, of course, I have never been forgiven and never will be. In my mother's mind, every misfortune they have suffered is as a result of that. She is unshakeably fixed in the notion that it was my fault that she quarrelled with Aunt Emily which meant they had to leave Sibley and thus, instead of inheriting that very comfortable living when the aged incumbent died, my father had to move away from his family's sphere of influence and hence the gradual but inevitable decline in their fortunes.

"And now they are left with me crippled and pretty well useless and I really don't know what to do," Robert sighed. "I apologise. I don't usually bore people with family history. Maybe I'll go abroad and make my fortune in India or wherever, as far away as possible."

"It does have its attractions," said James. "To live in England with expensive tastes and no money, is constricting."

They were riding through a field of ripened barley; in the distance, stooping figures collected the sheaves in the wake of a line of men who, with neat, economical strokes, scythed through the glowing barrier of stalks stretching to the horizon. The golden sun of a September morning poured down on the toiling figures.

"The trouble is," added James, "I really do not want to live anywhere else. I just need money. Without it, our lives are as constrained as those labourers over there, never changing, stuck forever in a rut."

"You exaggerate. Things do change; they are changing all the time. With the new ideas in agriculture, these people will stop being peasants tied to particular parcels of land. They will be labourers free to move to better masters if they wish."

"Robert, you're being a sentimentalist. What happens is that the new improvements meant that fewer labourers are needed and so they're thrown off the land into the cities, penniless and starving."

"Are you saying that there should be no change, no improvements?"

"No, they've started and can't be stopped. People like Mr Harries will see to that."

"This is his land, I believe," said Robert. "It looks as if he's going to have a very good harvest."

"A pity his obvious efficiency hasn't been passed on to George."

"I suppose when Lucy marries George, Sophie is going to be left, stuck as you say, in a rut."

"I think Caroline should be able to help there," said James, who like many selfish people, firmly believed that everyone else had a duty to give a helping hand to those in need.

Robert had spent every waking hour of the past twenty-four hours thinking about Caroline Firth, so he seized on this.

"Mrs Firth? How could she help?"

James laughed. "I'm sure you don't believe the story that she's the impoverished widow of some tradesman?"

"No, it didn't seem likely."

"I told her yesterday she's going to have to drop that pretence so I don't think I'm betraying a confidence. Anyway, Benedict knows her. She's the Countess of Firth."

"Oh." Robert's heart sank. She was completely unattainable.

"Her late husband was a despicable creature and my beloved grandmother and her spineless daughter and son-in-law forced Caroline to marry him when she was just seventeen. She was sold to the highest bidder, and by God, she had to pay for it.

"Fortunately, Firth died before he completely destroyed her. He forbade her to see me, but we occasionally managed to do so. We grew up together and although we quarrelled frequently, we were united by our feelings for our grandmother, so the bond was close. Although she's said very little about it, I know she was abominably treated by Firth and there was nothing I could do to help her."

They rode on in silence, each absorbed by his own thoughts. Robert was in despair. Caroline Firth was part of a world that he would never be able to aspire to, and it was pointless his even dreaming about her. He immediately fell into a fantasy of having met her some years previously and with great derring-do, saved her from her wicked husband. He knew, while he daydreamed that he was being ridiculous, but it was pleasant all the same, and dreams would be all he would ever have.

James' thoughts did not veer off into fantasy. One solution to his penury would be to marry Caroline but it would be disastrous as they would end up quarrelling unceasingly. He had too much affection for her to prejudice their friendship. He looked sideways at Robert's gloomy face and unable to stop himself, said laughing, "There you are: Caroline could be your rich heiress. All your problems solved."

Robert gave him a furious look; lips tightly pressed together in a thin straight line. James cursed himself. He should have known better than to joke with a besotted lover.

"My stupid tongue. It was a silly thing to say."

"Yes."

They went on in silence until they reached a vantage point where the countryside opened out before them. The view was quite exceptional; immediately below them, the ground fell steeply down to a twisting, shining river and steeply rose again on the other side. Opposite them, on a promontory made by a wide loop in the river, stood a huge, many-gabled house, its walls rising sheer from the rocky outcrop: a fortress secure from invaders. Beyond, the land rose and fell in comfortable curves, gentle undulations in striking contrast to the dramatic plunge of the river valley.

"That's Millington," said Robert.

"Oh, lucky, lucky Benedict. I envy him this from the bottom of my heart."

Robert laughed. "So do I." The constraint between them disappeared as they moved on.

"Is Mr Rivers married?" asked Robert. "I'm not sure why but I've somehow assumed not."

"You're right. When he was a poor, struggling barrister – it's all comparative as he was always better off than me – he was far too shy of the ladies to even think of marrying. I wonder whether he's changed, now he has all this."

"Perhaps we should introduce him to Sophie," said Robert, to show he really could take a joke about marrying money, provided it did not refer to Caroline Firth. "Or Mary and Anne Harries, of course."

"Those two would eat him for breakfast. One could not be so cruel."

They laughed and conversation turned to another form of hunting as a fox shot across the road in front of them.

The approach to Millington Hall was through high, rusty gates into a drive which led its winding way through a tunnel of overgrown trees, opening out before the house into a wide circle. Everywhere there was evidence of neglect: stones were missing from the roof, the mullions of the windows were cracked and damaged, and glass was missing from many of them. Grass had been cut roughly, as a meadow rather than a garden.

As James and Robert rode up, two men were standing in the centre of the circle, looking up at the roof. They turned as the riders came near and the taller of the two, a slightly built fair-headed man with a long thin face, cried out, "James! What on earth are you doing here?"

James swung off his horse and he and Benedict Rivers gripped each other's hand, laughing with pleasure at their reunion.

"Pure chance. I'm staying with Robert here – may I introduce you – Robert Latham, Benedict Rivers. My cousin, Caroline Firth, has rented a house close to Robert's parents in the Darkleigh Valley. Caroline mentioned you were here, taking stock, you lucky fellow."

Benedict groaned: "Welcome to Castle Threadbare. There is so much needing to be done, I don't know where to begin. Josiah was just telling me that the main roof timbers have dry rot, wet rot and death watch beetle and on top of those, the tiles are crumbling away. My uncle and his father can't have spent a penny on repairs in fifty years."

"Poor Benedict," said James, unsympathetically. "The problems of being a man of property. Not something I would know about."

"Still fighting your grandmother?"

"If a total lack of communication can be called fighting, yes. I came to these parts in the hope that Caroline would intercede for me, but there is no communication between them, either."

"How is your cousin?"

"Very well. She would, I'm sure, be pleased to see you."

"How kind." Benedict looked anxious. Then he said, "But come along in."

Josiah had summoned a stable lad to take the horses. Benedict thanked him and added, "Look, you know what needs to be done and who would be best to do the work.

Carry on and get it done as quickly as possible. If we can get the house watertight before winter, at least that's a start."

Josiah beamed. After so many years of suffering under a grudging penny-pinching master, he still could not believe his good fortune. Robert was amused to note that Benedict's diffident manner and general air of indecisiveness was merely a façade.

They went into a cool, cavernous hall and into the library, a lofty room with long windows looking out over the valley. As if drawn by a magnet, James and Robert went across to them. Immediately below them, the rocky crag plunged down to the river in a dramatic fall.

"No one seems able to resist that view," said Benedict behind them.

"It's amazing," said Robert.

"And it's all yours, as far as the eye can see?" asked James.

"Pretty much so. Some of the land is poor and all, of course, is badly neglected, like the house. Come and see the rest of it, if you dare risk the woodworm."

Benedict's enthusiasm for his inheritance meant a protracted tour of the house, gardens and stables, and a major part of the five hundred acres of the home farm, to James' protestations. Robert was fascinated by the house and James' complaints were ignored as he and Benedict enthusiastically discussed improvements.

They adjourned for lunch, Josiah's wife producing a meal consisting of an enormous quantity of cold meats, fresh bread, and ale.

"This is perfection," said Robert, leaning back on his chair, replete.

"Delighted you came over. After six weeks of inspecting dilapidated buildings and decrepit tenants, I was in need of company. I hadn't realised how much."

They left, with some reluctance, shortly after, having extracted a promise from Benedict that he would come over to Darkleigh on Thursday. Benedict, in turn, made James promise that he would join him the following week. Robert listened wistfully and then consoled himself with the thought that the rectory was considerably nearer Middle Darkleigh than Millington Hall.

Benedict's easy, untidy male household reminded him of life in his regiment and as they rode back to Knight's Darkleigh, he was afflicted with nostalgia for a lost way of life.

* * *

Mid-afternoon, and Sophie had managed to escape from the wedding preparations upon which Mrs Latham and Lucy had embarked the moment George had departed. As she walked up the valley to Middle Darkleigh, she realised that she was still unaccountably upset with Major Howard's deviousness and she wanted some sort of reassurance, though quite what, she couldn't work out.

Caroline greeted her with warmth.

"I understand that Mr George Harries and your sister are now formally betrothed. I hope they'll be very happy."

"How do you know?" asked Sophie, surprised.

"This," said Caroline and handed Sophie the carefully written invitation she had received shortly before Sophie's arrival.

"Goodness, they've been quick!" said Sophie. "Mother is going to be upset." Her heart sank at the thought of Mrs Latham's Hurt Feelings.

"I suppose they've upstaged your parents." But Caroline was unable to repress a laugh. Sophie smiled reluctantly.

"It's stupid, I know, but my mother is inclined to take offence." She struggled to be loyal. "She's suffered so many slights over the years and perhaps sees them now when they aren't intended. She is very easily upset and that affects her health."

"Oh, poor Sophie."

"Never mind. Anyway, it will be such fun to have a party. And how brave of the Harries' to do so in the teeth of Mr Freeman's opposition."

"Oh?"

"Of course, you didn't hear Mr Freeman telling us yesterday of the evils of parties and idle frivolity."

"Tell me more." Which Sophie did with gusto. Hearing Caroline's laughter, she thought perhaps Mr Freeman would not be able to cast a total gloom over the valley as she had so fearfully imagined.

After Mathilda had produced tea and delectable cakes, Sophie said, "This is so pleasant. I must confess I've escaped from wedding preparations. Mother and Lucy are enjoying arguing over every conceivable detail. Robert and Major Howard escaped much earlier this morning to go to Millington Hall."

"Ah, to see Benedict Rivers."

"Do you know him?"

"Yes, indeed. He stayed two or three times at my grandmother's house when we were children. Poor boy, he had to act a peacemaker between James and me as we quarrelled over the slightest thing. We still do," Caroline added ruefully. "Yesterday was the first time we had seen each other in two years and within half an hour, we were arguing. He's arrogant, selfish, and unprincipled. He says I'm interfering and bossy and off we go at each other."

"You seemed to be very pleased to see each other yesterday."

"We were. We're very fond of each other; we just don't see eye to eye most of the time. It really is very stupid, but at least we usually make amends, as we did yesterday.

"One of the few things that unites us is our feelings for our grandmother. And I know James is here because he wants to persuade me to see her and try to beg her to give him what is rightfully his. He'll cajole me into going to Cheltenham and she will be rude and spiteful, and it won't be the slightest use as she won't change her mind, and it'll end up with me being upset and annoyed."

She broke off, nearly in tears. "Oh, Sophie, you just can't conceive of anyone like my grandmother. She's excessively rich, excessively mean, and excessively unpleasant."

"Goodness," said Sophie, inadequately. "I had been curious as to why Major Howard had come here and perhaps unreasonably annoyed that he was using my family."

"Oh, you had every right to be. He should be my grandmother's heir but years ago, she said she had disinherited him, she would not support him, and she would never change her mind. As time has gone by, various relatives and advisors have summoned up the courage to suggest to her that this is wrong, but she's always refused out of hand to reconsider.

"The main property is in Hampshire, in the New Forest. It's a beautiful house in a beautiful setting looking across the Solent to the Isle of Wight. James was banished from it when he was sixteen and I think it almost broke his heart. I can entirely understand that he wants to regain his inheritance, but he shouldn't use people the way he does in his pursuit of it. While he was in the army, his grievance was pushed into the background; but now, what has he got to think about? But let's forget James and his problems as I have a confession to make."

Sophie stared at her in surprise.

"It's alright, it's nothing too dreadful. It's just that I'm not Mrs Firth. I'm the Countess of Firth. James said yesterday that I should drop the pretence, though truly it wasn't really a pretence. I merely said my name was Firth and everyone assumed I was plain Mrs Firth. And I said I had come down from the North of England, which was true, but again everyone assumed that it was from one of the big cities and therefore my husband had been in trade. And as I wanted to live in a very modest house, the assumption was that he had died leaving me in straitened circumstances. I wanted to live quietly, and these misunderstandings meant that I was able to do so."

Sophie blinked as she adjusted to all this.

"But Mrs Firth," she said and stopped in confusion. "My lady, I mean. Oh dear."

Caroline laughed. "Please, call me Caroline. I really refuse to allow you to even think of calling me 'my lady'."

"It does seem a little grand for this little house."

"Much too grand. Quite ridiculous. I suppose I shall have to let it out as unobtrusively as I can."

"Major Howard, Mr Rivers and, I expect, Robert, by now, all know who you are so it won't be long before it's widely known. Mrs Harries will be overwhelmed with having a real Countess at her party."

"Oh dear," Caroline shuddered and Sophie laughed.

As she took her leave, Sophie said: "One thing I'm grateful to Major Howard for, and that is his kindness to Robert. He helps him so easily and casually without making any fuss, but he notices when Robert needs assistance and can give it at times when, if I tried, it would be humiliating and it would be resented."

"That's James at his best. He does have his good points, though often they're hard to find."

Caroline watched as Sophie walked away, a slight figure in an old-fashioned dress, but her thoughts were on Robert Latham. James' taunt about his being too young for her had touched a raw nerve.

Over the years, she had become used to young men falling in love with her and she had become adept at letting them idolise her until their infatuations had run their course, leaving nothing but friendliness on both sides. Her jealous, suspicious, and evil-tempered husband was always watchful, and he was reason enough for her never even to think of embarking on an affair. She had been truly frightened of him and only Mathilda knew how she had suffered through her marriage. The day he had died was the happiest day of her life. For months after his death, unable to adjust to the intensity of the relief in no longer having to live in perpetual terror, she had slept and slept as the long healing process began.

It therefore was not surprising that when she re-entered society, she allowed herself to respond to a handsome, charming young man and she still burned with humiliation at how she had let herself become so foolishly infatuated with a fortune-hunter, ten years her junior.

She had woken up in time, but not before her acquaintances had gleefully observed her folly. Unable to face the mockery, she had fled to Middle Darkleigh and now, even in this backwater, there was another attractive young man, apparently enchanted. Six months ago, she would not have questioned the sincerity of Robert's feelings, but now she was much more wary and on her guard.

James, it would seem, had heard the gossip; it was hurtful that even after four months, their mutual acquaintances were still talking about her lapse, and it meant she would remain out of London for some time to come.

As she went indoors to reply to Mrs Harries' invitation, she smiled at the thought that she, who was used to moving in the most exalted circles in the land, was now looking forward to the bucolic delights of the Harries' party.

* * *

Sophie thought about Caroline Firth as she walked back to Knight's Darkleigh. She wasn't surprised that Caroline was a member of the high aristocracy: pleasant and friendly though she was to everyone, there was a definite air about her that set her apart. But she had no idea why Caroline had come to the Darkleigh Valley. Sophie felt that under the charm and seemingly unforced humour, there was a sadness, and she could only assume it stemmed from the death of her husband. And yet, Caroline never mentioned him. Maybe the loss was so unbearable that she could not speak of him. But that didn't ring true. Sophie was a little ashamed of her curiosity and walked on more briskly. Her absence would soon be commented upon, but as she drew near the turning to Millington, she slowed down to look up the track.

She saw, with some consternation, that Mr Harries had taken matters into his own hands by fencing in the strip of disputed woodland. He had cleared enough of the undergrowth to make it accessible but had left sufficient ground cover for the pheasant with which he had now stocked the wood. Mr Harries, she thought, was determined to become the epitome of the sporting squire. It would be yet another thing to irk her parents.

In the distance, she could just see two horsemen approaching in a cloud of dust and she waited for them, delighted that her secret wish had been granted.

As Robert and James drew near, the sun behind them outlined them in gold and she was infused with a happiness such as she had never felt before. The two men looked down at her radiant sun-washed face and smiled with her.

"Why are you looking so pleased with life?" asked Robert.

"No particular reason," she said and looked down in some confusion. There was warmth in Major Howard's bright blue eyes, which was having a devastating effect on her heartbeat.

She said quickly, "I've been admiring the way Mr Harries has fenced in the woodland before the Rector could do so."

"He doesn't miss many tricks, does he?" agreed Robert. "George should have some good shooting this winter."

"I hope he's a better shot than he is a horseman," murmured James.

"Mr Harries has bought him a beautiful horse as a welcome home present," said Sophie as they moved on.

"Don't rub salt in the wound," said Robert. "What a waste."

"Don't be unkind," said Sophie. "George is so proud of it. He and Lucy have become engaged, of course, so talk at home is entirely of wedding preparations."

"I'm going to enlist. I won't be able to bear it," said Robert, striking an attitude.

"The Harries' are indeed having their party, despite Mr Freeman, so you must wait until after Saturday. Mrs F—, I mean Caroline, she's asked me to call her Caroline," Sophie said with some pride, "showed me the invitation she's just received from them."

"And she proposes to go?" asked James, amused.

"I believe so. It will be the pinnacle of Mrs Harries' career to have a Countess in her home so she will have to endure being treated with awe."

"So Caroline has told you who she is," said James.

"Yes." Sophie darted a quick glance at Robert's gloomy expression and then looked up at James and saw the amused understanding in his face. She said hastily, "Did you have a good day with Mr Rivers? What is Millington Hall like? I've only seen it from across the valley."

"It's beautiful, utterly neglected and needs a fortune, which luckily Benedict now possesses, to put it right. I believe he showed us over every rotting inch of it, encouraged I may say, by your brother who rivalled Benedict in enthusiasm for the tottering heap."

"I'd love to see it; it looks so romantic."

"Benedict is coming over on Thursday. We'll ask him then."

"Oh dear, I really didn't mean to suggest that I was… I was…"

"Angling for an invitation?" said Robert. "Sophie, we may believe you're not scheming to ensnare the County's most eligible bachelor, but we can't be too sure."

"Don't be horrid," said Sophie, crossly.

"No-one would ever suspect you of such intentions, Miss Sophie," soothed James. "And I'm sure Benedict would be delighted to show you his house."

"And he may fall in love with you anyway," added Robert.

This remark did not please either of his companions.

* * *

The Harries' invitations were all delivered by late that afternoon and, with the exception of Mrs Latham and the Freemans, were received with unequivocal pleasure. The Harries' were noted for their generous hospitality and the reasons for the impromptu party were ones that all could happily celebrate.

As Sophie had expected, Mrs Latham was outraged at what she saw as the Harries' wicked plan to demean the rectory family by holding this party.

"It is vulgar and unnecessary," she fumed and retired to her bedroom with instructions that as soon as Sophie returned, she was to go immediately to her mother.

Sophie endured some minutes of complaint about disappearing whenever she was needed but was allowed to be forgiven by brushing Mrs Latham's hair. The threatened migraine receded as Sophie gently brushed and soothed by agreeing that Mrs Harries perhaps did not understand social niceties.

"Lucy will be able to help her and George's sisters," said Sophie. "Just as you have been able to explain them to us."

Mrs Latham was pleased with this flattery. She had a vision of herself as the arbiter of taste in the combined Latham and Harries families. The vision faded as she remembered that Mrs Harries had never taken any advice from her during the past five years and her spirits were again lowered by the thought that this situation was unlikely to change. Mrs Harries had not disguised her opinion that Mrs Latham was an ineffectual, complaining woman who, as the daughter of a mere attorney, gave herself airs and graces above her station.

Mrs Latham put her hand to her head. Sophie decided that if a migraine was inevitable, then she might as well get some news which would be unpalatable to her mother over now.

"I went to see Mrs Firth, this afternoon."

Her mother stiffened.

Sophie went on quickly, "You know you've always said that she is a lady of taste and refinement."

Mrs Latham had never said any such thing; her opinion was that Mrs Firth was cold and reserved and had an unsympathetic nature.

"So," said Sophie, "you will not be surprised that she isn't just Mrs Firth. She is the Countess of Firth."

Mrs Latham sat bolt upright. "The Countess of Firth," she said incredulously. "The Countess of Firth. What, pray, is the Countess of Firth doing here?"

"I don't know. She's recovering from the death of her husband, I suppose."

"He was one of the richest men in England," said Mrs Latham. She lapsed into thought and then with a wail, said, "And Mrs Harries will be having the Countess of Firth to her party!"

With that, she burst into tears and had to be helped to her bed by Sophie.

* * *

"It will be a worldly, pleasure-seeking occasion," pronounced Mr Freeman.

Mrs Freeman said nothing. She sat on the edge of her chair and waited. Years of marriage to Mr Freeman had taught her that silence was her only option. If she were to say that she would like to go to the party, she would be berated for her lack of moral fibre. If, on the other hand, she said she did not want to go, she would be accused of being socially incompetent. So, she said nothing.

Mr Freeman gave one of his long-suffering sighs.

"All around me I see wickedness and vice. It's a hard struggle I wage against the forces of Satan. And yet I must persevere. I must not be disheartened in my solitary fight, my lonely battle against evil. I must be the sword; but I must also be the shield. I must be the protector against the ravening wolves of sin. To shirk this duty would be very wrong. I must be positive and go forth into the den of iniquity and use all my strength to purge, to cleanse, to purify it."

Long acquaintance with her husband's oratorical style enabled Mrs Freeman to interpret that they were to go to the party. She was pleased, though no-one seeing her pale, anxious face would have realised it. But did that include Richard? For herself, Mrs Freeman was never able to summon up the courage to ask her husband directly for anything, but for Richard: that was different.

"Do you think Richard should go?" she asked timidly.

"It is a problem, I confess. It is wrong for him to be tempted and sullied by pleasure, particularly in view of the calling to which he is destined. But if he never comes face to face with temptation, how is he to be tested? How is his moral strength to be tempered, to be perfected?"

Mr Freeman pondered deeply. "Yes. I have decided. Richard should come as well. You may reply to the invitation accordingly."

Dismissed, Mrs Latham left her husband's comfortable study and went to her dark, shabby little sitting room. She sat at her writing table and dutifully wrote her reply. Twenty years ago, she had been a pale, anxious young woman whose only attraction was her small fortune. Now she was a pale, even more anxious, prematurely aged woman whose fortune had long since been dissipated by her husband. She lived in a state of silent despair, her only joy, her beautiful, changeling son. She could not admit even to herself that Richard showed her little respect or affection and that he had caused her unceasing worry with his strange moods and spiteful nature. She fiercely believed that it was just boyish high spirits, thwarted by his father's ponderous moralising, that made him as he was; that with a less heavy hand upon him, he would be a normal, carefree, happy boy.

She went in search of him to tell him about the party. He made little response in her presence, but as she went back to her room, she heard high, excited laughter.

Polly, wearily cleaning windows in the dining room, also heard him and scowled.

Chapter Five

Mrs Latham's migraine lasted for the rest of the week. Sophie had to be the dutiful handmaiden to her afflicted mother and apart from breakfasts with Robert and James, her days were spent in numbing boredom. She would watch enviously as the two men disappeared off, exploring the surrounding countryside and returning via Caroline Firth's cottage to sample Mathilda's baking. For both men it was a pleasant escape from having to consider their futures and for James also, an escape from Lucy.

As the days went by, Lucy was finding that her awareness of James Howard was increasing with an almost unbearable intensity. Even though she realised the impropriety of her behaviour, she was unable to prevent herself making small physical contact with him. If he held a door open for her as she left a room, she contrived to brush against him. They seemed to meet surprisingly often on the stairs, and it was impossible not to touch as they passed. James was all too aware of the effect he was having on her and as he found her soft, curvaceous body very much to his taste, the temptation she was presenting to him did try him sorely. He just hoped that the other members of the Latham family did not see what was happening. He felt it was fortunate that Sophie had to spend so much time with her mother as he had come to respect her clear-eyed observation of those around her.

There was a respite from Mrs Latham's migraine on the Thursday, which enabled her to leave her sick bed and to meet Benedict Rivers, but it returned with renewed severity as soon as he left. Mr Rivers had been silent and awkward with Lucy and Sophie and had departed with James with all too obvious relief.

As he and Benedict rode over to Middle Darkleigh to call upon Caroline, James said, in some exasperation, "You really do not change, Benedict. You were terrified of those two girls. In heaven's name, why?"

"It's all very well for you. You have always been able to say the right things. I just get tongue-tied and angry with myself which makes it worse. Do you think I like sitting like a dummy in front of such a beautiful girl?"

James blinked at his vehemence.

"Miss Latham is betrothed, Benedict," he reminded him.

"I'm not talking about Miss Latham," Benedict said scornfully. "Miss Sophie, of course."

James blinked again.

"Of course," he echoed.

"I'm not saying that Miss Latham isn't very pretty, as indeed she is, but Miss Sophie is something quite different, quite exceptional." Benedict turned to look at James and his usual good humour re-asserted itself as he saw James' stunned expression and he laughed.

"I'll grant you she has considerable charm," said James and then stopped and shrugged. "Anyway, here we are at Middle Darkleigh, the domain of the Harries family."

Caroline greeted Benedict with easy friendliness and his anxious look receded as they indulged in childhood reminiscence.

"And Slepe is all closed up?" he asked.

"Yes," James said bitterly. "Grandmother does not want to live there herself and doesn't want anyone else to, either."

The frustration he felt ebbed and flowed as ceaselessly as the tides of the Solent that swept passed Slepe. At that moment, it was in full flood, and he realised that pleased as he was for Benedict's sake with his good fortune, he felt a sour envy, which if he let it, would poison their friendship.

Caroline said dreamily, "Do you remember the time you took the rowing boat out one night and you vanished for all the next day and no-one knew what had happened to you both."

"How could we forget?" asked James, glad to be diverted from his thoughts. "We were trying to prove our theory that the tides were of identical strength and therefore we would get back to Slepe before dawn."

"It would seem you forgot little factors like the wind when you made your calculations," said Caroline.

"I was convinced," said Benedict, "that the wind followed the tide, but I've no idea where I got that particular idiocy from."

He smiled as he remembered the enchanted moonlit world as they had been borne away silently on wind and tide down the Solent, past the Beaulieu River and on to Calshot Spit. And then the long, hard row back against a freshening westerly wind. James, always the physically tougher, had done the lion's share of the rowing. And had endured the beating when they had returned wet and exhausted and starving in the late afternoon.

"Caro," said Benedict, impulsively, using her childhood nickname without thinking, and then stopped.

"Oh, all right, I will," she said, exasperated and angry with herself for weakening. "But it won't be any use. She will probably refuse to see me."

"You mean, you will go to see grandmother?" James was unable to believe his ears.

"Yes."

"Dear Caroline," he kissed her. "You truly are my favourite cousin and I love you."

"I have three conditions," she said.

"Anything you want."

"First, you go to Cheltenham and find out where she is staying. Second, you find suitable lodgings for me. And third," she stopped. "And third, you persuade Mr and Mrs Latham to let Sophie come with me."

"The first two conditions are no problem at all. The third may be more difficult. I accept."

They solemnly shook hands as they had as children when entering a pact. Then they all laughed, and Mathilda brought in tea and a formidable selection of cakes. Benedict Rivers had always been a favourite of hers; his thin figure a challenge to her motherly instincts and she considered it her duty to feed him up. She hustled out into the kitchen and she and Fred agreed that it took one back seeing those three together again.

When he returned to the rectory, James sought out Robert and found him in the cellar, fury in every line of his body as he tried to disentangle fishing line and tackle with one hand.

"There are times when life is impossible," he said.

"An hour ago, I would have entirely agreed with you," said James, who carefully did not make the mistake of offering to help. "But things are happening and I've come to ask your assistance."

"Oh?"

"Caroline, may the heavens bless her, has agreed to see my grandmother. She is the only person of whom my grandmother takes the slightest bit of notice, so I have to put my faith in her. It means I must go to Cheltenham tomorrow. Would you like to come? We could stay overnight and be back on Saturday for the great party."

"I'm not sure but that I'd prefer not to go to it," said Robert, grumpily.

"It's partly in honour of the returning heroes, remember. That's us."

"Oh no. We're merely minor attendants; background for the Great Hero, George."

"Very likely. But never mind that. Will you come to Cheltenham and help me look for grandmother and find lodgings for Caroline?"

"Oh yes, of course."

"Now, the other condition that Caroline has laid down is that Miss Sophie goes with her. Will your mother be well enough to allow her to go?"

"Probably not. We'll have to see what we can do. Sophie deserves a treat."

"Maybe Miss Lucy could help," James said, doubtfully.

"I somehow don't think so," Robert grinned. "I say, could you hold this line for me? I want to get that weight through there."

* * *

On receiving Caroline's polite little note the next morning, Mrs Latham instantly said that it was quite impossible for Sophie to go to Cheltenham. Her fragile state of health would not permit it, and she was surprised that Sophie could be so unfeeling as even to consider abandoning her mother at this time.

Sophie drooped with disappointment. She could see no way to persuade her mother to change her mind.

However, Lucy also received a note: this was from Mrs Harries asking if she and Mrs Latham would like to spend a day, early the next week, to discuss furnishings for Hill Farm and to go into Cirencester and choose materials. Lucy bridled at the thought of Mrs Harries having a say in how she should decorate her home, but a basic shrewdness told her that she would get her own way far more easily by seeming to be compliant, rather than conflicting with those who, no matter how generous they were, held the purse strings.

Mrs Latham was torn between wanting to join the furnishing discussions – since her opinion as Lucy's mother should be of great importance – and continuing to be the suffering invalid, with Sophie anchored to her side.

Mr Latham added to her dilemma when he said, "It is a great compliment that Lady Firth has befriended our little Sophie and if you do feel able to spare her, I'm sure she will be a credit to her upbringing. Perhaps she will also meet Lady Theodora Howard." The titles rolled pleasurably off Mr Latham's tongue. He added, "It cannot go unnoticed that of all the young women in this valley, Lady Firth has found Sophie the most congenial."

Lucy sulked for a while on hearing this, but the excitement of setting up her own home and the suggestion by George of a wedding trip to London were sufficient for her soon to ignore Sophie's doings.

Robert added the pressure on Mrs Latham by saying, as he bade her goodbye before leaving for Cheltenham, "I wonder what the Harries' will think when they hear that Sophie has been invited to be Lady Firth's companion. Anne and Mary have always been condescending towards Sophie, so this will be some revenge for her."

Mrs Latham looked thoughtful, and Robert said to Sophie as he and James were leaving, "Don't say anything, but I think mother is preparing to change her mind. Another day and she will be convinced that you should go to Cheltenham."

Sophie gave him a hug and said, "Thank you, oh thank you, I do so want to go."

She waved goodbye to them from the front door, just as she had done the past few mornings but this time, James happened to look back and laughed when he saw her dance a little jig of joy. She stopped, blushed and then laughed, waved and vanished indoors.

She was definitely charming, thought James, and he liked the way she treated him with unaffected friendliness. Indeed, he enjoyed looking at her face with its changing expressions and she had lovely eyes. But was she beautiful, as Benedict thought? He, himself, had immediately seen Lucy as the beauty and Sophie just as a pretty girl, whereas Benedict had considered Lucy as a somewhat commonplace pretty girl and Sophie as something special. He felt an unprecedented loss of confidence. Was he only attracted to the superficial and the easy? Then he shrugged. He had never had any difficulty in attracting any woman who took his fancy and when he recalled some of the luscious, accredited beauties who had undoubtedly found him agreeable, why was he worrying about the merits of two country girls?

* * *

Mrs Latham did indeed spend a thoughtful twenty-four hours. She was inclined to refuse to go to the Harries' party, saying that her health would not permit it and of course Sophie must stay with her. She lay propped up on her pillows on the Saturday morning and contemplated her unhappy situation.

People really did not appreciate how ill she was. Lady Firth had been most thoughtless and unfeeling to have asked for Sophie's company when her mother was in such distress. A tear rolled down her cheek. The weather had at last broken, and she looked out through a gauze of scudding rain on a dismal landscape. Another tear rolled down her face as she reminded herself of how much she hated this valley and how neglected she was by everyone.

It was fortunate that before she could sink into total misery, Sophie and Lucy appeared. Lucy, oblivious of her mother's woebegone face, said: "Mama, I want to wear this dress tonight, but Sophie says I should wear that one. What do you think?"

Mrs Latham looked at the bright blue dress Lucy was holding against herself and the cream one on Sophie's arm and although she sighed, a discussion on what they should wear that evening was really rather more interesting than being a solitary sufferer. She sat up straighter and, forgetting the fadeaway tones she had used for the past five days, made her decision.

"Sophie is right. You should wear the cream."

Lucy pouted. "It's so old. And this one is much more striking. Anne and Mary will be wearing new dresses, and this blue will really show up against them."

"No it won't," said Sophie. "It will look as if you are all fighting for showiness."

"It really must be the cream," said Mrs Latham. "But why not have a sash or some ribbon to give it a little colour. Sophie, let's see what we've got in my sewing box."

Sophie carried the box over to her mother, saying: "What am I going to wear?"

The morning passed very amicably in deciding what they all should wear and without noticing it, Mrs Latham committed herself to going to the party. She discovered in the back of her closet a dress in a very pretty silver blue which suited Sophie, and they happily continued into the afternoon, reshaping it to make it a little more fashionable and to fit Sophie's slimmer figure. Lucy trimmed her dress with her favourite pink ribbon, and they chatted and laughed as they sewed.

"Do you realise," said Sophie, "that it's only a week ago yesterday that we went into Cirencester and saw Robert and Major Howard arrive on the coach? It seems much longer, as if they've been home for weeks, not days."

Lucy was standing, looking out of the window. A week ago, she and Major Howard had looked at each other in a way which made her shiver when she recalled it. Had she been too precipitated in becoming betrothed to George? If Mrs – Lady – Firth was able to persuade his grandmother to make Major Howard her heir, he would be rich, he would not need to marry money. He was attracted to her, of that she had not the slightest doubt, and she was just as sure she could fan the interest into something more. She slid over the snub in the churchyard as something she must have been mistaken about. She felt a strange excitement at the thought of dancing with him at the party organised to celebrate her betrothal to George.

As she looked down the garden, she smiled a secretive smile and watched Major Howard and Robert, damp and muddy on their tired horses, ride up the drive.

Chapter Six

"Is Cheltenham very elegant?" asked Sophie.

She and James were in the drawing room, attired in their party best, waiting for the others to appear.

"Yes, it was a surprise to me how attractive it is. My grandmother is ensconced in a pleasant house in the Royal Crescent, to the north of the Royal Well and I've hired lodgings for Caroline and you, I trust, in the Royal Parade, to the south of the Well. An easy distance apart, but not too close, was my intention. Very tactful of me, I thought."

"Oh, indeed, remarkably so," said Sophie, her eyes twinkling.

He laughed. "Miss Sophie. I can always rely on you to mock my pretensions."

"Maybe tactful was the wrong word. A military manoeuvre would be more accurate, perhaps? Positioning your troops for the final assault."

"A very accurate analogy. No wonder I feel as if I'm on the eve of battle," he sighed. "Ah well, we will see whether Caroline manages to melt that stony heart. If grandmother has a heart, which I often doubt. But never mind that, tonight we are going to celebrate the heroes' return and the alliance between two of the important families of this valley. I'm looking forward to this major event in the social calendar."

"Don't jeer at our country ways," said Sophie, nettled by his tone. "You have, no doubt, been to many grand occasions, but for us, it's a special and important one."

He was silent. Unhappy that she had damaged the easy friendship between them, she said, "I'm sorry, that was unnecessary of me."

"No, no, it's for me to apologise. I did not mean to sound condescending. It's just that I can't help thinking it's going to be a strange mixture of people."

Happy to meet him halfway, she laughed and said, "You are very right. And I can't wait to discover whether the Freemans have been asked – and whether they will be there."

"I hope they are. Robert has whetted my appetite to meet Mr Freeman."

Robert appeared and they waited for the others, reading and chatting in a desultory manner.

"Come on," muttered Robert after about fifteen minutes. "Why does it take Lucy twice as long to dress as it does you, Sophie?"

"Because it is twice as important to her as to me," said Sophie and added a little wistfully, "and the effect it has, twice as good."

It was an opportune moment for Lucy to appear, and she looked ravishing.

"I see what you mean, my poor Sophie," said Robert, laughing. "You look splendid, Lucy. George is a lucky fellow."

Lucy acknowledged his compliment with a gracious nod. She knew she deserved it and waited for Major Howard to say something. But he just smiled appreciatively, and she sat down on the sofa next to Sophie. He wondered whether she had done so in order to use Sophie as a foil. But she did look lovely and there was no denying he wanted her. Despite Benedict, Lucy was definitely the prettier of the two though he would be the first to admit that so far as character was concerned, Sophie shone in a way that self-absorbed Lucy never could. But as his relationships with women were almost invariably based on physical attraction, personality was of minor importance.

Mr Latham bustled in, for once the expression of petulant irritation was absent from his face and he even looked the proud, fond father as he looked down on his daughters. In an emotional voice, he said: "My little Lucy has grown up while I haven't been looking and now, suddenly, she is to be married." He bent down and kissed her, and this very rare demonstration of father affection brought tears to Lucy's eyes, which added to the charming picture she presented.

"I'll go and see if mother needs some help," Sophie said and slipped out of the room.

* * *

Jarvis Harries stood with his back to the fire and surveyed with huge satisfaction his family and his guests. The extensive alterations to the house had included enlarging what he was used to calling the parlour but must now remember to call the drawing room, making it a very handsome room. It was, he reckoned, nearly twice the size of the rectory drawing room. He had refused to allow his wife to raise the ceiling or change the ancient, mullioned windows for new sash ones, but he had allowed her to install a smart new fireplace, so the room was still snug and comfortable and, much to his taste, a happy compromise between the old and the new.

The same, he thought, could be said for the guests: old friends and new mixing agreeably and enjoyably. He looked indulgently at his cheerful, good-natured daughters and his comfortable wife, all in new dresses of dazzling colours – large, homely birds in exotic array. The old friends, he was pleased to note, could not rival his family in the elaborate details of their dresses.

Lady Firth was talking to Mrs Brigstock, whose face was going red and whose voice was becoming more raucous, and he frowned. Widow of a sea captain Mrs Brigstock might be, and flattered that they had been to make her acquaintance when she first came to Laine, but now she was becoming an encumbrance, her coarseness in embarrassing contrast to Lady Firth's quiet elegance. She was smiling at something Mrs Brigstock had said, and Jarvis was annoyed with himself for not having immediately appreciated how handsome and how much the great lady she was. He, like everyone else in the valley, had made the wrong assumptions and had consequently been blind to her undoubted quality. His daughter, Mary, appeared at Lady Firth's side and he was suddenly aware that Mary's strident, fussy dress was quite, quite wrong.

He looked across to George, who was trailing around after Lucy like an overgrown, very happy puppy. George was, of course, unaware that Lucy's progress inevitably led to Major Howard, who was standing with Robert Latham. Again, Jarvis recognised the restrained good taste of Major Howard's coat, compared with George's expensive but showy one. Lucy, he was pleased to note, looked good enough to eat. His family, if they wanted to improve their social position, must cultivate the tastes of their new friends.

Major Howard, escaping Lucy's attentions, joined Jarvis.

"George tells me, sir, that your wife is from Cheltenham. Robert and I have just come back from a brief visit; it is a handsome town."

"And growing fast, Major Howard, growing fast. Where my wife lived as a child in the country is now one of the best parts of that town. And all because of the springs. Did you take the waters while you were there?"

"No," said the Major, firmly. "I did not think I had the need."

"Quite right, quite right. They taste so dreadful, one has to be at death's door to force a glass down."

"Either that, or like my grandmother, convinced that if something is unpleasant, then it must be good for you."

"Strange how many people's philosophy that is. Not mine, I may say. I like people to be happy and then I believe one gets the best out of them."

"That is certainly the case this evening, sir."

"Thank you, Major." Jarvis beamed with pleasure. Robert joined them.

"Well, young man," said Jarvis heartily. "It's good to see you again."

"It's good to be home again, sir," said Robert politely. "I've been admiring the improvements you've made to the house."

He could not have said anything that would have pleased Jarvis more and he was promptly invited to a tour of the house.

James gracefully declined the invitation and went to rescue Caroline from Mrs Brigstock.

He need not have troubled, as his cousin was enjoying Mrs Brigstock's stories of some of the outlandish places she had been to on her husband's ship. Gradually, the group around Mrs Brigstock extended as Lucy and George and young Richard Freeman joined it, and they listened in enthralled silence as Mrs Brigstock graphically described how she had helped fend off pirates in the South China Sea.

"I was so angry," she said, "that they dared to try to board my Dick's ship, that I picked up a sword and the next thing I knew, I was in the thick of the fighting. And I've got a scar to prove it."

Lucy and Mary shuddered as they were shown the puckered red wheal on Mrs Brigstock's large arm. Richard Freeman stared at it with an intense fascinated interest.

"Still want to be a soldier, my boy?" asked George. "That's the sort of injury you could suffer."

Richard looked up at him with a strange shining look and then smiled, and again, as at their first meeting, George was unable to resist it.

Lucy turned towards James and in the confidential voice she was inclined to use when speaking to him, asked whether he had suffered any injury in the war. Hearing the insinuating tone, Caroline turned away to hide a smile and caught Mrs Brigstock's shrewd and very knowing eye. She hastily looked away and was dismayed to see Sophie obviously in some distress.

Sophie was having a dull party. Mrs Latham may have allowed herself to be persuaded to go to the party, but she was not yet reconciled to the idea of Sophie going to Cheltenham and had insisted upon Sophie sitting next to her "in case I find it all too much for my nerves." Sophie therefore found herself trapped in a corner of the room, unable to do anything other than watch the chattering groups. Mrs Freeman, with a timid smile, came to sit next to Mrs Latham and proved to be an exceptionally good listener. Within five minutes, Mrs Latham was pouring out all her woes and as Mrs Freeman seemed honoured and flattered that she should be the recipient of these confidences, they were soon on their way to becoming firm friends. Sophie sat bored and a little sorry for herself but when Mr Freeman loomed over her and drew up a chair in front of her, she couldn't feel that this was in any way preferable.

The Harries' were generous hosts, liberal with their wine and brandy and Mr Freeman was enjoying the latter with relish.

"Well, Miss Sophie," he said in an avuncular manner and leaned forward so that she was forced back in her chair to avoid the brandy fumes and his cold, fishy eyes. "I hear you teach the village children their numbers and letters. A laudable effort, I'm sure and well-intentioned, but I have doubts, serious, even grave doubts, about the wisdom of introducing any form of education to the lower classes. It will make them discontented with their station in life and that we must never allow. The Lord has ordained that they be labourers and that is what they should remain. The privilege of education should be received only for those in the higher echelons of society, otherwise it is merely, my dear Miss Sophie, casting pearls before swine."

Quite overpowered, Sophie managed to summon up enough spirit to ask, "But surely, Mr Freeman, they should be allowed the opportunity to learn to read the Bible?"

"I do not see the necessity. They should be guided by their betters. But why do you look so troubled, Miss Sophie?"

He leaned forward again, and Sophie felt sickened and frightened by his large, fleshy face, so close to her own. His tongue like a fat, red slug, slid over his thick lips. He put a hand on her arm, and she felt a fear bordering on terror that she was imprisoned, unable to escape from this monstrous man.

"Mama," she whispered, but Mrs Latham, deep in her conversation with Mrs Freeman, had turned away and did not hear her.

Then she heard a cool, clear voice saying, "My dear Sophie, what are you doing, monopolising Mr Freeman's attention? For shame on you!"

Caroline stood smiling down at her and Sophie could have wept with relief and gratitude at her deliverance. Mr Freeman turned round and seeing Lady Firth, hastily arose, and gave her a deep bow. Sophie was forgotten for the time being with this far superior quarry in sight. He was expertly drawn from Sophie, who felt she could not stay a moment longer in that corner. She stood up and coughed to get her mother's attention.

"Would it be alright, Mama, for me to walk around for a little while?"

"Yes, yes, child," said Mrs Latham impatiently and went back to telling Mrs Freeman the fascinating history of her migraines.

James had watched Caroline's efficient rescue mission with amusement, but he was just slightly put out that he had been less observant than she and thus slower to react to Sophie's predicament. Again, detaching himself from Lucy, who had a hand just touching his arm, he went up to Sophie and said quietly, with mock gravity, "You really should be more adept at avoiding being trapped in corner, Miss Sophie."

"I know," she said. He saw she was shaking and only then realised how upset she had been by Mr Freeman. He felt a surge of anger against the man but before he could say anything to try and comfort her, Robert and Mr Harries approached.

Robert had enjoyed his inspection of the house and had made some bright suggestions for further improvements which had impressed Jarvis.

"So you've been let out, have you, Sophie?" Robert said cheerfully. She smiled and nodded.

"Has Robert persuaded you to remodel the rest of your house, sir?" James asked Jarvis, drawing attention away from Sophie.

"He's given me some ideas I wouldn't have thought of myself, that's for sure," said Jarvis.

Overhearing the conversation, Caroline, who was wearying of Mr Freeman's unctuous compliments and was irritated by his obsequious manner, turned to join them.

She said, "I hear he did the same at Millington Hall. You should make it your profession, Mr Latham."

Robert blushed and dissolved into speechlessness under her smile.

"Not before he comes round next week to talk to me again about his idea of where to put in a back staircase," said Jarvis

"I will do that willingly, sir, as a thank you for your hospitality tonight."

"Ah, the young men home from the wars," said Mr Freeman, not wanting to be left out.

"Indeed yes," said Jarvis. "And much we have to thank them for. Without them and our Navy, we would now be overrun by the damned French."

"Our military and naval effort was, of course, of some degree of importance," said Mr Freeman. "But without our Protestant religion and without the great cultivation of our moral qualities, that effort would have been as of nought."

"I would have thought it was the cultivation of our industries and agriculture which was of more importance," said James. "They were the essential reinforcements to our military effort."

"My dear young man, you are truly misguided. Without the great fight against moral turpitude, without the guarantee of our social order, of our national greatness, all of which are ordained by God, there would have been no victory against the immoral, popish French.

"I have been privileged to fight the spiritual fight, at first at a lowly level, as a common foot soldier, shall we say, but I have risen to a position of command and I know that without the steady march of moral progress, fighting the endless battle against sin and wickedness, without these, my friends, there would have been no victory."

Jarvis was put out. Mr Freeman was denigrating the courage of his son and his friends in the long and bloody war, but remembering his duties as a host, restrained himself from retorting sharply.

"Come, come, let's not argue about it. Just rejoice that they are home. Now, where is George? I reckon we should drink a toast to the soldiers of the King. George, George, come here, my boy."

George was deep in conversation with Richard Freeman, explaining the intricacies of the manoeuvres before the Battle of Waterloo (and how his strategy would have been far superior to Wellington's) but broke off and with a good-natured smile, said, "I suppose I'd better obey the commanding officer," and moved towards his father. Lucy, he saw, was the centre of a circle of some of the more elderly gentlemen and was enjoying their admiration. He looked at her fondly: she was going to be a credit to him, of that he had no doubt.

Jarvis called for silence. After a little time, the chattering stopped, and he had everyone's attention. He stood large and expansive, with his round ruddy face and untidy grey hair, the epitome of the English yeoman. His wife and daughters had gravitated towards him, and they led the laughter at the witticisms and compliments in his little speech of welcome. The way the Harries' were so pleased with themselves was tiresome, thought Sophie, but there was no denying that they were a quite remarkably devoted family.

A toast was enthusiastically drunk to the gallant heroes and then Jarvis called again for silence.

"And now, a second toast. Lucy, my dear, come here, don't be bashful."

There was applause as Lucy, looking demure and sweetly innocent, emerged from the crescent of guests and put her hand into Jarvis' outstretched one. She was drawn into the Harries fold between Jarvis and George and was like a dark, beautiful butterfly among large, overblown roses. She captured all eyes.

"I have it on good authority," Jarvis bowed to Mr Latham, "that the Banns will be read tomorrow and all will know officially that our George has been made the luckiest young fellow in the valley. In four weeks' time, Lucy and George will be wed, and we will be the luckiest family in the valley for having such a lovely and charming girl as Lucy joining us. I know it's too early, but I can't resist saying it," he bent down and gave Lucy a hearty kiss and said, "welcome to my new daughter."

Lucy blushed and smiled shyly and then to great cheers, stood on tip toe and returned Jarvis' kiss. He gave a roar of delight, and the laughter and applause continued.

"And now," said Mrs Harries, "let us go in for supper and afterwards, for those who are young and energetic, there will be dancing. Your Ladyship, will you do us the honour of sharing our small repast?"

Chapter Seven

Robert yawned and helped himself to an apple.

"I'm getting old," he said. "All that gaiety last night, my constitution can't stand it. This is a good apple," he added as he took a large bite out of it.

"I picked them yesterday. You're suffering from eating too much supper," said Sophie, unsympathetically.

"I couldn't resist all that food. What temptation."

"I enjoyed the dancing," said Sophie. It was the first time she had waltzed and to do so for the first time in the arms of Major Howard was the ultimate in happiness. And although he had very properly stood up with Mary and Anne Harries in the early country dances, he had danced the first waltz with her. Then he had danced with Caroline and then with Lucy. Here Sophie's dreams wobbled precariously as she remembered the way those two had danced silently, a little too close together. She hoped no-one else had noticed.

"Did you enjoy waltzing?" she asked Robert.

"I was not at all happy with the idea. I was very annoyed with Anne for insisting I danced with her, but it really wasn't so bad after all."

"It was nice, dancing with you. You didn't trample all over my feet."

"What, like George and young Freeman did?" Robert laughed.

"Poor boy, he was so frightened that his father would be angry with him for dancing, he could not concentrate."

"He needn't have worried. Mr Freeman was far too keen on enjoying Mr Harries' brandy to be concerned with anything else."

The thought of Mr Freeman sent a shiver through Sophie. "I don't like Mr Freeman. I'm a little scared of him," she confessed.

"Scared of him? There is no need to be. He's an out and out hypocrite and a pompous windbag but there is nothing to be frightened of in him. The man is a fool."

Sophie did not agree but did not argue.

"And best of all," she said, "Mama has agreed that I can go to Cheltenham. I can hardly believe it. Oh, Robert, aren't I lucky?"

"You call it luck? It was a carefully planned operation carried out with military precision."

James appeared in the doorway and made his way rather limply to the table.

"Had a good party?" asked Robert, grinning.

"You might think it's Mr Harries' brandy that's my problem this morning, but you would be wrong. It was dancing with Miss Anne and Miss Mary. What energy!" He groaned. Sophie and Robert laughed.

"A military man vanquished by two mere females," said Sophie. "It's a sad sight to behold."

"Mere females!" he said in a broken voice. "I have never met anything their like before. My self-esteem drained out of me as they instructed and bullied me through the dances."

"They always do know best. And are so wretchedly good-natured when explaining to you how you've gone wrong. As if to an idiot," said Robert, remembering.

"You poor, feeble creatures," said Sophie. "But never mind that. Tell me how you persuaded Mama to let me go to Cheltenham."

"We let her talk herself into it," said Robert. "We made sure that she and Mrs Harries were together and then I mentioned to Mrs Harries that Lady Firth had invited you to go with her to Cheltenham."

"And I said how much Caroline was hoping you would be able to go," said James. "Ever tactful, I asked Mrs Harries if I had chosen the right part of town for your lodgings."

"Mrs Harries said it was quite the best area and she was obviously furious that it was you and not one of her girls who would be able to boast about it in the future. So, she said that it was a pity that mother wouldn't be able to spare you, meaning of course that she hoped she wouldn't. Of course, mother had to say that you would be going and before she could change her mind, James told Lady Firth, who thanked mother in such a way that it made it seem that she and mother were on the same social level and therefore it was right and proper and natural that it should be you that would accompany her. Mother became very gracious indeed and that was it. Mission accomplished."

"Not entirely," said James. "Caroline then had to soothe Mrs Harries' ruffled feathers. I'm not sure what she said but it worked well enough as Mrs Harries definitely preened herself afterwards."

"And I will accompany you," said Robert, happily.

He had been unable to summon up the courage to ask Caroline to dance with him and was bitterly regretting his cowardice. But to be in attendance on her for three or four days was a reward beyond his wildest dreams.

Sophie was surprised. "But what about you, sir?" she asked James.

"Caroline says I would be a hindrance rather than a help. That if grandmother knew I was in Cheltenham, she would insist on seeing me and that would be that. Caroline is probably right," he added grudgingly, "so I will do as arranged – go and stay with Benedict and await news. It is not a situation I'm going to enjoy."

"Your fate in the hands of two women," said Robert.

"Something like that. I think by Thursday, I shan't be able to stand it any longer and will persuade Benedict to go with me into Cheltenham." That wouldn't be too difficult, he thought, if Benedict knew Sophie was there.

Sophie was pleased. When James had said that he was going to stay with Benedict Rivers, she felt a sudden piercing sense of loss. He was going and perhaps she would never see him again, other than fleetingly. Never again in the easy, informal way that she had so much enjoyed this past week.

Robert stood up and stretched.

"I must give myself some air before having to listen to Mr Freeman and his moral crusade."

James and Sophie watched as he went out through the front door and walked down the lawn: a tall, upright figure, still thin but less haggard than he had been a week ago. They had both observed that he had not asked Caroline Firth to dance with him.

"What's he going to do?" she said, thinking out loud.

"Become the expert in remodelling houses. Practice on Mr Harries and Benedict as a start and then do it on a professional basis."

"Do you think he could?"

"Of course. He's got a gift."

"Wouldn't it be terrible, though, if the house fell down because he didn't know enough about building."

"That would be no problem. He'd just explain that it had been in imminent danger of collapse, and it was fortunate that he was there to oversee the rebuilding."

"Would you let him loose on your house?"

"Oh, yes. If I ever do get Slepe." He lapsed back into gloom. "Ah well, according to Mr Freeman, all I need is to say I have moral authority and then all will be given to me."

"Did he really mean that?"

"It's what he said. It seems a very easy philosophy to me. All you have to do is to convince people of your moral superiority and then you can do what you like."

"Like chiding the Harries for suggesting having a party and then not only coming, but also eating and drinking more than anyone else."

"Precisely. It's splendid. He gets the best of all worlds."

"I don't think it's splendid at all."

"Ah, but then you allowed him to overawe you."

"Yes. I don't know why he frightened me so. I was sitting next to my mother in a room full of people I know, and yet he made me feel helpless and terrified." She hung her head, embarrassed at having admitted this so openly.

"It's not surprising. He's very skilled and very practised at dominating."

"Robert thinks he's a fool. I don't think I do."

"No, he's not a fool. He's a cunning, self-indulgent hypocrite."

At that moment, Mr Latham came in and heard James' last words.

"Good gracious, Major, who are you talking about?"

"Mr Freeman."

Mr Latham gasped. "Those are very strong words to use, Major, and especially of one who professes a great and energetic faith."

"In my opinion, sir, Mr Freeman may profess those things but he doesn't practice what he preaches."

Mr Latham was aghast. "But he is preaching today, in an hour's time, in the church. And you are suggesting he is unworthy to do so. I can't believe it: his moral principles are so firm, so definite."

"All I suggest, sir, is that you consider what Mr Freeman says and what he does. I myself, am going to listen to his description of the Spiritual Barometer with great interest."

"Oh dear, I really don't know what to think." Mr Latham wrung his hands.

Sophie felt sorry for him. He did so hate having to make judgements or decisions.

"Never mind, Papa, it's too late to do anything about it now. The good thing is that Mama and Mrs Freeman seem to be becoming good friends."

He cheered up. "Yes, it will be good for your mother to have another sympathetic friend."

"I feel sorry for Mrs Freeman, she looks so anxious," said Sophie and added, inconsequentially, "and their son is so handsome but he seems very shy."

"Shy?" queried James.

"Yes. But no, that's not the right word. He's wary, as if ready for flight. Oh dear, I can't explain it, but he is a little strange, I find."

"You were the only one he danced with," said James and Sophie was delighted that he was sufficiently interested in her to observe such things.

"Mr Freeman had strong words to say about waltzing," said Mr Latham.

"I'm sure he did and does about anything that gives pleasure to anyone other than himself. It's no wonder his son is so scared of enjoying himself," said James. "He must have learnt to be a little sly."

"I'm sure you're wrong. The lad has an open and honest look," said Mr Latham.

* * *

Mr Freeman stood, large and impressive, in the pulpit holding in his left hand, unfurled down the front of the pulpit, a long sheet of paper on which there was drawn an elegant stick barometer.

"You will observe, my friends," he boomed, "here at the highest point is written the word, glory. Here," he tapped with a long pointer, "at the lowest, is death and perdition."

There was complete silence as he looked down at his audience, broodingly, assessing where each member fitted into the scheme.

"And the barometer falls steadily and inexorably if one indulges in such evils as theatre going, parties of pleasure, wine and spirits, levity in conversation, love of fashionable clothes."

He hit the paper as he spoke in a steady beat, like a drum.

"Behold here, halfway down this terrible decline, is the sin of indifference and thus begins the side down into neglect of family worship. You may think that coming to church once a week is enough. But you would be wrong, dreadfully wrong. My friends, to worship as a family on Sundays only is the start of catastrophe: it leads to the omission of private prayers and then of family religion altogether. And that, as we all know, my friends, inevitably means death and perdition."

A larger thwack than ever made everyone jump. A considerable proportion of the congregation were feeling the effects of the Harries' hospitality and Mr Freeman's thumps were painfully received. Considering that he had imbibed rather more than most, there was also a vague feeling of resentment that he seemed not to be suffering at all, and indeed radiated energy and life.

"In order to prevent this terrifying descent into the abyss, it is necessary to always fight for moral progress, to stamp on wickedness and sin, to show people the errors of their ways and to guide them back to the paths of righteousness. It is for their own salvation that they must be persuaded, exhorted, and rebuked. This, my friends, is what, in all humility, I do here today.

"All I ask, is that you remember that you must be forever on your guard, to prevent lapses into the yawning chasm of indifference to the great moral standards ordained by the church. I am here to be your guide. Trust me, my friends, and I will lead you on the straight and narrow way to glory." This was roared and the pointed thumped the barometer with tremendous vigour. He took out his handkerchief and mopped his brown, overwhelmed by his own oratory.

"Yesterday evening, I shared in the celebrations for the home-coming of our young men from the War and the betrothal uniting two of the families of this parish. I may tell you, my friends, that I wrestled for many hours, weary, lonely hours, to decide whether I should join the merriment or whether I should avoid the risk of contamination."

There was a distinct stiffening in the Harries' pew. Mr Harries folded his arms and looked grimly up at Mr Freeman.

"But I decided my duty lay in joining the celebrations, to observe the demeanour of those present and to be there as a spiritual leader in the case of need. My presence would, I felt, be a shield and a sword against the pitiless might of sin and temptation. It was indeed a joyous occasion, a blessed occasion, my decision was vindicated, thanks be to God.

"Finally, my dear friends, I have many inspiring pamphlets developing my theme this morning and for a modest, a very modest sum, they are available to all who wish to join the great crusade. Amen."

"A very remarkable sermon," said James gravely to Mr Freeman who stood at the porch door, waiting for congratulations. Mr Freeman bowed in acknowledgement, but he was too experienced a speaker not to be aware that his peroration had been unenthusiastically received by his audience.

He was used to such a response. He would cast his net wider to other parishes in the neighbourhood. There was sure to be one which had a leading family zealous to join his moral crusade and who (for a while) would be happy to contribute to his expenses as their guide. The Lathams and the Harries', he accepted, were not of that inclination: the Lathams from lethargy and the Harries' from too great an enjoyment of the good things of life. In a few years' time, Mary and Anne would be likely material when their natural bossiness increased with age and their youthful good nature decreased, but at present it was not worth trying to rouse enthusiasm for a spiritual life in the Harries' family. Besides, if they embraced it too warmly, it would inevitably mean a loss of a nearby source of remarkably good food and wine.

Jarvis Harries was still looking annoyed and his wife bewildered. Robert went up to them and said, smiling, "Thank you for your hospitality yesterday. I don't know when I enjoyed being contaminated more."

"Ha," snorted Jarvis. "If he thinks he will again eat and drink us out of house and home after that, he's got another think coming to him."

Mrs Harries had not understood much of Mr Freeman's sermon, but native wit – and Jarvis' scowl – had told her that it was not entirely complimentary.

"I reckon we didn't ought to have invited them," she said. "Though to be sure, Mrs Freeman and the lad seemed to appreciate it. So did he, so why is he now saying he shouldn't have come. I don't understand."

"Don't you worry about him, my dear," said Jarvis. "Look, here comes her ladyship."

Caroline made her thanks and compliments in such a way that Mr Freeman's aspersions became of little significance. If the widow of an Earl had found all that was right with their hospitality, who was a mere Mr Freeman to cast doubts? Other people came up to add to the chorus of thanks and Caroline and Robert moved away.

"Why did you not ask me to dance last night, Mr Latham?" she asked, teasing him.

"I didn't have the courage," he admitted.

"For shame on you. You selfishly deprived me of pleasure."

"Would it have been?" he asked eagerly.

"Now, how do I know whether it would or not – you wouldn't let me find out."

"Then I promise I shall ask you at the Assembly Rooms in Cheltenham."

"Oh, so you propose that we go to them, do you?"

"We'll have to do something to celebrate the success of your mission."

"And if it doesn't succeed?"

"Then to cheer us all up instead. But you will succeed, I'm sure of that."

"I wish I had your confidence. I have very little hope of success. Every appeal to grandmother's generosity has failed in the past, so why should it succeed now?"

"Then don't appeal to her generosity. You must find some other way, be as ruthless as she. Attack her where she's weakest."

"You know, I hadn't thought of that. I admit, it does open up possibilities. Though putting undue pressure on one's grandmother cannot be regarded as anything other than morally questionable."

"It will mean a big fall in the Spiritual Barometer. Does that worry you?"

"Not at all."

"You disappoint me, ma'am," said Robert in mimicry of Mr Freeman. "Grievously, sadly, there is a want or moral leadership in our aristocracy. It is a tragedy and one that I, in my own unworthy way, must do all that I can to avert. A hard task, a challenge, but one that I will not shirk."

Caroline struggled not to laugh out loud. "Please don't, I really would be in utter disgrace to be caught giggling in the churchyard. I think it would take a large number of Mr Freeman's tracts to redeem me."

"That would be a foretaste of perdition."

James joined them, holding one of the tracts.

"Look," said Caroline, "James has been won over to the side of the righteous."

"A conversion bordering on the miraculous, I would have thought," said Robert.

"Mr Freeman pressed it into my unwilling hands. He thought I was persuadable to his shoddy morality."

"It was the rapt look on your face, as he preached. It was most convincing, I thought," said Robert.

"Oh good, you saw the look of an earnest seeker after truth. One of my more useful accomplishments, I have found, but to be used sparingly."

"What with Mr Latham here suggesting I should somehow blackmail my grandmother and with you admitting guile and deceit, I feel that Mr Freeman's sermon has fallen on stony ground," Caroline said.

"Blackmail?" James looked at Robert with approval. "What a splendid idea. But there's a problem; she may be a disagreeable bully, but she is the soul of icy rectitude. No falsehood, and certainly no kindly white lie, has ever passed her lips. No scandal has ever been attached to her name. She is quick to attack other people's mistakes and misdeeds but very careful never to be seen to make any herself."

"An impregnable fortress, in fact."

"Yes. But Caroline has a thoughtful look in her face. What will your strategy be?"

"I don't know. Why I let myself in for this, I just do not know."

Chapter Eight

Two days later, as she waited to be ushered into her grandmother's presence, Caroline was still thinking about the same thing. Why had she allowed herself to be persuaded into being James' emissary? She felt very alone and vulnerable. Robert and Sophie had walked with her to Royal Well and, waving cheerfully, had left her at her grandmother's door while they carried on to investigate the delights of Cheltenham.

Her grandmother, of course, kept her waiting. Her heart thumped and her hands were hot and sticky, and she was back to being twelve years old and terrified of the coming ordeal.

Simes the butler appeared. He was another figure from her past that she would have preferred not to have had to meet again. His face was its customary inscrutable mask, but she knew the depth of the disapproval that lay behind it.

He preceded her up the flight of stairs.

"Her ladyship has suffered an injury," he said portentously.

"I'm sorry to hear it. I trust nothing too serious?"

Simes reached the curve of the stairs and turned to look down on her. The disapproval seeped out.

"A housemaid spilt some boiling water on her ladyship's hand. She has been in considerable discomfort but has borne it with the fortitude her ladyship has always shown in the face of adversity."

"I'm sure she has." Caroline translated this to mean that her grandmother was in a vile temper, so this visit was going to be a complete waste of time. She scowled at Simes' rigid back as he continued up the stairs. As usual, he made her feel that it was all her fault.

She took a deep breath as he opened the door and announced, "Lady Firth, my lady."

Lady Theodora sat large and unmoving in a huge wing chair, one side of an empty fireplace. A damn chilliness pervaded the lofty room but despite her injury, Lady Theodora was not going to succumb to the comforts of a fire until it was absolutely necessary. She preferred to save on the outrageous cost of fuel by adding another layer of clothes, black upon mountainous black. Hunched over, she had more than a passing resemblance to a vulture.

"I am sorry to hear of your injury, ma'am," said Caroline, walking towards her and curtseying.

Her grandmother grunted. "Hm," and lapsed back into unmoveable silence.

Caroline was left standing, awkward and unnerved. It was a deliberate ploy and one which her grandmother used successfully many times before. She saw Lady Theodora's left hand, lightly bandaged, lying upon the arm of the chair in such a way that it cried out to be noticed, to be the recipient of much sympathy. As Caroline looked at it, a long slumbering rage and resentment woke within her, and with it, the knowledge of how she was going to fight this dreadful old woman.

Calmly, she sat down in a small chair opposite Lady Theodora's throne-like one. The black eyes glared.

"I do not recall inviting you to sit down," she grated.

"You will recall that one result of your selling me to Firth is that I am the widow of an earl. You may be the daughter of an earl, but you are the widow merely of a knight. I think, therefore, that precedence allows me to sit."

"You are impertinent. Any more of this and I will summon Simes to throw you out."

"Oh, I don't think you will." She stood up and unloosed her cloak and let it fall. Before her grandmother's furious stare, she turned her back and allowed her dress to fall, joining her cloak in a heap. Lady Theodora could see, in the small of her back the letter 'F' burnt into her skin. It was about three inches high, and it showed red and puckered on the smooth white skin.

Still with her back to her grandmother, Caroline said, "You will see, grandmother, that I do understand how painful your burn is. This is what Firth did to me on our wedding night. 'I brand my cattle,' he said, 'so why should I not brand my wife?'"

Her voice shook with remembered pain and fear. She took a deep breath and quickly drew her dress back on. She was shivering and she wrapped her cloak tightly around herself as she sat down.

"He tied me down on the bed and used a poker." She looked at her grandmother and leant forward as if to put her hand on the bandaged one. Her grandmother gave a little squeak and snatched it away.

Caroline leant back and laughed. "Don't worry, I won't touch it. But I'll tell you what Firth did after that. He untied me, turned me over on my back and lay upon me." She shuddered. "I'll spare you further details. But now you know, if you didn't anyway, what sort of man you forced me to marry."

"I didn't force you to marry him. Your parents…"

"My parents. They were too frightened of you to dare go against your wishes. Ever. And your wish was to marry me off to that evil old man."

"He was a man of impeccable pedigree. How was I to know…"

"That he was a sadistic horror? Oh really, grandmama, are you trying to tell me that you, with all your connections and knowledge of the world, that you did not know anything about his reputation?"

"I may have heard one or two rumours. But that was all they were. Rumours, unsubstantiated rumours, nothing more. He was a great catch for you."

"I begged and begged you not to make me marry him. Why did you insist?"

"It's all a long time ago. Why do you bring this up now, when I'm not feeling well? It's all in the past."

"That is too easy. Do you really expect me to forgive and forget?"

"What do you mean?"

"You made me marry Firth to spite James. I doubt if we would have married, but to make sure, you sold me off as quickly as possible to a rich, unpleasant old man – the complete antithesis to James."

"Nonsense. That had nothing to do with it. Firth demonstrated that he adored you – the fortune in clothes and jewellery he lavished upon you. He was proud of making you worthy of being the wife of one of the greatest noblemen in the country. But you didn't give him what he most desired, did you? You failed to give him a son."

"I failed to give him a son?" Caroline laughed harshly. "Does it not occur to you that it might have been his fault?

That despite the pleasure he got out of beating me – oh, he did that frequently – he could not… he was impotent."

Her grandmother was silent. But for once, it was not the silence of formidable power.

"I came today to suggest that it was time you gave Slepe over to James."

"Never. Never."

"I think I can make you change your mind."

"Do you indeed. Huh."

"You pride yourself that, unlike other people, you do not make mistakes. You do not commit the follies and stupidities of ordinary mortals. You believe implicitly that your judgement is always, always right. You enthusiastically point out to people the foolishness of what they have done. To put it vulgarly: you rub their noses in it and seem to find enjoyment in humiliating them. I don't think you realise how many people you have hurt and angered in this way and therefore how many people would be very happy to see the great, censorious Lady Theodora humbled and mocked.

"You're contemptuous of mothers who have not been able to marry off their daughters, and you crowed when you were able to ensnare Firth for me."

Lady Theodora shifted in her chair but otherwise gave no sign that she was listening.

"So, if it now comes to light that he was the sort of man that no-one in his right mind would let near a young girl, the question must be asked: why did Lady Theodora allow such a match? There must have been a good reason, some pressure – even blackmail, perhaps? – to force the great Lady Theodora into selling her granddaughter.

"But that's ridiculous, the thought of anyone trying to blackmail the upright Lady Theodora. But a whisper goes around that there had been a liaison between her ladyship and Firth. That ever-popular subject of mockery: the older woman and the younger man… she would have wanted to keep that quiet, wouldn't she? Maybe it is old history, but so amusing, don't you think?"

"You wouldn't dare," Lady Theodora was purple with rage. "You would not dare to spread such lies and scandal about me. No-one would believe it."

"Are you willing to risk testing it? All I need to do is drop a confidential word or two to one of my dear friends and then we'll see. If I'm wrong and everyone ignores it, then I've wasted my time and no harm done. But if I'm right, the scandalmongers are going to have a wonderful time."

Caroline rose and looked down at her grandmother with unpitying eyes.

"I'm staying in Royal Parade and will be there until Friday."

"Where is James?"

"I believe staying with Benedict Rivers, at Millington, about twenty miles away."

"I don't want to see him."

"He doesn't want to see you."

"A fine thing: a grandson hiding behind a woman. And demanding something to which he has no right."

"James knows I'm here, but he doesn't know what I've said. And he does have a right to Slepe, and you know it. Good day to you, ma'am."

Her fighting spirit carried her back to her lodgings, but once there, safe inside the cosy little sitting room, she collapsed, weeping in Mathilda's arms.

Chapter Nine

"So, we sit and wait for a summons from your grandmother?" asked Sophie at supper, some hours later.

"We wait, but we certainly do not sit about while doing so," said Caroline.

"But you really think you've won her over? By fair means or foul?" asked Robert.

"Oh, foul," Caroline smiled unhappily. "At the time, I was full of righteous wrath and indignation and was thoroughly horrible. But now I feel awful. I never thought I could be as bad as she."

"It's the problem of having a beautiful nature," Robert said. "Nastiness doesn't come naturally."

"I'm not sure."

"Well, I am," said Sophie. "I know the ends are not supposed to justify the means, but there must be exceptions and this is one of them. Major Howard would, I'm sure, agree with that."

"And that makes me feel even more that it is morally wrong." But Caroline was feeling more cheerful. Sophie and Robert's easy company was consoling. And it was very pleasant to be told that you had a beautiful nature.

They fell into a discussion of what they would do the next day, until Sophie, seeing Caroline's tired face, said firmly to Robert that it was time he went off to his lodgings and let them have an early night.

"I must confess that I am very tired," Sophie said. "I was so excited I couldn't sleep last night and what with the journey and coming here and walking down the High Street and coming back and everything, it's been wonderful."

She laughed at her own enthusiasm and Robert and Caroline smiled indulgently at her.

After Robert left, she said to Caroline, "I do so hope that your grandmother summons you tomorrow and then when Major Howard comes, we can tell him what a mere female has been able to achieve."

* * *

Sophie's wish was granted: a letter was delivered at breakfast next morning requesting Caroline's attendance upon her grandmother at noon.

When she saw her grandmother, Caroline's conscience smote her. Lady Theodora had aged overnight, but more, the implacable self-confidence had been fractured.

"Sit down, child," she said. "I'll come straight to the point. I am deeply angered by your outrageous attempt at blackmail, and it is only for the sake of our family's good name that I am prepared to agree to your despicable demands. James can have Slepe. I'm giving it to him under duress. I do not consider that he deserves it in any way, and I will have the bitter satisfaction of watching him waste it with his wild extravagance. When he does, I will have great pleasure in saying to you 'I told you so'."

"If that happens, you'll have a perfect right to do so. Do you wish to tell him of your decision yourself, or would you prefer me to do so?"

Lady Theodora did not answer. She stared at the dead fireplace, her face turned away and in shadow. Caroline waited.

"How is he? I haven't seen him for eight years."

Caroline only just heard the muttered words.

"He is well. He came through the War uninjured. He looks… he looks too tired for someone of only thirty-three, as if he has been fighting for too long."

"Since he's been fighting from the time he was born, that isn't surprising," said Lady Theodora, tartly.

Caroline laughed. "He always will. And he's still determined to get his own way by cajoling, charming, and conniving."

"Completely lacking in all morals, just as he always was."

"That is perhaps not quite fair. The last time I saw him was outside a church with a religious tract in his hand."

"Good heavens!" said Lady Theodora in horror. "He hasn't caught this new religious disease?"

"No, I don't think it's come to that."

"I should hope not. Religion is all very well in its place and its place is in church and that's all that is needed."

A meeting between her grandmother and Mr Freeman would be a clash of the titans, Caroline thought, but her money would be on Lady Theodora.

There was silence. Then Lady Theodora said abruptly, "Why didn't you tell me? I could have helped you."

"I was too frightened. He threatened unimaginable retribution if I told anyone. And I felt so ashamed… that somehow it was my fault. There was nothing anyone could do to help. Nothing at all. James guessed a little and Firth forbade me to see him. But James anyway was far away most of the time. Without Mathilda, I don't think I could have survived."

"And then you made a fool of yourself over young Maitland."

"Yes." Caroline had guessed that her grandmother would have known about that.

"Don't look so shamefaced, child. Where did you run away to?"

"A small valley called Darkleigh, a few miles this side of Cirencester. James tracked me down. He knew you were in Cheltenham, though I didn't."

"Keeps tabs on us, doesn't he?" her grandmother snorted.

"Yes." Caroline hesitated and then summoned up courage. "He'll be coming to Cheltenham tomorrow, with Benedict Rivers."

"Oh."

Caroline left it there. She rose. "I have brought a young friend with me. She has led a very dull life in the depths of the country, and I thought a few days in Cheltenham would be a welcome change for her. I only hope it doesn't make her dissatisfied with her lot. Her father is curate of the parish I'm staying in."

"Ha. And as poor as the proverbial church mouse?"

"Yes."

"Bad thing to do: taking up poverty-stricken females. They cling forever, if you're not careful."

"Not Sophie. She's an independent soul. Her brother has accompanied us. He was wounded – lost an arm at Waterloo and is still coming to terms with it. I've promised to meet them at the Pump Room, so I'll take my leave, ma'am."

"Bring James. Tomorrow."

* * *

Sophie thought Cheltenham was wonderful. She was dazzled by it all: the handsome new houses, the grand public buildings, the shops filled with exotic goods, the elegantly dressed people. Everything exuded grace and wealth. She exasperated Robert by stopping every few yards and staring at the endless succession of delights paraded before her enchanted eyes.

"Sophie, come on," he said as she stopped before a milliner's shop where an enormous and elaborate confection was on display.

"Can you imagine anyone wearing that?"

"Not you, at any rate." He pulled her away. "Come on, otherwise we'll be late at the Pump Room."

And that would never do, she thought and grinned. She allowed herself to be hurried towards the Royal Well, knowing full well that Robert's anxiety would result in their arriving a good half hour before the time appointed to meet up with Caroline. It would be the stuff of fairy tales if Caroline, her best, perhaps her only friend, fell in love with him. But they were so far apart in their stations of life that it was an unbridgeable chasm. Caroline liked Robert, she was sure of that, but she showed no more than an easy friendliness towards him. There was none of the ardour that consumed him. Maybe it would just burn itself out, Sophie thought and felt sad.

Robert had spent many hours with thoughts similar to Sophie's. He felt as if he were a small boat on a stormy wave-tossed sea, so completely was he at the mercy of his unmanageable emotions. One moment, he would be in the heights of ecstasy if she smiled at him with what he was convinced was more than friendly warmth, the next in the depths of gloom as she treated him with everyday coolness. He could only pray that no-one, and she in particular, realised his predicament. He quickened his pace: she might come away from her grandmother earlier than expected.

Sophie complained. "Robert, you're making me run. Please slow down, we're going to be far too early anyway."

He stopped and laughed. "I'm sorry. You're right, of course."

She gave his arm a sympathetic squeeze but didn't say anything.

Some half an hour later, Caroline entered the Pump Room and saw them before they caught sight of her. Something in her heart contracted as she watched them talking together. They were neatly and soberly dressed but amongst the fashionable crowd milling around them, they had the unmistakable aura of genteel poverty. They were the sort of people she was used to regarding with the mild, indifferent contempt reserved by the fortunately placed for the Poor Relations hovering on the fringes of their world.

Robert saw her and said something to Sophie. As they came up to her, they both smiled their identical, heart-stopping smiles and she thought that it was a long time since she had last been welcomed with such open, uncalculated warmth and pleasure. She felt ashamed of her somewhat condescending pity for their straitened circumstances. But that such a discontented, complaining couple as Mr and Mrs Latham had managed to produce two such sunny-tempered children was one of the miracles of nature.

"We must go to the Assembly Rooms tonight," she said and laughed, suddenly joyously happy. She could begin to believe that the terrible years of her marriage to Firth would lose their power over her life. And her grandmother was no longer the terrifying ogre of her childhood, impregnable and all powerful. She was just a domineering old woman who could be fought against and vanquished and, surprisingly, one who in future might be talked to and even confided in.

* * *

"Do you know Cheltenham, Mr Rivers?" asked Sophie.

"No, I've never been here before."

"Then as we are old Cheltenham hands of all of two days, Sophie and I will show you the sights," said Robert.

Benedict said he was grateful to them for advancing his education and his rather solemn face relaxed. James had persuaded him to start for Cheltenham at an appallingly early hour that morning and they had consequently arrived at Caroline's lodgings while she and Sophie were still at breakfast. The landlady obligingly produced coffee and boiled eggs and toast for them, clearly succumbing to James' charm.

"How nice. Just like old times, Miss Sophie," he said. "One shouldn't criticise one's host, but Benedict has the wrong attitude to breakfast. His method is to eat it as quickly as possible, in silence, and then rush off to continue his war against the woodworm."

"You wait until you start finding all the problems there are with Slepe," Benedict retorted. "Then you'll discover there are not enough hours in the day."

At the mention of Slepe, James beamed like a happy schoolboy and said, "I still can't believe it. Caroline, you are a genius. How did you do it?"

"I don't give away the secrets of my success," she said and turned the subject. "When will you go to Slepe?"

"As soon as I can persuade Robert to come with me."

"Robert?" Sophie was surprised and very pleased. Then he had meant what he said.

"That's not fair," said Benedict. "I wanted to ask him to come and help me."

He was rewarded with one of Sophie's widest smiles. Compared with James, he knew his attractions were small and he had seen the way Sophie watched James. Maybe, he thought, that with James far away in Hampshire, he might have a slight chance of success. His spirits rose. He was improving, there was no doubt about it; here he was, having breakfast with two beautiful young women and he was coping adequately. More than that, he was thoroughly enjoying the experience.

Robert joined them. The landlady, who, from the moment they had arrived, had divined Robert's lovelorn state and had been thrilled by the romance of it all, produced a cup for him and yet more coffee.

It was agreed that Caroline and James would visit their grandmother at noon, and it was then that Sophie asked Benedict whether he knew Cheltenham.

A serious discussion ensued between Sophie and Robert on the best way to show Cheltenham to Benedict. He was charmed by the enthusiasm with which they planned the excursion solely for his benefit.

"How is grandmama?" James asked Caroline quietly.

"Suffering from a burn on her hand but it seemed much better yesterday than it had been on Tuesday, as she even once or twice forgot to wince when she moved it."

"Apart from that?"

"Very well. Even larger than she was the last time I saw her, but otherwise unchanged. But she is, I think, a little lonely. So many of her friends have now died, she isn't able to get about much and I don't think many people call upon her."

"As she's mortally offended most of her acquaintances one way or another with her plain speaking, it's not surprising her company is not sought after."

"You will be patient with her, won't you? She is giving you what you wanted. Don't demand anything more of her."

"You're sorry for the old monster?" James was incredulous.

"I suppose I am, a bit. I… I wasn't very kind to her."

"What did you say to her?"

"Maybe one day I'll tell you, but not today. Come on, let's join the Latham Specially Conducted Tour of Cheltenham until it's time for us to see grandmama."

* * *

The first meeting for eight years between James and his grandmother was conducted with an icy formality which, Caroline informed him as they left the house, had reduced her to a shivering wreck.

"Why?" he asked. "We were both perfectly polite."

"That was the problem. It was painfully unnatural, and I kept dreading the façade would crack at any moment."

"You underestimate us. In the circumstances, to have done anything other than rigidly observe the proprietaries would have been a sign of weakness. Next time, no doubt, normal hostilities will be resumed."

"You haven't forgiven her?"

"No."

"Oh."

"She isn't doing it for me. She's doing it because you forced her to, in some way. Being contrary, she will always blame me that she was vanquished by you." He looked at her expectantly, but she shook her head.

"I'm not going to tell you. That is something between grandmother and myself."

"If I weren't feeling so pleased with life and so grateful to you, I would suggest you're being unnecessarily pompous and secretive."

"If I wasn't so pleased with having achieved what I came to do, I would take offence at that."

"Instead, I will ask if you and Miss Sophie will join us for supper at 'The Plough' this evening."

"I think I can safely accept on Sophie's behalf. Thank you, we will be delighted to come."

"Do you go back to Darkleigh tomorrow?"

"Yes. I promised Mrs Latham that Sophie would be returned on Friday."

"Back to your rural fastness?"

"Yes, for the time being. And you?"

"I'll stay for a few more days to make sure grandmother does write to Edwards, the attorney, with her instructions. Then I think I'll take the letter to London to deliver it personally and make sure he does draw up the documents. Then I will escort him back to Cheltenham to make sure they are correctly signed. Otherwise, I don't believe it'll happen."

"I think you're doing grandmother an injustice if you think she will go back on her word."

"I don't think she will. But I do think it could drag on and on and I will not feel safe. It would be just like her to die before the documents were signed."

"I wonder who she's made her heir."

"Maybe it was you. That would be splendidly ironic, wouldn't it? She would enjoy that."

"If that is the case, you most certainly can give me dinner this evening as some compensation for my losing her fortune to you."

Chapter Ten

Sophie had told herself to expect that her return to Knight's Darkleigh would be a severe anti-climax after the excitement of Cheltenham, but she had consoled herself with the happy thought that she would relive it in her memory, hugging the recollection to herself.

She had not anticipated that Mrs Latham, wanting to live the experience vicariously through her daughter, would demand a detailed minute by minute account of all her doings: what she had seen, what people had said to her, what she had said to them, a cross-examination that went on and on, leaving her tired and empty.

When they had gone to bed, Lucy asked questions about Major Howard regarding what he had said, what he was planning to do, and whether he was coming back. *Surely*, she said, *Sophie must know*. Sophie was being deliberately sly and secretive; she was making a laughing stock of herself by so obviously throwing herself at him. It was a disgraceful exhibition.

Incensed, Sophie retorted that that was the pot calling the kettle black, and unlike Lucy, she wasn't betrothed to another man. At that, Lucy burst into tears and turned her back on Sophie, taking most of the bedclothes with her.

What a homecoming, Sophie thought dismally, and tears trickled down her face. But Lucy's accusation frightened and worried her. Major Howard treated her with ordinary friendliness, nothing more, and she responded in kind. She didn't flirt with him and try to get his attention the way Lucy did. She was sure that nothing she had said or done could be interpreted in that way Lucy did. The thought that she might have made herself the object of ridicule was abhorrent: that Caroline, Robert, Mr Rivers and, worst of all, Major Howard, were seeing her as a silly lovesick miss, was unbearable. A nasty little voice inside her pointed out that this was precisely what she was, and she refuted it angrily. He was just a friendly acquaintance, that was all. In the same way as nice, shy Mr Rivers was. She cheered up a little when she thought about Benedict's silent but obvious admiration for her and she allowed herself to be tempted by the picture of herself as mistress of Millington Hall. It was tempting, but she would not let herself marry a man she did not love, for money, as Lucy was. Better than declining into poverty-stricken spinsterhood, said the little voice, as that is the alternative. The memory of Major Howard looking down at her from his horse in the Millington Lane rose up to comfort her. Maybe it wasn't just indifferent friendliness that he felt for her. She fell asleep, happily thinking about him.

* * *

A wind rose that night and it rattled and whistled through the old casement windows of the Chantry, waking Polly in her tiny attic bedroom. It was a chilly wind, and her thin blanket was little protection against it. Polly tried to pull it tightly around her and she curled into a ball, hoping her feet would warm up. If it was like this in mid-September, she couldn't begin to imagine what the winter was going to bring.

She thought about her employers, something she did frequently. Her initial wariness of Mr Freeman had deepened into something akin to fear. She usually managed to avoid him but when he did come upon her unexpectedly, she was scared. She was used to – indeed she enjoyed – men looking at her with lusting eyes, but the way Mr Freeman looked at her made her feel sick. What made his greedy lascivious stare so disturbing, she could not fathom. She just knew it was dangerous.

Mrs Freeman was so weak and feeble that Polly felt a vague desire to protect her from the contempt in which she was so openly held by every other member of the household. Mr Freeman's frequent savage criticisms of what she said or what she did would have demoralised a far stronger person; with Mrs Freeman, it crushed her into a hopeless submission. The servants took their cue from their master and rarely bothered to carry out the few hesitant orders she dared to give. She drifted around the house, a pale, sad ghost, looking for her son.

Between Polly and Richard Freeman there existed a secret state of war. What could have been regarded as a childish game was anything but when played with the hatred and loathing of the combatants.

The day after he had pushed her into the stream, Richard found a dead frog in his bed. His bare toes touching the cold, slimy skin as he lay down made him shriek with horror and his mother came rushing in panic-stricken that some terrible fate had befallen him. He didn't say anything about the frog, telling her that he had had a nightmare and demanding that she just went away.

He felt revolted by Polly. Her body exuding its earthy sexuality, her plump face with its round, knowing eyes, her slack red mouth an ever-open invitation, her coarse laugh, there wasn't a single thing that he didn't find disgusting. He enjoyed tormenting her: as soon as she finished cleaning a floor, he would walk mud into it; he put glass into her dusting cloth so she scratched the dining table; he hid in dark corners and tripped her up as she went by with a loaded tray and laughed and laughed each time she was berated for her apparent clumsiness. He stopped short of pushing her to the limit so that she would leave the Chantry or be dismissed for, that would end the game and that was not his intention.

Polly's retaliation was perhaps a little more subtle. With an animal instinct, she knew Richard Freeman found her repulsive, so she deliberately flaunted herself when he came near. His sick look of disgust and the shudder that went through him when she pushed her heavy breasts against him and touched him with her thick, dirty fingers was recompense enough for his petty spite.

Each kept watch, waiting for a moment of inattention in the other so an attack could be made and another victory chalked up. It kept Polly's spirit alive, as there was no letup in the relentless hard work or in the other servants' cold indifference. In her few hours of freedom, she took to spying on Richard. She knew how frequently he disappeared to go riding or fishing with George Harries when his father thought he was in his room, studying. And she knew when he climbed out of his bedroom window at night and ran like a wild thing into the woods.

The wind moaned and sighed, and rain splattered against the window. Polly shivered again. When she could get Mrs Freeman on her own, she would demand another blanket, and she knew she would get it. Fancy Mrs Freeman being frightened even of her, Polly thought with scorn, and drifted into an uneasy sleep.

* * *

The days slipped by, and Lucy spent many hours at Manor Farm with Mrs Harries, discussing curtains and furniture and chatting about fashions. Anne and Mary sometimes joined them but soon became bored with talk of servants and linen. Jarvis was delighted that Lucy and Mrs Harries were getting on so well; Lucy had started out by treating Mrs Harries with careful courtesy, purely out of self-interest but she soon began to enjoy Mrs Harries' comfortable, gossipy chatter and shrewd observation of the world, so unlike her mother's ceaseless lamentations. She enjoyed even more trying to teach Mrs Harries in the finer details of polite behaviour and did it sufficiently tactfully for Mrs Harries to become an eager student.

Hill Farm began to change into a cosy farmhouse, waiting for its young owners to take up residence. Sophie did not find Lucy's fussily pretty furnishings entirely to her taste but kept her opinion to herself. The breach between the sisters remained but so little did their lives impinge upon each other that it went unobserved by their family and largely unregretted by them. Sophie occasionally felt a spasm of conscience but not enough to obey its dictates.

With the harvest over, the village children came back to school and Sophie's mornings were occupied with trying to teach half a dozen unenthusiastic scholars the rudiments of reading, writing, and arithmetic. After some particularly difficult mornings, she did wonder whether there was something to be said for Mr Freeman's point of view.

Mr Freeman himself had taken soundings in the surrounding villages which might be receptive to his moral crusade and found one in a high, bleak village, appropriately called Cold Trenton. It was a poverty-stricken village, unattractive, and remote, and his call to follow him on the path to Heaven was an escape for the inhabitants in their miserable earthly existence. The Living was vacant, the squire had died many years before and his widow was pathetically grateful for Mr Freeman's interest in their moral welfare. It was thus an ideal situation, and he was soon being paid generous 'expenses' by the lonely old lady. In return, he spent many hours in front of her fire, drinking the fine old brandy laid down by her husband and the occupants of the Chantry breathed more freely in his absence.

The friendship between Mrs Latham and Mrs Freeman blossomed. By unspoken agreement, the ladies met for tea in one or the other of their houses only when Mr Freeman was away. So long as Mrs Freeman accepted the role of confidant to Mrs Latham's complaints, the relationship prospered but there was a small hiatus when she forgot and began to tell Mrs Latham of her wretched life. She speedily recognised her error and never again attempted to burden Mrs Latham with her problems.

As observed by Polly (and his mother), Richard spent much of his time with George, who provided him with a horse and taught him how to cast a line for fish. Jarvis, watching them one day at the lake, thought with satisfaction that his years in the army must have taught George the art of dealing with young people. He could not wait for George and Lucy to give him grandchildren. But he did feel a little uneasy at having seen George and young Freeman emerging from one of the less savoury hostelries in Cirencester one market day. He did not think it particularly wise of George. Mr Freeman would be outraged at his son being led into such places. On the other hand, it was part of a lad's education to be made aware of the dangers of such places – the excessive drinking, the brawling, the women, the general dirt and degradation they presented – under George's eye, this was perhaps the best way to experience them. Jarvis allowed his unease to subside.

* * *

Benedict, before James was able to do so, asked Robert to stay for a while at Millington and accept a commission to help plan the alterations he intended to make to make the house more habitable. Robert was delighted to accept and Sophie waved him off with conflicting emotions: she was as pleased as he was with his good fortune but very sad to see him go.

Caroline returned with pleasure to her little house but realised that her time in retreat was running out. She had the suspicion that when the formalities of the transfer of Slepe had been completed, her grandmother would begin a campaign to persuade her to spend the winter in Cheltenham. It was a prospect which did not fill her with the horror it would have done two weeks before and she accepted that in return for giving in to her, her grandmother would extort recompense and that she would be prepared to give it. James called in on his way to London, but her usefulness was at an end, and his visit was brief.

She had said as much to Sophie one afternoon, a couple of days before the wedding.

"One has to accept that James uses one, he makes no secret of it, and as soon as he has what he wants, off he goes. But it is a little hurtful, all the same." She stopped. There was a stricken look in Sophie's eyes which dismayed her. She had been amused by Lucy's efforts to attract him but hadn't thought about Sophie, which was extremely unobservant of her. It was inevitable that exposure to James' charm would have had a disastrous effect on Sophie's heart, and she thought it was admirable the way Sophie had hidden her feelings under her friendly manner.

Her dreams, her golden ridiculous dreams, crashed around Sophie. He had visited the valley, probably ridden past her door, but had not bothered to see her, so little was his interest in her. She felt like a wounded animal; she wanted to creep away and hide in a dark corner, to protect her pain from mocking, prying eyes.

"I didn't know he had been back here," she managed to say through a constricted throat.

"It was a very fleeting visit," Caroline said apologetically. "Just to let me know that grandmama had signed all the documents and he was on his way to Slepe."

"Then he won't come back again." It was the cry of an abandoned child.

"I don't think so." Caroline thought it kinder to be honest. "Though I'm sure he will be writing to ask your brother to go there soon."

"Yes, of course," said Sophie dully and then said abruptly, "I must go."

Caroline watched from her front gate as Sophie went down the steep slope towards the river and stayed there until the small figure, trudging like an old woman, was hidden by the curve of the valley. She shivered and went in. She must think of some distraction to occupy Sophie so that she didn't brood too much. After the wedding, there would be little to keep Sophie's mind off her woes.

Chapter Eleven

The Harries' made the wedding a cheerful, boisterous occasion. Lucy looked a little pale but lovelier than ever and made her vows in a sweet, hesitant whisper. George, standing very upright, made his as if repeating orders before battle. The wedding breakfast was perhaps a little on the frugal side, but Mr and Mrs Latham had tried to be hospitable to the best of their limited means and imagination could encompass.

The night before the wedding, Lucy had, with great satisfaction, told Sophie that their wedding trip was to be a short stay in London, thereby totally eclipsing Sophie's Cheltenham holiday. Sophie expressed suitable envy and warm congratulations so that Lucy was able to forget that she was not speaking to Sophie and as they prepared for bed, chattered away on what she hoped to see and particularly, to buy.

Sophie was pleased that they were back on friendly terms and tried hard to enjoy the wedding, but she felt a strange coldness within her, cutting her off from the warmth and laughter around her. She would not have believed that she could grieve for a person as she did for James Howard. The past two days had revealed to her the depths of her feelings for him. Through inexperience, through circumstance, she had allowed a friendly acquaintance to deepen into something considerably more.

He was a shadow, always just out of her reach, an echo reminding her of things he had said, how he had laughed, the way his eyes looked at her when he smiled. She was plagued by memories of him which came unbidden, but when she was able to forget him for a few minutes the anguish she felt at not having him near, even if it was just in her memory, was even more painful.

"Mr Latham," said Caroline to Robert, as she watched Sophie's attempt at laughing as she caught Lucy's posy of flowers, "I think after this is over, Sophie and your mother are going to need a little cheering up. I'm thinking of asking Benedict if we could visit him. Do you think that would be a good idea?"

Robert saw Mrs Latham wiping away tears as she waved farewell to her daughter and then looked at Sophie who, now his attention was drawn to her, did seem somehow diminished, quite unlike the bright sparkling person of Cheltenham.

"They do look a bit down in the dumps," he agreed. "We start work on remodelling the East wing in about two weeks' time, so do come before then so you can see what has to be done."

He heroically restrained himself from launching into details of the scheme; he had discovered when helping Jarvis Harries and his new staircase that apart from his patron, other people, surprisingly, did not seem particularly interested in the minutiae of the work involved.

Robert could not believe his good fortune that he had chanced upon an occupation which fascinated him, and which would pay him handsomely. Jarvis had spoken loud and long of his delight in Robert's help and there were already tentative enquiries from rivals to the Harries' in the fraught business of climbing up the social ladder. In the meantime, Millington was proving a somewhat daunting challenge, but one made enjoyable by Benedict's unfailing good temper and enthusiasm.

Mr Latham frowned upon Robert working as a glorified tradesman. It was not the occupation of a gentleman but felt powerless to stop it. Robert's modest funds from selling out his commission were disappearing, and he had to do something to keep himself. When this was pointed out to him, Mr Latham was unable to think of anything else Robert could do, so was reduced to his habitual state of irritability whenever he happened to think about it. With Robert staying at Millington, this fortunately was infrequent.

"I'm going back to Millington tomorrow. Would you like me to ask Benedict?"

"I'll write him a note, if you would be so kind as to deliver it."

"For you, anything," said Robert, unable to stop himself.

She smiled and moved away, leaving him furious with himself.

Later that evening, he and Sophie sat in a glum silence in the drawing room. The fire was lit and Robert, looking at Sophie's downcast face in the flickering light, was distressed at how unhappy she looked.

"What is it, Sophie? What's wrong?"

She shook her head, sure that if she spoke, she would cry. He went over to the sofa.

"Move over, so I can put my arm around you and you can cry on my shoulder."

She tried to laugh but it ended in a flood of tears as she wept her heart out.

As a very good-looking young man, Robert had sufficient experience of lovelorn young girls to guess Sophie's problem.

"Is it James Howard?"

She nodded, her face still hidden in his shoulder.

"Oh dear, oh dear. There's no future in it, my poor Sophie, you know that, don't you?"

She nodded again, gulped and a fresh fountain of tears soaked into his coat.

"I'm being so stupid, I know," she eventually said, "and he gave me no reason to think that he regarded me with anything other than friendliness."

Robert was relieved. If James had set out to capture Sophie's heart, then he would have been angry enough to have broken off their friendship – and thus lose a lucrative commission. He gave her a hug and said, "What are we going to do with you?"

"I don't know. The past few weeks, since you came home, have been so different, so much more has happened. Now, to go back to my usual dull life is a dreadful thought. I'm sure Caroline will soon be leaving, and you'll be gone as well, and I'll be left with poor Mama and Papa."

"It doesn't seem a cheerful prospect, does it? I, at least, know I can leave and become rich and famous as an architect. I'll be the architect who persuades his patrons to spend fortunes on houses which would have been far better left alone."

Sophie managed to laugh at this. "The more you persuade them to spend, the more fashionable and popular you'll be?"

"Of course. Though how prepared I'll be to bow and scrape to prospective patrons to get my commissions, is another matter."

"Does Mr Rivers expect you to do that?"

"Good lord, no. Neither did Jarvis Harries, for that matter."

"There we are, then. You make them accept that you're a gentleman of superior skills and they're gentlemen with superior money, so you're equal."

"It's a nice thought but not quite the way of the world. Father is upset that I'm employed as something akin to a tradesman. Which is what I am and which I'll have to get used to."

They sat for a while in silence, which Sophie broke. "I've been very selfish, burdening you with my problems when you've got your own, with Caroline. But I don't mean to pry," she added hastily.

"I suppose it's obvious, for all to see," Robert said, mortified.

"No, no, not at all," she lied. "I expect that it's because I'm in the same situation that I've noticed."

"We're a fine pair, aren't we?"

"At least Caroline is worthy of being loved. I don't know that Major Howard is particularly admirable as a person. Which should help matters, but it doesn't."

"She's going to ask Benedict if you and she and mother could come to Millington to see the house. Will you come? I'd like to show you what is to be done."

Show Caroline, she thought, but cheered up a little at the prospect of going to Millington.

* * *

They went in Caroline's discreetly elegant carriage on one of those rare sunny autumn days when the countryside is defined with sharp clarity and colours are jewel-bright. For Sophie, the days since the wedding had crawled by, the feeling that she was existing in a cold, dreary world of her own had intensified and she was unable to sleep, unable to eat, unable to do anything but sit in a state of dumb, debilitating unhappiness. She lost weight and her eyes, heavy and shadowed, looked dully out onto a grey world.

Mrs Latham had noticed that Sophie seemed in low spirits, but, true to form, avoided finding out what was the matter. She alone had the prerogative to be ill.

Caroline was infuriated with this attitude and while they were preparing to set off, she said quietly to Mrs Latham that Sophie did not look well, hoping that perhaps a concerted effort by them to lift Sophie's spirits would have some effect. Mrs Latham merely stared, affronted, and said that Sophie had not complained of any illness, whereas she herself was suffering acutely from neuralgia, though of course she didn't want to make a fuss about it. She would suffer in silence and could only feel hurt that Sophie did not try as hard as a daughter should to help her poor mother.

As they set off, Sophie silent in her corner of the carriage and Mrs Latham complaining of the brightness of the sun, Caroline seriously wondered why she had bothered to arrange this expedition.

Benedict's greeting, a little nervous but openly showing his pleasure, restored Caroline's good humour which had been further tested on the journey by Mrs Latham's grumblings on the state of the lanes, the advent of winter and the lack of charm in the landscape. Even the distant view of Millington Hall failed to please her, though

Caroline was pleased to note that Sophie did rouse herself to remark appreciatively and from then on to seem more interested in her surroundings.

As Benedict handed her out of the carriage, Sophie smiled her thanks, but he was dismayed and disappointed at the change in her. Since receiving Caroline's note, he had thought little of anything except seeing her and showing her his home. *Damn, James*, he thought, *what do I do now?*

"Come into the library for some refreshments after your journey," he said diffidently to Mrs Latham and Sophie. Robert, with a proprietorial air, was already showing Caroline the main features of the house.

Mrs Latham found the madeira provided by Benedict very much to her liking and preferred to stay in the library with a second glass while the others did a tour of the house. They went from one damp, neglected room to another, laughing as Robert was teased by Caroline and Benedict for his enthusiasm. Sophie allowed herself to forget her broken heart and to enjoy the moment.

"We intend to open these two rooms into one to make a good-sized drawing room," said Robert, "and the present drawing room will be made into the dining room. It's nearer the kitchen, so there will be only half a mile instead of a mile of passages in which the food can get cold."

"Don't exaggerate, Robert," said Benedict. "It's not that bad."

"It seems a very thick wall to cut through," said Sophie. "What if the whole house falls down?" She remembered with an ache the breakfast conversation she'd had with Major Howard.

"It won't," Robert said positively. "We'll put a large beam across and that will hold everything up."

"I'll remember not to stand under it – just in case," said Caroline, laughing.

"You haven't seen the massive oak that's to be felled. A beam from that will hold anything up. But, just in case, I'll stand ready to take the weight of the collapsing house on my shoulders, a veritable modern Atlas." Robert gave a comical look of anxiety upwards.

"I think you'd become the ghost of Millington Hall, if that were to happen," said Caroline. "A strange scrabbling in the night when all that was left of the house were a few walls and a heap of stones."

"More likely a voice, eerily like Robert's, saying 'if we just put a window in here and move the door there, we'll be able to make an amazing difference in this room!'" said Benedict and everyone laughed.

Sophie stopped by one of the windows and looked out across the lawn and sunlit meadows. Caroline and Robert, with one accord, continued into the next room.

"Is there a ghost?" asked Sophie.

"No, I'm certain there isn't." Benedict stood behind her, looking down at her.

She turned away from the window and said, "Even if there was, I'm sure it would be a happy one," and Benedict felt the first glimmerings of hope.

"I'd like to think so, too. I still cannot quite believe my good fortune in having inherited Millington. I hadn't been very successful at the Bar and was beginning to despair that I was ever going to get any reasonable briefs. Then on the very day that I heard about Millington, I was offered one that would make my name."

"Did you take it?"

"Oh yes. I had to prove to myself that I could succeed and then give up gracefully. Fortunately, we won the case and my client, a very rich and influential man, was acquitted and I was paid my fee, the largest I had ever charged, without demur. My colleagues told me my career at the Bar was made. Whether justice was done in that particular case, is something about which I have my doubts."

"What was he accused of?"

"Oh, murdering his wife," said Benedict cheerfully.

"Good Heavens! But you say you think he did it – but you helped him get acquitted."

"Are you very shocked?"

"I think I am. But I think it would be worse if he were innocent and had been convicted."

"That does happen."

"Has it to you?"

"Perhaps once, I'm not sure." Benedict remembered one case with unease. To change the subject, he said, "And now I'm a gentleman, though with Robert around, I cannot say of leisure, thankfully I am no longer dependent on my profession for my keep."

Sophie smiled up at him. "I'm sure the Bar has lost a brilliant member, and Robert is very lucky to have found such a kind patron."

Benedict blushed and stammered, "You really are too generous, Miss Sophie."

Sophie later admitted to herself that there was a great satisfaction in reducing a man to a state of stuttering confusion, and it was a balm to her wounded feelings.

Caroline and Robert strolled out into the garden, feeling pleased with themselves.

"It would be a most perfect match," said Caroline. "Sophie is just the sort of girl that Benedict should marry."

"And you organised this expedition entirely for that purpose?"

"Yes, of course. And to get her mind off James."

Robert wanted to say: *Did you not want to see me? Didn't I come into your plan at all?*

They had reached a low wall, separating the garden from the steep slope of the valley. They looked down into the shadowy depths to the river which ran dark and swift through overhanging willows and elders.

Misunderstanding his silence, she said, "I thought you would have known that Sophie is eating her heart out for James."

"Oh yes, I know that."

"And you blame him?" she asked, thinking that this must be the cause of his sudden moodiness.

"No, no I don't think he gave her any encouragement. At least, that's what she says, and I saw nothing to the contrary."

"I'm relieved to hear it. I'm not James' keeper. I've no reason to feel responsible for his behaviour, but I do. It's stupid of me, but I always have, and I expect I always will."

And you think about him more than about anyone else, Robert thought bitterly. *You may quarrel with him, criticise him and complain about him, but if he so much as raises a finger, you will be there, ready to wait upon him. No-one else can get near you.*

"Oh, do look," she exclaimed. She put her hand on his severed arm as she leaned across the wall to point at two deer who had run up the bank opposite them and had taken up positions in a clearing in the scrub. Robert was intensely aware of her hand, appalled that she should touch his disfigured arm but full of gratitude that it did not seem to disgust her.

They watched the two stags circle one another, their heads with their great sets of antlers lowered, ready to fight. When it came, the viciousness of the clashing of the antlers made Caroline gasp and she turned away, inevitably into the circle of Robert's arm. For a moment, they stood together, her head on his shoulder; then he felt her stiffen and, the hardest thing he had ever done, dropped his arm and moved away from her. The stags were locked together in an ungainly tangle of antlers, one slowly sinking to its knees in battered submission.

Robert and Caroline walked back towards the house in silence. When they reached the front door, he said, "I must go and see if Josiah needs some help, if you will excuse me."

She, far more practised at hiding her emotions, went into the house and joined the others.

Chapter Twelve

Mrs Latham was jubilant; it was quite obvious that Mr Rivers was very taken with Sophie, and she had no doubt he would soon be asking Mr Latham for her hand. She reduced Sophie almost to screaming point by her talk of Millington and its splendour, of Mr Rivers' enormous fortune and of what a catch he was.

Sophie would never have believed that she would find a topic more tiresome than her mother's complaints about her health, but this premature, triumphant boasting horrified her. Benedict Rivers was attracted to her, even she could see that. But he was far too shy to push his suit, even if he wanted to, and in her present dismal state of unrequited love, she could give him no encouragement. She liked him and she had been touched by the way he had spoken to her and pleased that he had lowered his defences. She would be sorry if she never saw him again, but that was all. Nothing like the all-consuming ache she felt for James Howard.

When Caroline told her one morning after church that her grandmother had asked her to stay with her in Cheltenham, Sophie's first thought that another link with James Howard would be lost to her, and as a second thought, how much she would miss Caroline. The third was: poor Robert.

"I'll miss you," she said. "When will you go?"

"In about a week's time. I'm keeping the cottage on, as an escape if I need it but I expect to be in Cheltenham for the winter."

She looked out from the church porch over the damp churchyard; the landscape was dank and grey under low cloud. A raw wind blew across the valley and rustled the yellowing leaves. No birds sang and she felt the countryside closing in on her.

"I don't like the country in winter," she admitted.

"It hasn't much to recommend it, has it?" agreed Sophie. "If one hunted – but do you?"

"Oh yes, but I must confess to being daunted by your stone walls."

"I doubt if our small local hunt would compare with those you have ridden with."

"Perhaps not." Caroline recalled with some nostalgia, days with the Quorn, the Pytcherly and the Belvoir.

"I'll return your book before you go."

"Oh, please keep it. But come to tea later in the week and take some away with you. They'll just be left otherwise, neglected and unread."

Sophie was truly grateful. Reading until she was exhausted had been her only way of getting to sleep some nights. No longer having to share a bedroom with Lucy was a considerable relief.

"Lucy and George return tomorrow," she said.

* * *

Lucy chatted as she poured a second cup for Sophie.

She's changed, thought Sophie. *Lucy never bothered to talk so much to me before. But now she doesn't seem to be able to stop.*

"… and we went to the theatre at Drury Lane, it was quite wonderful. Oh, Sophie, the ladies' dresses, their jewellery and the hairstyles, you just couldn't imagine them. I can't recall the name of the play for the moment, but it was very amusing. But Sophie, you'll never guess who was there!"

Lucy looked exultant. Sophie, with a sinking heart, said, "Major Howard?"

"Yes, indeed. Wasn't that a coincidence? He was with a party of friends, but he came over to talk to us in the interval." Lucy smiled. "He was very attentive."

"I thought he was at Slepe."

"He said he was in London on business." Again, Lucy smiled her secret smile. "I saw quite a bit of him after that. We twice drove in the Park, and he escorted me to a ball and…" Lucy stopped abruptly, seeing Sophie's angry face. "Whatever is the matter?"

"I can't believe what you're saying. Whatever was George doing, allowing you to flirt so openly with him? You've only been married two weeks."

"You're just saying that because you're jealous. It's different when you're a married woman," said Lucy, loftily. "George didn't mind. He was busy with his friends, and he knew Major Howard would look after me."

She did not tell Sophie that George's friends were members of a seedy gaming club or that Major Howard's "looking after her" had included many passionate encounters.

George had seemed unable, or unwilling, to make love to her unless he was drunk and the ensuing couplings had hurt and disgusted her. Her senses told her that there was more than this to lovemaking and she was therefore all too ready to fall into the experienced arms of James Howard. In the final week of her honeymoon, she and George saw each other only briefly as they went their separate ways and she lived in a delirium of love and frenetic gaiety with James. She was too unsophisticated to know that the elegant houses to which James took her, were not ones which women who wanted to keep their reputations should enter. He justified his behaviour by saying to himself that in all probability she would never visit London again, and certainly not enter that particular circle of raffish but high society in which he moved.

As for seducing her, he was happy to give her as much pleasure as she gave to him and since George all too apparently was neglecting his marital duties, he, James, felt free to step into his shoes. Or bed.

Lucy wrenched her thoughts back from their tumultuous leave-taking when, with tears streaming down her face, she begged him to come down to Darkleigh so that they could have one last hour together, just one, just once. He had said no, it was too risky, but the way he couldn't stop kissing her as he said it, made her confident of her power over him, and sure he would return.

"He was the perfect escort," she said to Sophie and thought, and I was the perfect mistress.

Sophie felt a great weariness descend upon her. *I can't cope with this*, she thought. *I don't know what to think, what to believe.*

"You haven't told anyone else about your... meeting with Major Howard?"

"No, I didn't think it would be of interest to anyone else." Lucy scored her hit with some glee.

Sophie flushed and didn't answer.

Lucy looked at her with scornful pity. "Forget James Howard, Sophie. He's not interested in provincial little girls like you."

"Then what are you, if not a provincial little girl?"

"Maybe I was once. But not now, not anymore." Lucy smiled complacently and then laughed as Sophie rose and ran out of the room.

Sophie half walked, half ran away from Hill Farm as if she was fleeing some horror. The implications of Lucy's words were just too dreadful. How could Lucy, how could he... she should have guessed that he was a libertine; she hoped she would never see him again. She didn't want to see Lucy again either, for that matter.

As she approached the ford, she slowed down to a more decorous pace, but her steps seemed to say, *how could she, how could he*, as she toiled up the steep hill away from the snug little empire of the Harries'.

If she had looked back, she would have seen George, with a sulky look on his face, emerging from the Manor Farm. George had endured an uncomfortable interview with his father about the money he had spent in London. Jarvis Harries was outraged when he heard that George had lost a thousand pounds gambling and the tongue-lashing he was given had pierced even George's complacent attitude towards the way he conducted his life.

George plodded up the muddy road, trying to avoid getting his expensive new boots too dirty and wet and felt aggrieved. Dammit, the old man must know that a fellow had to be a sport. It was just as well that he'd had that run of luck the night before they returned, otherwise the losses would have given the old boy a heart attack. He had been tempted to carry on playing that night; the others were egging him on, the excitement was intense, it would have needed one more throw of the dice to win it all – or lose all. Why caution, ancestral peasant caution, had made him so suddenly stop, bewildered him as much as it disappointed his now jeering friends. He had lurched out of the gaming house on his own and trailed back to the lodgings where Lucy, pretending to be asleep, was heartily relieved when he climbed heavily into bed and instantly fell asleep.

And then they had come home to the usual enthusiastic warming Harries' welcome and to the usual indifferent Latham reception. George stopped at a gate and looked down at the green valley towards Knights' Darkleigh. A pheasant clattered in the woods, and he began to cheer up. There would be some good shooting this year, particularly in the newly annexed copse. Dull and damp though the day was, it was good to be home. He didn't really like London, he decided, and if it was a choice between gaming and sport, then he knew which he would choose. His spirits lifted even more when he remembered that the hunt was having its first meet of the season on the following Friday, only two days away, and he would be trying out his new horse. He must get hold of young Freeman: he would like to introduce the lad to the excitements of the hunt. The boy rode well, with an easy, natural grace, and George derived unexpected pleasure in enlarging the boy's narrow existence. Yes, Richard must come hunting with him on Friday.

His self-esteem fully restored, he joined Lucy in the sitting room and was pleased to see that she also was looking more cheerful. He had noticed that she had looked a bit dismal since they came home. They had a comfortable, if rather silent, evening together as George visualised riding hard across the country, baying hounds and Richard, his acolyte, beside him, and Lucy visualised in equally happy anticipation, her reunion with James Howard.

Chapter Thirteen

Sophie spent some time trying to work out how she could get a message to Robert to tell him of Caroline's imminent departure to Cheltenham. She would have been delighted if she had known that the same thought was exercising Caroline. After their passage of arms in the garden, she and Robert had avoided speaking to each other again that day. Caroline felt that she could not just disappear into Cheltenham without saying something to him. But as she wasn't at all sure what she wanted to say, she felt thoroughly confused and annoyed with herself.

On the Friday morning of the hunt, she stood at her little garden gate and watched the hounds working the wooded slope of the valley. There was the sudden, magical moment when the fox broke cover and she saw it running swiftly along the valley floor towards Middle Darkleigh. Soon afterwards came the hounds, baying and wildly excited and behind them, the riders urging their horses down the slope, slithering and slipping dangerously as they charged down through the trees.

The fox abruptly changed course and darted back up through the trees and she could see it running towards her and then, in a tawny flash, it was gone, leaping over the wall into the woods behind her house.

The hounds yelped and cried and followed, panting and frantic as they raced up the steep slope. One hound over-enthusiastically jumped onto her wall, squealed and then turned and followed its fellows.

The riders came up the hill, the master directing them to the further side of the wood and she watched, more than a little critically, the large country squires and farmers on their strong, clumsy horses, puffing and blowing their way past her. The whole scene was the Grand Old Duke of York in reverse, she thought, and really all hopelessly undisciplined. Towards the rear of the field, George went by and she noted that his horse was one of the few good-looking animals there. She saw with some astonishment young Richard Freeman coming up behind him. George turned, giving him a grin of encouragement and slowed to let him catch up. She could hear Richard's high, excited laugh and then they vanished. *I wonder whether Mr Freeman knows about this,* she thought. George must have lent him the horse and kitted him out. Although the horse had looked a little elderly and the jacket was badly fitting, there was no doubt that Richard Freeman had the best seat and the lightest pair of hands in that motley field. And George the worst.

In the aftermath of the hunt, the little valley seemed quieter than ever. It was a still, mild day, not quite raining but with a clinging dampness in the air. Sophie decided it would be a good afternoon to walk over to Middle Darkleigh and take up Caroline's offer of her books.

Caroline welcomed her with her usual warmth and was pleased to see that the wounded look in Sophie's eyes had lessened and that she had more life in her.

"Did you watch the hunt?" Caroline asked. "I did for a while as they came up from the valley into the woods behind the house."

"Was I right in thinking it was a little different from what you're used to?" Sophie asked, laughing.

"Just a little." Caroline smiled at the recollection and then said, "It's made me realise the difference between living in the country as we are here, and my former way of life. Then, one was transported to a large house with many of one's friends and acquaintances and continued life a little different in substance from that which one led in London. You strolled in the grounds of the house, instead of the Park, hunted across country instead of a decorous trotting along the Row and entertained and socialised in the same way, merely on a smaller scale. We were insulated from our surroundings. If the weather was wet, we turned our backs on it and played cards or whatever. We weren't part of the country around us, that was unknown territory, only interesting when it was ridden across, flat out after a fox. The people who lived in the villages, those who worked the land, year in year out, were an alien race, to be avoided. After the hunt, we retreated back into our great houses and ignored everyone else."

"What was your home like?"

"Huge. And beautiful. It was light and airy, with glorious rooms wonderfully decorated, everything of the most excellent quality, all on a vast scale. It was surrounded by gardens and parklands as beautiful as the house. It was as near to perfection as one could imagine. And do you know, Sophie, it is the unhappiest house I have ever known. There was something so wrong with it, I cannot describe it, but it was a house which had retained all the tragedies and hates of generation after generation of Firths, but there had never been any love for it to absorb, so it emanated malice and anger."

Seeing Sophie's astonished face, she laughed. "Don't worry, I haven't gone mad. I was very unhappy there – my husband was perhaps the human equivalent of the house: extraordinarily handsome but something terribly wrong behind the façade. Anyway, that's all in the past, thank goodness, and I never have to go back there again." She shivered as if an old ghost was haunting her and Sophie changed the subject.

"Even Cheltenham is going to be rather provincial and… and commonplace compared with what you're used to. I thought it was wonderful, but then it is rather different to Knight's Darkleigh or Cirencester. But you're used to the best society and that's surely London, not Cheltenham."

"Yes, I feel that Cheltenham is very worthy, perhaps not the glittering cynosure of high society it hopes to be and perhaps a little elderly, but never mind, I'll survive a few months there while I decide what I'll do. I've needed to mark time for a while and living here has been ideal as it's been so completely different from my former life. And wouldn't my life have been far, far poorer not to have met, for instance, Mrs Brigstock, or Polly, or Mr Freeman?"

"I could have done without meeting Mr Freeman."

"Young Richard Freeman was out hunting. He and George passed by me, here."

"Goodness, I'm sure Mr Freeman wouldn't approve of that."

"We need your brother to mimic him pontificating on the evils of the chase."

"I hope Robert will come over soon."

Caroline didn't answer and they went on to talk about books.

* * *

George and Richard were remembering the glories of the day.

They lay sprawled on hay bales in the loft above the stables, the warm smell of tired horses mingling with the sweet scent of the hay. It was dark and warm, and the spell cast by the hunt continued to bind them. Every fence and wall was recalled in infinite details, their achievements boasted about, other people's mishaps mocked and derided. Richard had a turn of phrase to describe others' discomfiture that kept George convulsed with laughter.

"Do you remember the last run, in the fields above Prior's Darkleigh," said George, "when that woman on the big black horse stormed past us and then went a purler over the next wall – did you see what happened to her?"

"You didn't see? You missed a treat. She must have winded herself as she landed, as she lay on her back, legs in the air, habit and petticoats over her head, and she was trying to get them off her face, so you had arms and legs waving about, like a beetle on its back. Except the legs were rather podgy for a beetle and being clothed in white underdrawers, a most unusual species."

George giggled. "The greater female hunting beetle."

"An awesome spectacle, determined to push her way ahead and suddenly, with a high pitched scream," Richard crouched on all fours, "waiting to pounce," and he shot out a hand and punched George on the chest.

George lay back, laughing and grappled with Richard as he tried to land another one. Richard collapsed on top of him, his head lying on George's chest. The laughter vanished. As if of their own volition, George's arms went round the boy's slim body, holding him tight.

* * *

Sophie, laden down with books, was delighted, on arriving home, to see that Robert was there. However, she didn't realise until she had actually entered the dining room, when there was no escape, that she had walked into a row between her parents and Robert. Her mother was sniffing into her handkerchief.

"I really do not see any reason at all why you should feel obliged to write to *that woman*," she moaned.

"I told you, Mama, I believe I should pay back as soon as I can the cost of my commission. It was most generous of my uncle to pay for it. Surely, the least I can do is to offer to repay him."

"It was his duty. You are his nephew and godson," said Mr Latham, peevishly.

"And you should be his heir," wailed Mrs Latham.

"Mama, Aunt Emily did not produce Harry just to spite us."

Mrs Latham dissolved into further floods. "You've always taken her part against me. To tell his mother that he didn't love her. It was a wicked, wicked thing to say."

"I didn't say that. And you know it. Good God, Mama, I was only nine at the time."

"Don't take the name of the Lord in vain, Robert," commanded Mr Latham.

"I apologise, father."

There was a glowering silence, broken only by renewed sobs from Mrs Latham. Sophie decided it was time to intervene.

"Mama, why don't you come up to your bedroom to lie down, otherwise you'll get a migraine. Then Papa and Robert can talk it over by themselves in the dining parlour."

Mrs Latham allowed herself to be led weeping from the room and up to her bedroom. There, Sophie listened in amazement to her mother's diatribe against Robert. It would seem that all the problems of the Latham family could be laid at his door. With great difficulty, Sophie restrained her impatience to hear Robert's version of events while she brushed her mother's hair and coaxed her into bed. The complaints and tears continued until Mrs Latham exhausted herself and gradually drifted into sleep.

Sophie tiptoed out of the room and ran down the stairs. She listened at the dining parlour door, and with some relief, heard a murmur of voices. At least there wasn't a battle royal going on between them. She went into the drawing room and taking up her embroidery, waited for Robert.

He appeared some half an hour later and dropped onto the sofa with a sigh.

"Well, father and I are still on speaking terms – just – but I think it would be a good idea if I kept out of mother's way for a while."

"Whatever did you say to her that caused such a rift?"

Robert groaned. "I thought you must know. But I suppose there was no reason for you to be told."

"It was always obvious that there was something wrong between you and Mama, but I never knew what. Tell me."

Robert did so, ending, "… and of course what was so unfortunate is that I did so very much prefer Sibley Hall to our home. Aunt and Uncle were so happy and wanted everyone else to enjoy life as much as they did and particularly to share their joy when Harry was born, so they were deeply hurt by mother's attitude. Sophie, it was unbelievably shameful. I still can't bear to think about it. It was a gesture of great charity for Uncle Henry to purchase my commission. When I told him this, he just laughed and said that he was sorry it couldn't have been into a better regiment, but he had suffered some bad losses that year."

"You've seen them since we left Suffolk?" Sophie was surprised.

"Of course. Father and mother don't know and for heaven's sake, don't tell them. If my just mentioning in conversation that I intended to write to them could raise such a storm, Lord only knows what admitting I'd stayed with them would create."

"It all seems quite ridiculous and rather sad."

"Yes, it is and there is nothing that can be done to change matters. I wish you could go to Sibley, then you would understand what it means to me."

"Some of the times when you said you were visiting school friends, were you in fact staying at Sibley?"

"A few times. I haven't been there for three or four years, and I must try to do so. I've been luckier than you, as I've had a second home and one so much more enjoyable than this."

"I never knew. How strange."

"Not really. We're not a family that confides in each other. Five individuals connected by blood and not much else."

"Not you and me now, surely?" Sophie was distressed.

"No," he smiled affectionately at her. "No, we've become good friends which is the best of things and more than I could ever have wished for. But think, mother and father live in their own solitary worlds, each convinced that he or she is suffering the most from the disappointments of their lives. Lucy lives in her own dream world, and I have never fathomed what, if anything, she really feels or thinks."

Sophie shivered, remembering Lucy's revelations.

"What's the matter?"

When she hesitated, he said, "Come on, tell me. Something is worrying you about Lucy."

"She saw Major Howard in London. A number of times." She found she couldn't say any more but she had no need to; Robert had little difficulty understanding the implications of her words.

"Oh dear, oh dear. Let's just hope it ended there, in London. Otherwise there really will be problems."

"Yes." Sophie struggled with the hurt anger that rose within her, but was unable to stop herself saying bitterly, "I hope I never have to see him again." And tried to believe it.

"Poor Sophie. Life hasn't been fair to you. I'm sorry I brought him here."

But Sophie, feeling contrary, wasn't sure that she wished that she had never met James Howard.

"Why are you here today?"

"Benedict needed to go into Cirencester on business so we went in together. He's dining at the Mansion this evening and staying overnight and will return this way to Millington tomorrow."

Sophie smiled at the thought of Knight's Darkleigh being considered on the way between Millington and Cirencester and was flattered that Mr Rivers was prepared to go on quite a detour to see her. She also noted that Robert had not answered her question and to make it easier for him, she said, "Caroline leaves for Cheltenham on Monday."

"Oh." Robert digested this unwelcome but not unexpected news.

"Then Benedict, no doubt, will want to say goodbye to her tomorrow."

"No doubt," agreed Sophie.

* * *

When George had not returned home from the hunt by six o'clock, Lucy, in some irritation, decided she should walk down to the Manor Farm to see if he was there. As her boots squelched along the muddy road, the annoyance deepened. George was neglecting her; he spent too much time with that Richard Freeman, or with his family, and he did not give her the attention which was her due. That she did not particularly want his company was entirely beside the point. He should be there when she wanted him there and then go when she wanted him to go. His neglect of her meant that if – she corrected herself – when Major Howard came, she would be completely justified in seeing him.

She turned into the short driveway to the house (now altered so that it no longer passed through the farmyard as it had done for centuries) and her tranquillity restored, presented her usual placid face to her in-laws.

The Harries' greeted George's absence with noisy anxiety. Jarvis roared for a lantern so that he could go down to the stables to see if George's horse had returned. As he strode down to the stables, Mrs Harries – who was standing at the front door – cried after him to let her know immediately if the horse was there.

Joining in with the chorus of commotion, Anne and Mary disturbed them well before Jarvis had reached the stables, which was fortunate for George and Richard – George frantically tidied himself up and slid down the loft steps, leaving Richard shaking with silent giggles, hiding behind some bales in the farthest corner of the loft.

Jarvis entered the stable and in the light of his lantern, saw his son standing near his horse, dishevelled and embarrassed.

"What the devil, George," he spluttered, relief making him angry.

"I – I fell asleep in the hay loft, after stabling Captain," George muttered.

Jarvis snorted. "You've upset your mother, your sisters, and your wife. Really, you should know better."

They walked to the house, Jarvis still huffing and puffing, but when his mother and sisters saw George with his clothes awry and hay in his hair, they laughed and hugged him and then Jarvis joined in, slapping him on the back and saying, "Well, it must have been a fine day's sport."

"It was," George said, smiling sheepishly. He saw Lucy, standing a little apart. "I'm sorry, love, if I worried you."

She acknowledged his apology with a small nod and a gracious smile and none of the Harries' were aware that a slither of ice had slipped into her heart as she watched him come into the room. She had seen a clumsy, awkward, unkempt… peasant. Her husband. She, refined, beautiful Lucy Latham was his wife. He did not deserve her; she was absolved from all duty and responsibility towards him. When Major Howard came to claim her…

* * *

Captain whinnied as Richard stole away into the dark night, but nothing else stirred as he ran through the meadows back to Knight's Darkleigh and the Chantry. He vowed that if not in the next hunt, then in the one after, he, not George, would ride that beautiful horse and show the world how it should be ridden. He gave his high, wild laugh as he vaulted over the wall into the Chantry's neglected garden. In darkened windows in different rooms, Mrs Freeman and Polly, each with her own reason for watching out for him, saw him return.

Chapter Fourteen

Benedict appeared at the rectory in the middle of the morning. Mrs Latham was most impressed when she heard that he had dined at the Mansion and she hurried downstairs to greet him. Her fulsome welcome embarrassed him but he was rewarded by Sophie's friendliest smile. Under Robert's prompting, he described the Mansion, none of the Lathams having seen more than a glimpse of it.

Mrs Latham had determined never to speak to Robert again, but when he said to Benedict, "I haven't told them. I thought I'd let you."

She said sharply, "Told us what?"

"I'm thinking of holding a ball at Millington, just before Christmas."

This made Mrs Latham and Sophie gasp with excitement.

"The main alterations should be finished by then and although people have been truly kind in inviting Robert and me to dine over the past few weeks, I know that they're all curious to see what we've done. So, I thought a ball would be the best way of replaying their hospitality and satisfy their curiosity. It has been a recluse's house for so long, few people have been inside it. My mother wrote a few days ago saying she was coming down to inspect our efforts at the end of November, so it all seemed to fit together."

"Confess, Benedict," said Robert, "it was the thought of her comments on our bachelor way of life that has been the spur to your determination to get things finished."

"She will tell us exactly what she thinks of us and our work," Benedict smiled. "But if I tell her that I'm going to hold a ball, she'll be so relieved that I'm not going to become the third successive Millington hermit, she'll take over all the organisation of it, which suits me very well."

The exciting thought of a ball had, he saw, brought back much of the sparkle to Sophie's eyes and that was reward enough for the work that the ball (not a form of entertainment which he much enjoyed) would inevitably entail.

It was decided that the three of them would walk over to Middle Darkleigh to make their farewells to Caroline. Mrs Latham waved goodbye, well pleased with the way matters were turning out. She had abandoned her original intention of spending a suffering morning in bed and went into the dining parlour to acquaint Mr Latham with the plan for the ball, and also her firm belief that by then, Sophie would be betrothed to Mr Rivers and soon would be the mistress of one of the great houses of the neighbourhood.

Mr Latham received the news cautiously, but said, "Perhaps we were too hasty in agreeing Lucy's marriage to George Harries. I cannot help but feel that she would make a more suitable chatelaine of Millington than little Sophie, dear girl though she is, of course," he added hastily. "But she does allow herself to be rather enthusiastic about things, whereas Lucy has a calmer, more mature approach. And one has to say it: Lucy is so much the better looking."

Mrs Latham wouldn't go so far as to equate Lucy's self-absorption with a mature outlook on life, but she did agree about the beauty.

"Yes, Millington would have been a splendid background for her," she sighed, "whereas I feel that Sophie will be overwhelmed by its grandeur."

"Not that we can do anything about it," said Mr Latham.

Mrs Latham sighed again and left him to the wearisome task of composing his sermon.

Sophie, showing the liveliness which so distressed her father, regaled Robert and Benedict with the exploits of her pupils in their efforts to avoid education. This encouraged the two men to cap each other with recollections of some of the outrageous things they had done as boys.

"I'm amazed that any education was drummed into either of you at all," said Sophie as they walked across the little bridge at the ford in Middle Darkleigh.

"Wha 'do that mean, edication?" demanded Robert, in a broad Suffolk accent.

"Oi reckons it be bad for Oi," said Benedict in an equally broad Gloucestershire accent.

Sophie was reduced to giggles. Very happy to give her so much amusement, they continued in a similar vein until they reached Lucy and George's farmhouse. Then, in unspoken agreement, they walked quietly by it. But they were too late: Lucy heard them coming and flung open a window.

"What a dreadful row you were making," she said, manifesting a true Latham disapproval her father would have applauded.

"I'm sorry if we disturbed you," said Sophie coldly. It was the first time she and Lucy had met since their tea party.

She could not yet admit that Lucy's revelations had delivered what should be a fatal blow to her infatuation with Major Howard but now, jealousy and anger rose up within her and she felt a dreadful desire to scratch Lucy's lovely face, to spoil its perfection. Horrified by this reaction, she walked on but stopped without turning when Lucy said, "Wait, I'll come with you," in response to Robert's explanation as to where they were going.

"Well, don't be too long, then," he said, less than graciously.

Caroline greeted them with pleasure, hiding her surprise at seeing Lucy, who had not previously visited her. Indeed, Lucy had avoided being in Caroline's company; Caroline might be rather old, but Lucy recognised a rival beauty, less obvious than her own, but potent nonetheless. Now that Caroline was leaving, she could afford to be friendly.

By careful strategy, Robert managed to sit next to Caroline.

"Sophie tells us you're deserting us for the glittering social whirl of Cheltenham."

"To describe a visit to my grandmother as a great social event is perhaps a slight exaggeration."

"It's Mr Rivers who is proposing to give us the great social event," said Sophie, still not quite believing the wonderful idea of a ball, which would be the first one she had ever attended. She had found the Assembly Rooms in Cheltenham very splendid, but they would not compare with a private ball in a great house.

"I'm thinking of having a ball before Christmas," explained Benedict.

"What a wonderful idea!" said Caroline.

Lucy had met Benedict only the once when he had been at his most tongue-tied. She had not been impressed with him but now his worth shone forth. She gazed raptly at him, edged a little closer and in her soft, sweet voice, sad, "How very kind of you, Mr Rivers." She managed to make it sound as though he was holding the ball for her, and her alone. Benedict, stunned at being the focus of Lucy's attention, gave Robert a harassed look. Robert grinned.

"Lady Rivers will be organising it," said Sophie, somewhat put out. Mr Rivers was too nice a person to fall prey to Lucy in predatory form.

"Then it will be beautifully managed," said Caroline. "Lady Rivers is a genius at organising social gatherings."

"My mother's great mission in life is to manage and organise," said Benedict. "Which, no doubt, is why I'm untidy and disorganised."

"And anti-social," said Caroline. "Your mother's soirees are the most sought after in town, but how often do you appear?"

Lucy was bored with talk of parties which she knew nothing about and to show off her London sophistication, she said, "When I was in London, I went to a soiree at a most elegant house. It was at Lady Cray's." She turned to Caroline. "Do you know her?"

"I know of her," said Caroline in a rather odd voice, which made Sophie and Robert look at her. Thus, they did not notice the dismay on Benedict's face. Lucy noticed nothing. She was recalling that evening of sparkling company where lively flirtations were enjoyed by all and witty malicious gossip was bandied about. She had not understood most of what was being said but smiled and laughed when others did and she had felt more beautiful and more in her element than ever before.

"How did you come to be introduced to Lady Cray?"

A faint pink came to Lucy's cheeks. "Major Howard – we happened to meet him at the theatre one evening."

"I see," said Caroline flatly. The next time she saw James, she would murder him.

Unable to allow Lucy to expose herself further, Sophie asked abruptly, "Did George enjoy the hunt yesterday?"

"Oh, yes," Lucy said indifferently and thought that Sophie must be jealous of her success with Major Howard, in London.

"I must sometime call and admire his new horse," said Robert. "I understand it's very handsome."

"It is, indeed. I saw him on it yesterday. It was by far the best looking horse in the field," said Caroline continuing the conversation a little desperately. If James had taken Lucy to Fanny Cray's, all London would know that he had taken a rustic beauty as his mistress. Lucy's behaviour towards him before her marriage had been unwise and silly but James should not have taken advantage of her simplicity. From their embarrassment, it was obvious that Robert and Sophie knew about the affair and now she and Benedict did. None of them would spread the story, but how could they stop Lucy betraying herself any further?

"Lucy," she said. "I hope you don't mind my calling you Lucy? Lucy, a word of advice. I do not recommend that you mention again that you have been to Lady Cray's house. She isn't regarded as being entirely respectable. James should not have taken you there."

"Oh." Lucy was affronted but couldn't think of any retort. She was quite sure that Lady Firth was mistaken. The house had been on the best part of town, it was large and opulently furnished, and the people were the most elegant she had ever seen. Then she thought she knew what the problem was. Lady Firth was jealous as well. She was also in love with James and was angry that he had paid attention to her, Lucy. That must be it. She smiled her secretive little smile and didn't say anything more. Caroline felt strong misgivings about Lucy's discretion, but she had warned her and there was nothing more she could do.

It was with relief all round when a little while later, Benedict rose and said that he and Robert should be on their way.

Caroline gave Sophie an affectionate kiss which brought a lump to Sophie's throat. Somehow, Robert engineered it that Lucy, Sophie, and Benedict, went down to the garden gate while he remained with Caroline. He took her hand and kissed it. Still holding it, he said in a conversational tone, "You know I fell in love with you the moment I saw you, don't you? I know it's no use my hoping you could feel the same way about me, as what have I got to offer you? But I wanted you to know that I love you and always will."

He kissed her hand again and let it go. She found herself utterly incapable of speech and unable to meet his eyes. She looked down and with an enormous effort to get back to normality, he said, "Now I must go and try to drum some sense into that scatter-brained sister of mine."

He turned and blindly ran down the path to join the others as they stood at the door to Lucy's home. With false cheerfulness, he said, "Do you realise, Lucy, I've not yet seen your new home? Why don't Sophie and Benedict carry on and you can show it to me, and I'll catch them up."

Sophie's heart went out to him and she thought how much more courageous was his response to the loss of love compared with her own self-pitying one. Lucy looked sulky but could not think of any way she could avoid the quite unjustified and unwarranted scolding she knew Robert was going to give her and they went into the house.

Ten minutes later, Robert saw Sophie and Benedict in the distance; they were dawdling along and seemed to be talking happily together, so he slowed down his own pace. He had failed to make any impression on Lucy of the dangers at her position, and he felt immense exasperation with her. He caught a glimpse of Caroline's house across the valley and felt great misery settle upon him. His arm was aching, and it started to rain. He gave a groan and ran to catch up with Sophie and Benedict.

Chapter Fifteen

Sophie stood at the window of the dining parlour and looked out on to the blank greyness of a November fog. After some weeks of strong winds and heavy rain, the weather had abruptly changed and the fog had descended in the night, smothering the landscape in a cold cocoon. It could, she thought, symbolise her suffocating, limited existence. As usual, she had breakfasted alone and, in a few minutes, would be entering battle with her reluctant pupils for the rest of the morning. After a light, silent lunch with her parents, she would take a little exercise on her own and then she would sit in the cold drawing room with her embroidery, listening to her mother's complaints. If she were lucky, her mother would take tea with Mrs Freeman, and she would be free to read and re-read the books Caroline had given her. Then dinner would be endured and afterwards, yet more embroidery in the drawing room before retiring fatigued with boredom to the sanctuary of her bedroom.

The only rays which lifted the gloom were letters from Caroline. She could hear Caroline's voice as she read of incidents that had caught Caroline's fancy and which she knew would entertain Sophie. Sophie hoarded the letters and lived a vicarious social existence through them. Otherwise, nothing disturbed the relentless monotony.

Today was her birthday; she was twenty-three and she thought rather dismally that no-one would remember it. In the past, Lucy would have remembered, as her own birthday was a fortnight later and she did not want anyone to forget that. But now, she and Lucy had not spoken to each other for weeks and she didn't believe Lucy would use the occasion to break the silence. They had seen each other in church, on different sides of the aisle, and Sophie was interested to note that Lucy was looking plumper. Good, rich Harries' fare instead of the Rectory hard rations were having an effect on her figure. Sophie did, however, envy Lucy's smart new winter clothes and when George, equally smart, tucked his wife's hand under his arm, they looked the epitome of the devoted young couple.

Sophie turned away from the window and, looking martyred, put on her shawl and plodded up to the little schoolroom situated behind the house. While she waited for her unruly pupils to appear, she thought about herself and Lucy and Major Howard.

As if carefully prodding a scar to see it had really healed, she summoned up a picture of James Howard. She remembered how his intense blue eyes had laughed at something she said and it made her heart ache but in a detached way, she noted the former fierce pain had gone. She was almost cured of her infatuation, which is what it must have been, since it had so dwindled over the weeks through lack of nourishment. But if she were to see him again, then what? Would the overwhelming attraction she had felt come back again? Or, was it like the measles: once you had recovered from it, you were immune thereafter. She couldn't be sure until she did see him again and she fell to wondering whether he would be at the Millington ball. She had heard nothing further about that. Perhaps it wasn't going to happen, after all. That thought lowered her spirits even more and her pupils trooping in, eyed her glum face and wondered what was wrong.

"'er be in love," whispered one little girl.

"Na. No-one for 'er to be in love with," said her friend.

"She be miserable then 'cos she ain't in love."

Sophie glared at the whisperers who put their hands to their mouths to stop their giggles. Gradually, the noises of six pairs of scuffling feet in ill-fitting clogs and their owners' attendant sniffs and coughs died away and six pair of eyes stared at her.

How can I make the lesson interesting when I'm so bored with myself? thought Sophie. The silence became oppressive.

"It's my birthday today," she said.

The watchful eyes considered her.

"What's a berfday?" asked the smallest child.

"When a bubby is born, stupid," said her sister.

"Miss ain't a bubby, she weren't born today," pointed out the little one.

The others found this incredibly funny, and the laughter and jeers made the child cry. Sophie called them to order.

"Come on, Ellie, there's no need to cry. You were quite right; I wasn't born today. I was born on the same day – twentieth November – twenty-three years ago. Now, when were you born?"

There was silence. No-one was entirely sure when he or she was born and seeing confusion and even distress on some of the faces, Sophie said hastily, "Well, never mind. We'll get on with the lesson and do some numbers. Where are your slates?"

As a diversionary tactic, Sim Brown said, "Oi be leaving school next week, Miss. Oi be starting work."

"Really, Sim? Where will you be working? For Mr Harries?"

"Na, Oi'll be working for Mr Freeman at the Chantry. Wiv moi sis."

"We'll miss you," said Sophie sincerely. Sim had Polly's sunny good nature. The amount of learning he had assimilated was minimal and it was probably the best thing for him to start working. But at the Chantry?

The only other boy in the class looked gloomy. "Oi wouldn't work at the Chantry, Oi wouldn't ," he said.

"'e weren't asked, were 'ee?" retorted Sim.

"Do Polly like working there?" asked one of the girls and there were sly giggles. Sim looked worried but said defiantly, "Oi reckon she does."

"Mr Richard be ever so 'andsome," said the oldest girl.

"E don't bother 'er," said Sim.

"Na. 'E don't, do 'e? 'E and Mr George now, they be as thick as two thieves." The girl clapped her hand over her mouth. "Oi be sorry, Miss, beggin' your pardon."

Uneasily aware that the children's gossip had undertones that she didn't understand, Sophie said firmly, "Come along, down to work. Now, Sim, if you're going to be useful to Mr Freeman, you should at least learn to add some numbers together."

"Why?"

As she wasn't sure how to answer this, Sophie ignored him and ploughed on with the lesson. The reference to George she found unsettling and thinking perhaps she should be the one to bear the olive branch, she decided she would call on Lucy that afternoon.

* * *

Sophie had been correct in her assumption that her birthday would be forgotten by her parents and no mention of it was made at lunch. Her announcement that she was going to walk over to see Lucy did arouse some slight interest. Lucy had rarely bothered to call on her parents since she was married and this neglect was one more item in her mother's litany of complaints.

Mrs Latham said peevishly, "One day Lucy will remember where we live. Maybe you could remind her of our existence."

An hour later, Sophie reworded this to Lucy as "Mother sends her love and hopes she will see you soon."

Lucy looked a little ashamed. She was flushed and a little dishevelled and Sophie thought she must have interrupted an afternoon nap.

"It's been difficult, I've been so busy," said Lucy. "I've no idea where the days have gone. But I will come over soon, I promise."

"What have you been doing?" asked Sophie, making conversation.

"Oh, lots of things," said Lucy. Then realising this was inadequate, added, "We've become great friends with the Agars and Lewis' up in Darkleigh St Mary and we spent a good deal of time visiting and things. And you have no idea what time it takes to run a house, Sophie. One always has to be on at the servants to make them do their work properly."

"Yes, of course," Sophie avoided looking at the dust-covered table beside her. She cast around for another topic of conversation.

"I hope George is well."

"Yes, thank you."

"Is he out riding?"

"I expect so. He usually is." Lucy's indifference killed that subject. She lapsed into a dreamy contemplation of the fire and Sophie felt irritation with her. After all, she had made the effort to walk over to Middle Darkleigh; surely Lucy could respond with a little more energy. She was used to Lucy's day-dreaming, but this was infuriating.

A small devil prompted Sophie to rouse Lucy by saying, "I've been wondering whether Major Howard will be at the Millington ball."

It worked, as if by magic. Pathetically eager, Lucy exclaimed, "Oh, Sophie, do you think he will? I do so want to see him again."

She burst into tears. "I know I shouldn't be saying this, but you are the only one I can tell. Sophie, why doesn't he come to me? He promised he would. I've written to him, but he doesn't answer my letters. Sophie, it's driving me mad. What can I do?"

Lucy sobbed and sobbed while Sophie looked helplessly on.

"Lucy, I don't know. It's far too dangerous for him to come here. You should put him out of your mind."

Lucy raised a blotchy face, her eyes puffed and swollen, she glared furiously at Sophie. It was the first time Sophie had seen Lucy looking plain and unappealing and it dismayed her.

"You say that because you want him. But you can't: he's mine. He'll never be yours."

"I don't want him."

"Ha. You've suddenly changed your tune."

"It's true. It really is."

"I don't believe you."

"But, Lucy, what about George?"

"George? What has George got to do with it?"

"He's your husband."

"Are you comparing James with that... that clodhopper?"

"You're married to George. You seem to be forgetting that."

"James will arrange for us to be divorced. It can be done, you know, by Act of Parliament. Then he will marry me."

"Lucy, think of the scandal. His family, his grandmother…"

"It's nothing to do with them. It's just James and me."

"I think you've taken leave of your senses. Why should he bother to marry you? He seems to have had his way with you without the necessity of marriage lines so why should he bother to incur the expense and embarrassment of a divorce?"

Lucy burst into tears again.

"Go away, you horrible girl, go away. I never want to see you again."

"Stop being hysterical," snapped Sophie. "Don't worry, I'm going."

The clammy fog wrapped around her as she walked down the hill towards the ford. She could see only a few yards in front of her, and she seemed to be alone in a grey, silent world. Nearing the farm, she could just see shadowy, lumpy shapes in the field beside her, but the cows, huddled together, did not move as she, a ghostly figure in her grey cloak and bonnet, soundlessly went by.

As she passed the Harries' new barns, handsome stone buildings on the opposite side of the road from the farmhouse, she was distracted by a sound – was it laughter? – coming, it seemed, from the direction of one of the barns.

She peered through the fog but could see nothing. She jumped, startled, when she heard a whisper.

"Miss Sophie? Be that you?" Polly shambled towards her.

"Oh, Polly, you gave me such a fright."

"Oi be sorry, Miss, but you did the same to me. I thought 'ee was a ghost." Polly giggled and then raising her voice, said, "Oi reckons we best get back 'ome as quick as we can. This fog be getting worse. Can 'ee see – there be the ford? Look, Oi'll show 'ee."

Sophie was given the strong impression that she was being hurried away but she felt unable to resist Polly's determination to be helpful. They went across the bridge, Polly chattering non-stop.

"Oi be on my way back to the Chantry. Mrs Freeman sent me out to get eggs from Mrs Harries."

"Why come all the way over here for them? Surely Farmer Glover could provide eggs?"

Polly glanced conspiratorially left and right and lowered her voice. "Oi reckon Farmer Glover hasn't been paid these three months for his eggs and butter and milk. Oi reckon that's why."

"Oh dear. I thought… I heard… I mean…"

"You heard that Mr Freeman be plucking old Window Hardiman up in Cold Trenton. Oi reckons you heard right. But 'e's only bothered with his own comfort and poor Mrs Freeman has to make do the best she can. 'E'd be the first to complain if 'e didn't have his eggs for breakfast but he doesn't provide her with the money to get 'em."

"How are you liking working at the Chantry?" asked Sophie, guiltily aware that she should not be gossiping this way with the Freeman's servant.

"It be orlright," said Polly but she sounded evasive. "Our Sim be starting there next week."

"Yes, he told me so this morning. He didn't seem quite to know what he'll be doing."

"E'll be the gardener's boy and boot boy and stable boy." Polly cackled with laughter. "It'll be the first time in 'is life our Sim will have to work, lazy little bastard. Beggin' your pardon, Miss."

"Poor Sim. I'll miss him in school, though he was never very interested in studying."

"None of us Browns be that," said Polly cheerfully.

"Mr Richard is studying, I understand, to go into the church." Polly did not answer, and Sophie asked curiously, "What's wrong?"

"Nothing, Miss."

"Don't you like Mr Richard? He's very handsome."

"Aye, that he be." Polly was surly. "But looks isn't everything."

"No." Sophie sighed and thought of pretty Lucy. "I believe he and Mr George are good friends."

Polly again was silent and although Sophie couldn't see her face, she thought that Polly was embarrassed, and this impression was strengthened when Polly abruptly changed the subject.

"Did I heard you be doing to a ball over Millington way, Miss? That'll be ever so nice for 'ee, Miss. I reckon you deserve a little fun."

"Thank you."

"Tis a pity Oi can't come as your personal maid. Oi'd be ever so good and refined."

"I wish you could, Polly." Both laughed at the thought of Polly being a superior lady's maid.

A discussion of what Sophie was going to wear – a problem that weighed on Sophie's mind – lasted them to the rectory gate and their ways parted.

Chapter Sixteen

"Benedict, the invitations are going out far too late," said Lady Rivers severely. "They really should have been sent last week. It's just as well I've come down, otherwise I shudder to think how this ball would have been organised."

"You're right, as always, mother," said Benedict and then added gloomily, "I'm beginning to wish I'd never suggested the wretched thing."

"My dear boy, if you're feeling like that at this early stage, then Heaven help you when it comes to the actual day."

Lady Rivers looked at him, not unkindly, and added, "Don't worry, leave everything to me. All you and Robert need to do is to carry out my instructions to the letter, and then everything will be fine."

"Thank you," said Benedict meekly and then spoilt the effect by saying to Robert, "A difficult question for you: who was the general, my mother or my father?"

"Refuse to answer that, Robert," commanded Lady Rivers.

Robert laughed and obeyed.

Lady Rivers had harboured deep suspicions that Benedict was being duped by the young man overseeing the improvements to Millington Hall and this was one of her reasons for abandoning her comfortable London house for the cold winter winds of the Cotswolds. However, she soon discovered that Robert was her old friend Emily Latham's nephew and for her sake, she was prepared to suspend her suspicions. Within twenty-four hours, Robert had won her over entirely and a firm friendship had been established.

Benedict was delighted and left them happily arguing over arrangements for the ball while he carried on the battle of convincing obstinate tenant farmers of the benefits of his agricultural reforms. Even his hostile tenants were easier to confront, he thought, than the thorny problem of whether to invite James Howard and Lucy Harries to the ball.

He wanted to invite James, his oldest friend, and he did not want to invite Lucy, whom he believed could not be trusted to act with discretion. But he couldn't invite Sophie without her family and the ball without Sophie would be unsupportable. Robert had frankly said that if it were left to him, he'd leave out Lucy and George, but Benedict dithered and held off sending out the invitations.

Lady Rivers and Robert stood in the Great Hall. Loft and vast, bitterly cold and smelling of old damp stone, it was the heart of the original medieval house. They both shivered.

"The first thing to be done is to light some fires and try to get some warmth into the stones. At the moment, it's the most inhospitable venue for a ball I could imagine. And it's filthy," said Lady Rivers.

"The intention is that we start cleaning up in the next few days. We found some enormous tapestries in the attics to hang on the walls. Benedict wants as many candles as possible and with fires burning at both ends, it should be very splendid."

Lady Rivers looked unconvinced, and they returned to the warmth and light of the morning room. She returned also to her original grievance about the delay in sending out the invitations.

"These have been ready to send out for days. Why hasn't he done so? It isn't like Benedict to be so inefficient."

Robert picked his words with care. "He's in two minds over some of the invitations."

"What do you mean? Which ones?"

"Well, I suppose it's my family's fault."

"Of course your family is invited."

"That's kind of you."

"Then what's the problem? Come on, Robert. If there are going to be difficulties, I must know about them, so I can avoid or minimise them."

Undoubtedly, Lady Rivers was a general.

Robert said, "If I explain the position. James Howard…"

"Ah, James," she interrupted. "I see. Which of your sisters has he trifled with?"

"Lucy."

"The married one. I assume she's pretty?"

"Yes."

"And if James is invited, you think Lucy will be upset?"

"The reverse. She's besotted."

"Oh. He does have a way with silly young girls. You think she could cause an awkward scene."

"Yes. I hate to say it of my sister, but she is a very silly young girl."

"What about your other sister, what's her name, Sophie? Did she succumb also to James' charm?"

"To some extent, but James didn't trifle with her, he acted with complete propriety."

"I see." If this was the case, Sophie could have few attractions.

"Sophie is very different from Lucy. She has much more sense, for a start."

Lady Rivers translated this to mean dull.

"She and Lady Firth have become good friends," he added, wanting to talk of his beloved.

Lady Rivers was surprised. Caroline Firth did not make a habit of befriending plain dull girls. She let the matter rest, saying she must discuss food with Benedict's newly acquired cook but at the earliest opportunity she tracked Benedict down in the muniments room which he had made into his retreat. She came directly to the point.

"I hear your friend James has been up to his usual tricks. What are you going to do?"

"So, Robert told you the problem. I don't know. I feel I'm making a mountain out of a molehill."

"I think you are too. I know Robert is worried that Lucy will be indiscreet, but James is wily enough to contrive that she will not be."

"I hope so. But he hasn't been that discreet himself: he took her to Fanny Cray's."

This did make Lady Rivers blink. "I see. She must be exceptionally pretty, otherwise he wouldn't have risked the mockery of that set in showing off an unknown provincial. Is she beautiful?"

"Yes, I suppose she is."

"Well, all you can do is to invite James and between us we must make sure that Lucy is kept under control. Caroline Firth will help. I hope she'll come as it's time she came back into society."

"Why did she retreat to Darkleigh?"

"Didn't you hear? She made a fool of herself over young Maitland. Luckily, she came to her senses in time, but her pride was badly shaken, and she ran away. I put the idea of this part of the world into her mind. I felt sorry for her, as although she had been foolish, it wasn't too surprising after years of marriage to Firth."

"I can't say I liked him. Something unpleasant under the surface charm."

"Yes. Caroline was always discretion itself, but once or twice I saw her looking at Firth, and believe me, Benedict, she was terrified of him. I could never persuade her to talk to me. I'm very fond of her, you know." She looked hopefully at Benedict who laughed.

"No, forget that idea, mother. Anyway, Robert would murder me if he thought I was a rival."

"Robert?"

"Yes. Totally smitten."

"He's not the first. But Caroline?"

"I don't know. As you say, she is discretion itself. Robert thinks he successfully hides his lovelorn state but it's quite obvious. Caroline likes him, no doubt about that, but I don't know whether she feels anything more than friendship for him, poor fellow."

"No prospects?"

"None."

"So, we have Robert, who is in love with Caroline and Lucy who is infatuated with James. What about their sister, Sophie?"

A flush crept up Benedict's thin cheek.

"Sophie is very different from Lucy, I do assure you," and he smiled wistfully as he thought of Sophie.

So, Benedict was attracted to Sophie, thought his mother. And if shy, gauche Benedict had at last succumbed, it was inevitable that she would be a dim little nobody. He would be frightened off by anyone else. She resolved that she would call on Mrs Latham and inspect her future daughter-in-law.

* * *

Mrs Latham was so delighted to receive the invitation to the Millington ball that she was prepared to overlook the reference to Lady Emily Latham in the letter which accompanied the invitation and waited with keen anticipation to receive Lady River's promised call.

"If this isn't an indication of Benedict River's interest in Sophie, then what else can it be?" she declared jubilantly to her husband.

Lucy and George, having received their invitation, called in to share the excitement and it was agreed that Lucy should join Mrs Latham and Sophie in entertaining Lady Rivers. Sophie endured sly looks from Lucy and teasing references from George in a heavy humorous style that set her teeth on edge.

Lady Rivers, on meeting Sophie a few days later, breathed a sigh of relief. She had told herself that she was resigned to Benedict marrying a nonentity, but her gratitude that Sophie was so different from what she had imagined, made her realise how disappointed she had really been.

Sophie was not beautiful but when she compared her with Lucy's empty loveliness, she gave another prayer of thanks that Benedict had not fallen for a pretty, amoral nitwit.

Sophie regarded Lady Rivers with some awe: she was short, stout, not particularly handsome, but she radiated an inexhaustible energy and enthusiasm for life which was irresistible. It must be the basis of her success as a hostess, thought Sophie, hearing her mother and Lucy laughing, that one felt livelier, wittier and so much more interesting than one ever had before.

Lady Rivers was saying "… and you can imagine: the pair of them thought that all that was needed to make the evening a success was to clean up the Great Hall – and what a job that's turning out to be – light some fires and some candles and that would be it. No thought of a cardroom, a retiring room, of a supper room, indeed of any of the details that make all the difference to a social occasion."

"Men are so inclined to concentrate on one particular problem and ignore the fifty others of equal importance," agreed Mrs Latham.

To Sophie's amusement, she said this with a smile, her usual carping tones entirely absent.

"I hope they've remembered the musicians," said Lucy, whose heart was thumping at the thought of dancing the waltz again with James.

"They have been organised, if one could call it that. Benedict proudly told me that he had hired the musicians. I asked him if he had heard them play so you can imagine my horror when he said he had heard of them via a friend of a friend. Not my idea of a recommendation, I told him, so if they're terrible, I'll announce that they weren't my responsibility."

"It must be very different trying to organise a ball in a half-renovated house in the depths of the country, instead of London," said Sophie.

"I suppose one could call it a challenge," said Lady Rivers. "Myself, I regard it more as a nightmare. There is still so much to be arranged and it's only two weeks away."

"And only two men to help you," sympathised Mrs Latham.

Lady Rivers pounced on the opportunity thus presented.

"Exactly," she sighed and then, leaning forward, said, "Mrs Latham, it is, I know, a great impertinence of me to ask such a favour, but I feel we understand each other so well that I can venture to do so. Would you spare me Miss Sophie for the week before the ball? I feel I need help with all the little details that only we women can see need to be done."

Mrs Latham, highly flattered, graciously agreed to this.

"Oh Sophie, my dear," she exclaimed, when Lady Rivers had left. "You've made a hit with her Ladyship. I'm so pleased. I must tell your father. Now he'll believe me – our little Sophie, Mrs Benedict Rivers of Millington. It's more than I could ever have hoped for."

She rushed away, leaving Sophie prey to conflicting feelings. She was excited at the thought of staying at Millington and flattered that the redoubtable Lady Rivers believed she would be of assistance, but she also felt she was being lured into a trap.

Lucy voiced this fear: "Whether you like it or not, I'll bet you'll be married to Benedict Rivers by Easter."

"I feel I'm being manoeuvred," admitted Sophie.

"With no dowry and nothing outstanding in the way of looks, you don't have much choice," said Lucy who was admiring her reflection in the looking glass as she tied her bonnet ribbons. "But after marriage, things are different," and she smiled at the thought of the unsuspecting George.

* * *

Widow Hardiman of Cold Trenton died that night. Much to Mr Freeman's fury, he discovered two days later that, despite the numerous hints he had dropped and the nods and winks of understanding he had received from the old lady, she had not, in fact, altered her will in his favour. Everything had been left to her late husband's cousin who plainly told Mr Freeman that he was not welcome at the Manor and indeed had suspicions of the disinterested nature of Mr Freeman's visits to Mrs Hardiman.

Mr Freeman shook his head sadly and took comfort at the local inn and gave the landlord the benefit of his reflections on the perfidy of humankind. The cousin had not been near Cold Trenton for years, whereas he had been a constant, unfailing source of comfort to the poor old lady in her last months of earthly existence. All this out of the loving Christian charity of his heart, with no thought of any possible benefit to himself crossing his mind. To be accused of such base behaviour was the most cruel injury, particularly when he was deeply grieving the loss of a dear friend.

The landlord was unresponsive. After all, he had to consider his own position with the new owner of the Manor. Mr Freeman, recognising the lukewarm nature of the landlord's sympathy, sighed mournfully, finished his brandy and with a fulsome speech of farewell, left the inn without paying for his drink.

He rode slowly along the bleak high road, anger at the old woman's deceitfulness stripping the unctuous benevolence from his face. His temper was not improved as sleet, driven by a biting north-east wind, chilled him to the bone.

The Chantry was silent and empty when he returned. Mrs Freeman, believing he would be away all day as was usual when he went to Cold Trenton, was taking tea with Mrs Latham and being given a minute-by-minute account of Lady Rivers' visit. However, his wife's presence or absence was a matter of indifference to him, but he scowled when there was no sign of Richard, who was supposed to be studying.

The servants had made the same assumption as Mrs Freeman and had used the opportunity to take the afternoon off. The four newcomers had taken the trap into Cirencester, Sim had disappeared with one of his brothers to poach rabbits in Laine woods and Polly, as she had done many times before, had followed Richard.

* * *

After hearing Polly and Sophie talking by the bridge in the fog, George and Richard had decided that their meeting place should be more secluded and they were now using an old barn tucked in a fold in the valley between Middle and Priors' Darkleigh. They were also more circumspect in approaching and leaving the barn and Polly had lost track of Richard since then. But this time she was sure she knew where the meeting place would be as Sim had fearfully mentioned that the last time he and Tom had poached in the woods between Middle and Priors', he was sure they heard ghosts shrieking with laughter. Polly did not disabuse him and recommended that he should keep away as you never knew with hobgoblins and ghosts… Sim shuddered and turned his poaching attentions in the opposite direction.

The barn lay sheltered in its hollow, out of sight of prying eyes. Polly, who could poach as well as Sim, allowed Richard time to reach the barn and then walked silently up to it and peered through the slit window in one of its massive walls.

She gasped and crouched down below the slit. Disgust and curiosity warred within her at the sight of the tangled limbs, white and gleaming in the dark. Curiosity won and she again looked down at the two men. She had realised the relationship between the two was an unnatural one but seeing it in the flesh disturbed and excited her. She crouched down again and her cunning mind thought of what she could do with her knowledge. She stayed there, listening to the men's groans and sighs (the noises were a little eerie: it was no wonder Sim had been scared) and then to the soft talk of love which made her feel quite queer.

Then the mood suddenly changed, and they were quarrelling.

"I don't see why I can't ride Captain," said Richard sulkily. "You have all the good things, why can't I have just a little sometime?"

"It would cause talk, you know we can't allow that," pleaded George. "It's dangerous what we're doing, we must be careful at all times."

"You don't care about me. All you care about is your position. You want to finish with me, you're tired of me."

"Of course I'm not. You know that very well."

"Why can't we go away? We could be ourselves in France or Italy. Let's get away from this dreary valley and its interfering people."

"What about my family… my wife…?"

"Your wife? Ha! You don't love her, you love me. You promised me you wouldn't touch her. Have you? Have you lied to me?" Richard sounded hysterical and George harassed as he tried to soothe him.

"I haven't lied to you. But we have to keep up appearances."

"Like going to the Millington ball? The handsome Mr and Mrs George Harries dancing and laughing and enjoying themselves. While I stay alone in my room waiting for your return." Tears rolled down his cheeks, and his eyes, huge and mournful, stared piteously at George.

George couldn't bear it. "Oh, all right, you can ride Captain. But not tomorrow, not in this valley."

Richard flung himself into George's arms. "I love you," he said.

"Love my horse, you mean," said George laughing and the voices dropped again to a murmur.

Polly stole away and walked quickly back to the Chantry. She was still so busy with her thoughts when she went into the house that she was not aware of Mr Freeman's presence until he came out of the study and stood in front of her, blocking her way to the kitchen.

"Light the fire in my study," he said and she hurried away to get kindling. As she laid the fire, he stood over her and she felt trapped.

"Will that be all, sir?" she asked and tried to move crab-like away from him. He pushed her over with his boot, so she fell in a heap at his feet.

"You're dirty, you smell, but you'll have to do," he said and threw himself down onto her.

Afterwards, she painfully got to her feet, and he watched her stagger to the door and disappear. Restored to his usual self, he poured a large glass of the brandy from one of the bottles he had taken from Cold Trenton Manor and settled down to a nap in front of the fire.

Polly dragged herself into the kitchen and then out into the garden where she was violently sick. She had never before been treated with such savagery and she shivered uncontrollably with shock and pain. She was to notice the next day that although her body was black and blue with bruises, he had avoided marking her face, neck and arms. She had been raped, abused, and beaten with a calculating deliberation that terrified her, and she knew that if the opportunity arose, he would do it again. She had to get away, as far away as she could as she was not safe in the valley while he was there. No-one would believe he had taken her by force – she knew her reputation – and no-one would or could protect her.

She was on her own and she would fight her own battles. She would need money to go away, and she would get it somehow. She would use her secret knowledge but very, very carefully. While she worked out how best to go about it, she was going to make sure she wasn't alone again with Mr Freeman.

Chapter Seventeen

A thin winter sun bathed the old bricks of Slepe in a misty light and as James Howard rode slowly up the drive, and the house came into view, he stopped to feast his eyes upon it. It was what he had always wanted; a craving that had never lessened through the years of banishment and how it was his, all his. He had his house, his horses, enough money and to spare to indulge in whatever he fancied. He had the constant entertaining company of his friends, and he had good hunting and deep (and lucky) gaming. Everything to keep boredom at bay.

So why had he come out alone to brave a raw east wind blowing in from the sea? Why wasn't he sitting comfortably in front of a large fire playing cards with his charming witty friends, agreeably wiling the time away until dinner, and afterwards, to bed with the delicious Fanny Cray?

The invitation to the Millington ball had unsettled him in an extraordinary way. He would have shrugged off his brief affair with Lucy Harries, but her tear-stained letters were a persistent reminder of his folly. It had been stupid of him to succumb to the temptation to cuckold the yokel: it had added spice to his enjoyment of the liaison. But Lucy, unlike Fanny Cray, did not understand the rules and it was all too obvious that what had been for him, an idle dalliance, had become something considerably more for her. He shuddered at the thought of her letters with their wild words of divorce intermingled with sentimental dreams of eternal bliss and complaints of his lack of response. Each letter was the same and the last he had torn up unopened.

And now, Benedict had invited him to Millington and in all probability, with Robert staying there, Lucy and George would also be invited and thus, if he went, he would have to trust Lucy's discretion. Remembering her less than discreet behaviour when he stayed at the Rectory, he did not have a great deal of faith in that.

For the first time, he wondered whether she had been foolish enough to confide in anyone. Sophie, perhaps? That thought was distinctly uncomfortable. Somehow, young Sophie had managed to needle his slumbering conscience in a way no-one else, except maybe Benedict, was able to do. They would make a good pair, he thought, both with a steely core of moral rectitude.

On that demoralising thought, he clattered into the stable yard and swung off his horse. He nodded his thanks to the waiting groom and strode towards the house. Unbidden, there came the memory of Sophie dancing a jig of happiness before the door of the rectory; of riding with Robert across the high grasslands of the Cotswolds in easy, undemanding friendship; of tea and Mathilda's cakes and more companionship with Caroline.

No doubt it would have become tedious if he'd had to stay much longer in Knight's Darkleigh, but, as he looked sometime later down the long dining table at his guests, laughing and talking with the brittle cleverness which was their hallmark, he felt a spasm of irritation with them. Their company had grown stale, and he wanted them gone. He laughed with the others at one of the guest's mimicries of a mutual acquaintance – how often had he heard Edward Frane tell that same story? – and made the decision that come what may, he was going to accept Benedict's invitation.

* * *

"So you'll be leaving me and going off to young Rivers' ball," said Lady Theodora.

"For a night or two, that's all," Caroline replied.

"It'll be a well-run affair, if Eliza Rivers has anything to do with it," said Lady Theodora, grudgingly.

"Yes, I'm looking forward to it. And to seeing all the improvements that have been made to the house. It was in a shocking state. Old Mr Rivers can't have spent anything on it for years."

"He always was a strange man."

At Caroline's look of surprise, she cackled: "Oh, I knew old Joseph before he went off to India to make his fortune. I might say it was because of me that he went in the first place," she added with some complacency.

"Oh?"

"He wanted to marry me but I turned him down. I knew even then that there was a miserly streak in him."

Caroline tried to refrain from thinking about her grandmother's notorious parsimony and said, "Also, I'm curious as to whether Benedict will conquer his shyness and make an offer for young Sophie."

"Your church mouse?"

"Yes. They would be splendidly well-suited. One thing I must do is to write to Sophie to tell her not to worry about a dress for the ball. I'm determined to help there."

"All to further the ensnarement of Benedict?"

"I'd prefer to call it enchantment."

"Ha. I wonder what Eliza will think it is."

Caroline's letter arrived the morning Sophie left for Millington. Mrs Latham was inclined to take umbrage at Lady Firth's interference and Sophie endured a long complaint about how humiliating it was that the Lathams were regarded as being in need of charitable hand-outs.

"Pride should stop you from even considering Lady Firth's charity. I'm sure it's kindly meant, but it is deeply, deeply hurtful to me." Mrs Latham dabbed at her eyes. "However, I have no doubt that you'll accept the gift, despite my feelings, so I will say no more about it."

Having thus satisfactorily achieved the best of both worlds – a new excuse for a grievance and what would undoubtedly be an outstanding ball gown for Sophie – Mrs Latham felt invigorated enough to leave her bed and face the rigours of the day from her sofa in the drawing room.

Lucy appeared. George was out hunting, she said, and not having anything particular to do, thought she would come over to say good-bye to Sophie.

"Fancy, we'll be seeing you again in very different surroundings," she said. "Are you excited, Sophie? I am. You will not believe my new dress. George's father insisted on my having a new one specially, so the Harries' will shine, he said, in the best company in the County. I tell him he spoils me, but he just laughs and says I'll be the smartest and prettiest woman there."

"So you will be," agreed Mr Latham fondly. Lucy had put on a considerable amount of weight, and he liked her plump curves. His wife had become thinner and somewhat scrawny as she had grown older, and he was pleased to see his pretty Lucy was turning into a fine figure of a woman. Sophie thought Lucy was becoming blowsy and losing her looks and she was irritated with the Harries' complacency which Lucy had acquired.

"I'm having a new dress," she said. "But it's a surprise as Lady Firth is giving it to me."

Mr Latham frowned. "I think you should perhaps not mention that, Sophie. I agree with your mother that it is most generous of Lady Firth, but I'm sure she would prefer it to be kept a secret. Charity shouted from the roof-tops is not pleasant to hear and…"

He was interrupted by Lucy who was staring at Sophie with affronted astonishment: "Lady Firth is giving you a ball gown? Well, I've never heard anything like it. Why ever is she doing that?"

"She thought I would need one," said Sophie.

"Oh." Lucy was finding the thought of Sophie being as handsomely gowned as she, remarkably unpalatable. "Well, I personally don't think you should accept such an extravagant gift from a stranger."

"I said the same," said Mrs Latham, "but Sophie is so strong-willed, as you know."

It was fortunate that at this point the Millington carriage arrived as Sophie was close to losing her temper. She hurried to be off, a wave of excitement sweeping through her, banishing the oppressive weight of her family's sour disapproval. She smiled and waved as the carriage trundled down the drive and felt buoyant enough to ignore the tepid response: her father raised his hand as he turned away and her mother and Lucy had already retreated indoors. Well, it was a dreary, grey December day, she thought, and tucked her hands under the blanket the coachman had carefully laid across her.

She had enough vanity to be surprised that Benedict had not come himself to escort her to Millington, but she was glad to have the hour's journey to give her time to adjust to the prospect ahead of her. For the past ten days, since Lady River's visit, she had not dared allow herself to anticipate too keenly the treat of spending a whole week, the longest she had been away from her family, in a society that was not based on peevish complaint, in case for some unimaginable reason Lady Rivers changed her mind. Sophie didn't really believe that such a determined and decisive lady would do that, but now, sitting snugly in the carriage as it lurched and rattled its way along the rutted road to Millington, she could afford the luxury of day-dreaming of the excitements to come.

Benedict came out to greet her and hand her down from the carriage. By the promptness of his appearance, she had the pleasant suspicion that he had been watching out for her arrival. But, as they were walking towards the library, Sophie was suddenly afflicted with a panicky shyness and looked up in alarm to Benedict, who understood the symptoms all too well from personal experience.

"Don't worry," he said quietly. "If it all gets too much for you, just tell me and you can go home whenever you want. I hope you won't, as my mother is looking forward so much to having you as support in her battles with Robert and me. She has the lowest possible opinion of us as helpers. She complains we don't have the right priorities."

As if on cue, Lady Rivers could be heard from the depths of the library saying, "No, Robert, despite what you say, I think you're entirely wrong. It would be utter disaster to put the musicians at that end of the Hall."

"There, you see?" smiled Benedict, and as she laughed, Lady Rivers and Robert saw them approach in happy accord and watched with indulgent smiles.

* * *

Sophie soon discovered that being Lady Rivers' lieutenant was no sinecure and from a life of paralysing monotony, she was thrust into one where there were not enough hours in the day to carry out all Lady Rivers' exacting requirements.

She made a list of guests who were coming to stay, when they were coming and where they were to sleep; lists of additional guests who were coming to the dinner before the ball; lists of what servants needed to be hired for the evening and lists of what food was needed. Lady Rivers did not trust Millington's untried servants to know such matters and so Sophie then spent much time placating the butler, the housekeeper and the chef who went into high dudgeon over this slur on their professional abilities. By the questions they asked her, Sophie realised that Lady Rivers was correct in her lack of confidence in them, so Sophie became the face-saving channel through which they could obtain advice.

Most important of all, she was put in charge of the flower decorations which Lady Rivers decreed must be in every room "to cheer up this gloomy mausoleum".

"It's not a mausoleum," protested Sophie, who, within two days, had lost her awe of Lady Rivers. "It's a beautiful old house."

"My dear, you have no idea how much I'm looking forward to returning to my comfortable modern house. You're welcome to this gothic wonder."

Sophie laughed and said she must go up to the attics. Mrs Morgan, the housekeeper, had said that there were some immense brass pots, part of old Joseph's booty from India, somewhere in one of the many attics but she couldn't remember where.

"I think they sound as if they would be very impressive and just what we need in the great Hall."

"We certainly need something," Lady Rivers sighed. "Three days to go and nothing seems ready."

"It's much warmer now in the Hall with the fires going," said Sophie, consolingly.

"That's very true. My fingers merely go blue with cold, instead of getting frostbite. Off you go then and don't get lost."

The attics were bitterly cold but full of treasures, plundered largess from the East. Sophie found the two urns, five foot high and intricately engraved. With them were trays, tables, carved elephants, huge carpets and strange ornaments and statues of Hindu gods and goddesses, which she found somewhat uncomfortable. Venturing into a further attic, she discovered ancient furniture, oak coffers, dark with age, heavy solid tables and sideboards, and, startling her, two full sets of armour. In the many trunks, she found old clothes, heavy silks and velvets rotted by damp and moths. In his heyday, old Joseph must have been quite a dandy.

Slipped down in the side of one of the trunks, she found an old book, leather-bound and with an intricate clasp and lock. She took it to the low window and knelt down. In the poor light which filtered through cobwebs, she was excited to see that it was unlocked, and it was revealed to be Joseph

Rivers' journal, stated on his voyage to Bombay more than half a century before.

So absorbed was she that she didn't hear Benedict's footsteps and only became aware of his presence when he gave a little cough.

"I came to tell you luncheon is ready," he said.

"Good gracious, I hadn't realised I'd been here so long." Sophie realised she was cold and cramped. "Look, I found this." She tried to get up and give Benedict the book but was so stiff that she would have fallen if he had not caught her hand and helped her to her feet. Punctiliously, regretfully, he let go of her hand.

"It's your uncle's journal," she said, still in a trance with the book. "It's very sad, he loved a girl but she rejected him. He doesn't say who she was, but she seems to have been very unkind to him. So off he went to India, to try and forget his broken heart, vowing that he would never love another. It seems so romantic."

"Maybe. Although it could be said that he might not have loved another woman but became obsessed with money instead."

"And you benefit from that."

"Yes, it would be wrong of me to take a high moral tone with old Joseph." Greatly daring, he added, "and if I'm lucky, I'll be more fortunate in love, so get the best of both worlds."

He was pleased to see Sophie blush as she looked down in some confusion.

In the unromantic setting of a cold, dirty attic, full of the debris of five generations of his family, he summoned up courage to ask, "Do you think I will be?"

During her few days at Millington, Sophie had inevitably thought about Benedict and about Millington. At first, its great size had overwhelmed her but as she got to know it, spending hours exploring it, sometimes on her own, more often with Benedict, she had become fascinated with it and had come to appreciate the equally great social advantage there would be in being its mistress. Her liking for Benedict had deepened and strengthened, but it was a feeling of comfortable pleasure in his company rather than the intense excitement she had felt with James Howard.

Her fascination for the house and her regard for Benedict were so intertwined that she had difficulty in separating one from the other and she was distressed by this confusion in her heart.

In the muddle of emotions, she heard the anxiety in his voice, and it pierced her. She knew with total certainty that it was with Benedict, at Millington, where her future lay. In many ways, she would have to be the stronger of the two, protecting him from the agonies his diffident nature inflicted upon him. She felt a surge of joy and looked up at him with such a radiant smile that the next moment she was in his arms, being kissed with a fervour that pleased and surprised her. It was some little time before they were able to make themselves go downstairs and meet Lady Rivers and Robert, who had by then, almost finished their lunch.

"Wherever have you two been?" Robert asked and then roared with laughter as their faces crimsoned. He hugged Sophie and shook Benedict's hand. Lady Rivers beamed, kissed Sophie and said: "My dear, I am so delighted to have you as my daughter-in-law."

Sophie gulped back tears and said, "He couldn't have chosen a less romantic place to propose."

"These men have no sense of time and place," said Lady Rivers but Robert thought Benedict had been wise to secure Sophie's hand before James Howard's unsettling presence came amongst them.

"You'll be no use whatsoever, I can see," he said to Benedict. "So, I suggest you go tomorrow and ask my father for Sophie's hand."

Apart from the appalling thought of being without Sophie's company for a few hours, Benedict thought this was a good idea. He entirely trusted Sophie, of course, but like Robert, the thought of James was worrying. He rather wished he had not invited him to the ball, but it would be an opportunity to set at rest any lingering fears of James' effect on Sophie.

Chapter Eighteen

Within hours of Benedict waiting upon Mr Latham, Polly had heard the news of Sophie's betrothal and was generously pleased for her. Of all the people she knew, Miss Sophie particularly deserved good fortune and Polly, who didn't like Lucy, was especially delighted that Sophie had far outstripped her in the marriage stakes.

It was the only piece of good news in what was becoming an increasingly desperate situation for Polly; a few nights after his assault on her, she had been woken by Mr Freeman's heavy tread on the wooden stairs to her tiny room and she had been subjected to another savage rape. In the nights following, she had lain awake, terrified of hearing the slow deliberate steps and only getting to sleep a few hours before it was time to get up and face the day's grinding work. He would come every two or three days and the pain and the obscene humiliations he inflicted upon her increased with every visit.

Using Polly's body as a sadistic plaything had become a drug to him, a craving he found irresistible, and he was determined not to lose it. He gave instructions that she was not to leave the house, and the silent, dour servants entered into an unspoken conspiracy of not letting her out of their sight. Polly's brother Sim was discharged – a lazy good for nothing, said Mr Freeman, beyond redemption. Their feckless mother, preoccupied in producing yet another half-sister, did not notice she hadn't seen her eldest daughter for more than a fortnight.

In the late afternoon of the day before the ball, Polly was standing in the rear courtyard getting water up from the well. Her pail was full, and she was concentrating so hard on lifting it from the hook that she did not see or hear Richard coming up behind her. He pushed her and the pail tipped over and the water poured over her skirt and feet. He gave his high-pitched laugh and vanished.

Something broke in Polly; she could take no more, she had to escape. She had brooded long and hard over how she was to use her knowledge of Richard and George's guilty secret and had come to the conclusion that she would have to use the weakest member of the household. Mrs Freeman had a few pieces of jewellery left. They were not particularly valuable, but Polly reckoned they must be worth a few sovereigns, enough to get her far away from the Chantry. This would have to be tonight; Mr Freeman had come to her room last night and on previous form, he would not appear this night and therefore her absence would not be known until the morning.

She saw Mrs Freeman's shadowy figure moving across a window. Polly took a deep breath, wiped her hands on her apron, squared her shoulders and went off to find her quarry.

She tracked Mrs Freeman down in her little sitting room. She knocked briefly on the door and went in before Mrs Freeman could say anything.

The two women, ostensibly mistress and servant, but in reality, both victims of Mr Freeman, looked at each other. Mrs Freeman's nerve broke first.

"Yes, Polly, what is it?"

"Beggin 'your pardon, ma'am, for disturbin' 'ee, but there is a matter on which Oi need your 'elp and advice."

"Oh, yes?" Mrs Freeman looked alarmed. No-one ever needed help or advice from her.

"It's this friend of mine. 'Er master abuses 'er something cruel. Now she can't do nothing. 'E forbids 'er to go out of the 'ouse, 'e gets 'is other servants to spy on 'er and she's getting 'real desperate, she just don't know where to turn."

"Can't she leave, go away?" There was a sick look on Mrs Freeman's face.

"She ain't got no money and she reckons she's got to get a long way away, like Bristol, to be really safe."

"I haven't any money, you know that."

"You got them tidy jools."

"I can't give you them. They're all I have."

"Oi ain't got nothin', ma'am."

There was a silence and then Mrs Freeman, with a touch of triumph in her voice, said, "You can't prove anything. A girl with your reputation. Who would believe you?"

"Oi fort 'ee'd bring that up. But there's somethin' else Oi reckons 'ee should know about. Your precious son and Mr George."

"Whatever do you mean?" Mrs Freeman's hands clutched at her mouth.

"Unnatural goings on, that's wha'."

Mrs Freeman moaned and shrunk back in her chair.

"A hangin' matter at that," Polly added with callous relish.

"No… no…" the poor woman bleated. "I don't believe you. You're a wicked girl, telling such lies. It's not true."

"It is, and Oi reckons you know what sort of man your precious son is. And when Oi tells Parson and Mr

Wagstaffe, the Justice down in Laine, where to go tomorrow after hunting, they'll know as well what 'e and Mr George do get up to in the barn above Prior's Darkleigh. A hangin' matter, like Oi said."

"You wouldn't. You wouldn't dare."

"Oi be desperate, ma'am." Polly's matter of face tone was utterly convincing.

Mrs Freeman moaned. "What am I to do? What am I to do?"

"Give me that nice red pendant and Oi'll be on my way. You won't see me again, Oi promise you. And don't 'ee say nothin' to nobody," she added fiercely.

Mrs Freeman nodded like a puppet. "I'll go and get it," she whispered and dragged herself out of the room.

To give a reason for her presence in the room, Polly busied herself with tidying up the miserable little fire that Mrs Freeman was allowed and drawing the curtains against the December gloom. Mrs Freeman returned and gave her the pendant, a pretty piece with a garnet surrounded by pearls, looking away as she did.

"Thank 'ee, ma'am," said Polly. As she slipped it round her neck, she asked, "Will that be all?"

"Just go away," Mrs Freeman covered her face with her hands and rocked back and forth with soundless weeping.

Polly went.

Some hours later, when she was sure everybody had gone to bed, Polly crept out of the house and walked silently through the moonlit woods to Middle Darkleigh. She had 'borrowed' an old brown cloak belonging to Mrs Freeman and carried a small carpet bag containing an equally dingy dress, both similarly acquired. She proposed to sleep overnight at the barn above Prior's Darkleigh and half an hour later, let herself into it and snuggled down in the hay where a fortnight before, she had watched George and Richard in passionate embrace. The thought made her chuckle.

She stroked the pendant. It had been so easy; she had been stupid to have taken so long to pluck up the courage to confront pathetic little Mrs Freeman. And not to have got more out of her. But she had the pendant, and here Polly grew thoughtful. Her intention had been to walk to Cirencester and sell the pendant there, but she now felt that Cirencester was too close to Mr Freeman. She would walk up to the high road and go to Gloucester which was plenty big enough for her to hide in. Then she would go to Bristol, or even, and she hugged herself with excitement, London.

As she drifted into sleep, she thought it would have been nice to have had a young man's arms around her and a young man's body by hers to erase the memory of Mr Freeman's soft, moist skin and cruel hands. Robert Latham, she thought, he would do nicely. Polly slept, a smile on her face.

* * *

The same moonlight which helped guide Polly to her sleeping place looked down on George and Lucy in their pretty farmhouse. They had spent a happy evening with George's family, both lit by an inner excitement that was made more intense because it was secret.

For Lucy, the thought that she would see James Howard again in twenty-four hours made her delirious with happiness. She smiled and said little but her beautiful face glowed and Jarvis thought again how lucky George was and hoped for a grandchild soon.

George's happiness made him boisterous, teasing his sisters, and laughing uproariously at his own jokes. Tomorrow, he and Richard would be off with the hunt, in the high open country around Cold Trenton, and he would let Richard ride Captain. He would see his beautiful boy on his beautiful horse; even the thought of the exquisite pleasure this would give him made him want to cry with joy.

And then, slipping away from the hunt early, they would go to their own private sanctuary. And then to the ball with the cream of society. What a day it was going to be!

He and Lucy left the Manor Farm early to get a good night's sleep, and the moon fell on their faces as they lay side by side, not touching, in the big bed, each dreaming of a forbidden love.

* * *

At Millington Hall, the party had been increased first by the arrival of Caroline Firth in the early afternoon and then by James Howard in time for dinner. Her arrival was timely as all were beginning to feel tired and jaded with their efforts to make Millington presentable. Her delight in Sophie and Benedict's engagement and her praise for the transformation of Millington lifted everyone's spirits, so that by the time James arrived, all were quite convinced that the ball was going to be a great success.

Although James and Sophie were unaware of it, their meeting was watched with anxious, protective interest. He greeted Lady Rivers with his usual disarming grace, Caroline with a kiss and the comment that Cheltenham suited her, though he wasn't sure about her dress, and then Sophie with a smile of unaffected pleasure.

"My dear Miss Sophie, what a delightful surprise! I didn't expect to have the pleasure of seeing you here tonight. Does this mean we'll be able to have breakfast together, just like old times?"

Benedict moved closer to Sophie. She felt a little pang as she met James' bright blue eyes, but it was easily stifled and she said, laughing, "Alas, I've become used to the strict Millington regime of breakfasting. Maybe, though, we'll be able to persuade Benedict to give us dispensation tomorrow."

She thought she could feel tension draining away from Benedict as she turned to smile at him. His heart contracted with a surge of emotion, and he looked down at her with a beaming, idiotic smile.

Robert groaned. "You see how it is, James, we are awash with love."

"I do indeed. Congratulations, my dear Benedict, you are the most fortunate of fellows," James said enthusiastically, giving Benedict a hearty handshake. But Caroline, who knew him too well, thought he was actually rather put out; James had perhaps begun to realise that he'd let a prize slip through his fingers.

Later that night, the moon shone on a restless Robert, pacing the floor of his bedchamber in an agony of unrequited love; on Caroline, the object of his desire, equally restless, who sat at her window and looked across the dark valley to the moonlit slope beyond and who felt confusion that she was unable or unwilling, she did not know which, to let herself return that love; on Lady Rivers, who lay quietly composed in her bed, planning what and how things were to be done the next day; on Benedict and Sophie, both deeply, dreamlessly asleep; and on James, who was feeling a strange discontent and in his sleep, his face twitched and scowled as he dreamed.

Chapter Nineteen

Polly's escape from the Chantry proceeded with quite remarkable good fortune. She had woken before first light and trudged across the fields to the high road, munching a crust of bread. In the footsteps of where Roman legions had once marched, she set her face towards Gloucester and walked briskly away from the only place she had ever known.

She had not been walking more than half an hour when a cart rumbled up behind her, and the carter, a wizened little man with a twinkle in his eye, offered her a ride. Two hours later, in the shadow of the cathedral, and well before Mr Freeman was told of her disappearance, Polly jumped down from the cart and waved farewell to the carter. His disinterested kindness – to her surprise, he did not demand any favours – went some way towards restoring Polly's faith in mankind.

She decided she would explain her possession of the pendant by saying her mistress had had some misfortune, and not wanting the master to know about it, had asked the maid to dispose of it.

The first jeweller she went to in Westgate looked doubtful and offered her a guinea. Polly snatched the pendant away and stalked out of the shop.

The next jeweller she approached in Eastgate offered five guineas and after some spirited bargaining, he agreed to buy it for seven. Polly was highly pleased. Never had she had so much money, the equivalent of half a year's wages and here she was, in the middle of Gloucester, with the world at her feet. From that moment, Knight's Darkleigh and its inhabitants faded into an insignificant memory. *This is what life was all about.*

* * *

Mr Freeman had laid down strict rules to his household that he was on no account to be disturbed in the morning until he had summoned his man, Simkins. This was, he informed them, for the sole reason that he must have peace and quiet for the prayers and contemplation with which he started the day. Without those hours of solitude, when he communicated with his Maker, he would be unable to carry the burden of taking God's word to the people. To deprive the dwellers in darkness the benefit of a visitation by God's messenger would be a sin of the greatest magnitude. Woe betide any man who, for whatever reason, interrupted his profound and difficult meditations.

Consequently, it was well into the morning before Mr Freeman was made aware of Polly's absence. With spiteful satisfaction, Simkins said as he opened the curtains to reveal a cold, bright morning, "The girl, Polly, appears to have left in the night, sir."

Mr Freeman (who found meditation easier while lying supine in his large, comfortable bed) struggled to sit up, outrage making his eyes bulge.

"And what enquiries have been made of her whereabouts?"

"Only of her mother, sir, and she has no knowledge or, one may say, much interest in where her daughter might be."

Mr Freeman thought for a moment. "Don't make any further enquiries. I feel it is my duty to search for and find the girl and return her to this haven, this sanctuary, before she is even further steeped in sin. Expiration of her sins will be necessary, but she shall, if she repents, be forgiven."

Simkins hid a smile of sour glee. The servants hated their master but the hatred, instead of uniting them, caused discord as each manoeuvred for supremacy. On the principle of divide and rule, Mr Freeman fostered this poisonous situation by the judicious use of favours and punishment.

As he dressed, Mr Freeman thought about Polly. He was angry at her flight, and her disobedience would have to be punished. But the anger was diminished by the growing pleasurable excitement of thinking about what punishment should be meted out to match the enormity of her crime.

It whetted his appetite for a large breakfast, and it was noon before he was able to start his investigations. As he was leaving the dining room, he could see his wife standing on the small terrace, looking up the valley towards Middle Darkleigh. She was not wearing a cloak and with a white frost still on the lawns, she was shivering with cold. Why didn't the stupid woman put on a cloak, if she was going to moon around the garden in the depths of winter? A reason dawned upon him. He opened a window and bellowed: "Mrs Freeman, would you come to my study?"

She jumped in alarm and with a look of sick dread, went towards his study. He unlocked the door and strode in before her.

"Why weren't you wearing your cloak, woman?"

"I… I forgot."

"Where is it?"

"I don't know." The words came out in a thread of a whisper.

"You don't know? Pray, why don't you know? Have you lost it? Has it been taken with your knowledge? Or, as I suspect, has it been taken without your knowledge? In other words, stolen?"

"I don't know."

"Well, if my reasoning is correct and I feel sure you will agree that my powers of reasoning are normally superior to most peoples'…"

"Oh yes, indeed."

"Quite. As I was saying, if I am correct in my assumption that your cloak has been stolen, and if one takes into account the disappearance of one debased maid servant, then one comes to the conclusion that she has stolen it."

"If you say so," gasped Mrs Freeman.

"When did you discover your cloak was missing?"

"This morning."

"Has anything else been taken?"

"A carpet bag. That's all."

"A carpet bag. And what does that tell you?"

Mrs Freeman shook her head dumbly.

"It tells me she is intending to travel. To go some distance. That is what it tells me. And to travel some distance, what does one need?"

Paper-white, all Mrs Freeman could do was moan.

"One needs money. But the little slut had no money as she'd had, if you remember, her wages docked for the tray of china she broke. So where did she get money from?"

At this point, Mrs Freeman's legs gave way, and she crumpled to the floor in a faint.

In angry exasperation, he lifted her roughly and dumped her on a chair. With reluctance, he poured a glass of his precious brandy and forced it into her mouth. She revived, coughing and spluttering.

He watched with irritation until she stopped. "What did you give her?" he asked softly.

"My garnet pendant. You mustn't…"

"What mustn't I do?"

"You mustn't go after her."

"Are you out of your mind, woman? Maybe you will be so good as to inform me why you are giving me orders? Telling me what I must or must not do?"

Mrs Freeman was silent and then even more softly, he said, "In my pursuit of the truth, I will not hesitate to use any means at my disposal to achieve that aim. It is my right. It is your duty to obey me. I thought I had taught you that many years ago, but it would appear to be a lesson that you have forgotten and of which you need reminding." He went to a cupboard and took out a heavy whip.

She put her hands up as if to shield her face. "No, no. Not that…" Terror made her shriek.

"Stop that noise!" He tapped his boot with the whip, and she subsided into a grizzle.

"I'm waiting," he said.

"She came to me last evening and said that Richard…" she stopped, unable to go on, with tears pouring down her face.

"What about Richard?"

"That he and Mr George Harries…"

"Go on."

"That he and George Harries had a… had an unnatural relationship."

"And you believed that slut?" In a fury, he lashed her with the whip.

A red wheal crossed her face and as blood oozed out, she gabbled, "She told me that if you went to a barn above Prior's Darkleigh this afternoon, after the hunting, you would have your proof. If I didn't give her the pendant, she would go to Mr Latham and a Justice of the Peace. 'A hanging matter,' she called it."

The blood was trickling down her neck, staining her collar, but she was unaware of it.

"I don't believe it. Where is the boy?"

She shook her head and then lay back in the chair, her eyes closed, the picture of defeat and exhaustion. He lunged out of the room, banging the door behind him. She remained motionless until he returned, a few minutes later, and opened her eyes long enough to see his red, furious face and closed them again.

He shouted at her: "You knew he was gone from his room. Where is he?"

She did not answer and with a snarl, he left, calling for his horse. He and Jarvis Harries must have words. If the girl's allegations were true, the matter must be hushed up immediately. Damn the boy, damn George Harries. He rode along, swearing profusely, but as he approached Middle Darkleigh, he began to weigh up the situation and to see how he could take advantage of it.

He came to the conclusion that it would be best to let Polly disappear into the mire of one of the big cities, never to be heard of again. To find her and bring her back would be too dangerous.

So far as the Freeman family were concerned, they also would have to move on but a certain largesse from Jarvis Harries would be required to accelerate their going. The Harries' had far more to lose than they did, if any hint of the scandal leaked out. He remembered that the Michaelmas rent of the Chantry had not yet been paid, and the Christmas Quarter-day was looming. All in all, a quiet flit would be no bad thing, particularly with a sweetener of some Harries gold.

On this pleasant thought, Mr Freeman trotted up to the Manor Farm and in his usual lordly way, demanded to see Mr Harries.

Jarvis flatly refused to believe the appalling allegations: his son, his handsome, manly son, to be involved in such an affair, it was out of the question. All George had shown was a friendly interest in a lonely lad, one who had been shown little such kindness, and this was to be construed as something completely abhorrent. All on the word of a servant girl.

Jarvis shook with rage, but behind this was a deadly fear. Small things that he had ignored or passed off with a shrug crept into his unwilling mind; the times when George had stood unnecessarily close to the boy when showing off some new toy, a new fishing rod or gun; indeed, the amount of time George spent in the lad's company rather than with his wife and their friends. Jarvis' mind went blank with horror at the thought of what would happen if even a suspicion of this matter came to light. One thing was certain: this pernicious family must be gone from the valley as a matter of urgency. Polly's disappearance was a considerable relief. Then he pulled himself up. There could be no truth in her monstrous story.

"This is a complete lie. The girl wanted to frighten your wife into giving her the means to leave and she succeeded. There is not a word of truth in it."

"Where is this barn above Prior's Darkleigh? Does it exist?"

"Yes," Jarvis replied with a sigh.

"Then I shall go up to it and wait and see if what she says is true."

"Spying on your own son?" Jarvis was contemptuous.

"No, on yours. He is the one who has led my young boy into this despicable behaviour."

"My son is a married man. He adores his wife. There cannot be any abnormal behaviour between the two."

"Then come with me and pray God you are right."

Jarvis thought, irrelevantly, that this was the first time he had heard Mr Freeman speak with unadorned sincerity, and it made him more fearful.

"I'll come with you," he said, at last, and rose and went to the door and ushered Mr Freeman out before him.

They were met with a commotion in the hall as George flung open the front door and staggered in like a drunk, his eyes wild and crazed.

"George, whatever is the matter? For God's sake, what is wrong with you?" Jarvis cried out and shook him by the arm.

"He's dead. My darling boy is dead." George's voice was cracked.

"Oh my God, come in here." Jarvis thrust George into the parlour, Mr Freeman hard on his heels, and he slammed the door as Mrs Harries, Anne, and Mary came running down the stairs. Anne, always the boldest, opened the door and peered round. Her father snarled at her to get out.

Shocked at this unprecedented behaviour, Anne did as she was told, and the three ladies retired back to Mrs Harries' chamber in uncharacteristic silence.

George had sat down and was rocking back and forth, shaken with devastating sobs. Jarvis poured out three large brandies and after handing one to Mr Freeman, stood over George until the sobs started to subside. When he judged that George could hold a glass, he gave it to him. Jarvis was unaware that he avoided touching George's hand as he did so and he moved away to stand with his back to the fire.

"Now, what is all this about, George?"

George looked up, his face a mess of tears, and became aware of Mr Freeman. As he was still bereft of speech, Jarvis asked again, "What is it, George? Who has died? Is it Mr Freeman's son?"

George's face crumpled again and he nodded in dumb misery.

"My son, my Richard!" exclaimed Mr Freeman in deep, anguished tones. He sat down heavily, and taking out a large handkerchief, shaded his eyes. "My son," he repeated.

There was a terrible silence, broken by an acutely uncomfortable Jarvis. "What happened? Were you both out hunting?"

"Yes," whispered George. "He was on Captain and one moment they were going like a bird flying over a wall and next…"

"Go on."

"The next, he was on the ground, his neck at a funny angle." George's voice went up with hysteria.

"Now stop that, George. Take a sip of brandy and calm down."

George obediently took a gulp of brandy and, holding the glass in his large hands, stared down at the amber liquid. "My golden boy," he muttered into the glass.

"Where is he, where is my beloved son?" asked Mr Freeman.

"They're taking him to the Chantry. I... I couldn't bear to stay."

"Then I must immediately return to await the arrival of my poor dead son."

George shuddered.

"We will have to talk again," Mr Freeman said to Jarvis who nodded and ushered him out of the room in silence.

When he returned, George was still sitting hunched over his brandy but appeared a little calmer. He raised his eyes to his father with the stricken look of a wounded animal and Jarvis felt a bitter disappointment. All he had worked for, all his ambitions were centred on his children, and in particular, on George. George was to have been the instrument to thrust the Harries' ever upward in society: he had been educated as a gentleman, he had been an officer in a good regiment, he had married into a good family, his children would be accepted in a way that he, Jarvis, and his wife would never be. There had been no reason to suspect that anything could stop this progress. And nothing would, thought Jarvis in grim determination. It was as well that the lad was dead. George must act as it if were the death of an acquaintance, expressing conventional regret at the death of a fine young man, nothing more. No admittance, not a hint of any stronger feelings were to be mentioned again. The scene of a few minutes ago was never to be referred to. As far as Jarvis was concerned, he would deny, even to himself, that it had ever happened.

"A sad business. A fine young lad," he said. "I expect Mr and Mrs Freeman will decide now to leave the valley. It will not have pleasant associations for them. I can't say I'd be that sorry to see them go. Mr Freeman was, I think, hoping to borrow some money from me, which is why he was here. Ah well, it will all be for the best in the end, I've no doubt."

George didn't say anything. He didn't understand the drift of his father's remarks: at the best of times things had to be spelled out for him.

"Well, well," said Jarvis. "Now it's time you took yourself off home to your Lucy. Have a rest before the ball, don't you think?"

"Ball? The ball? I can't…" George buried his head in his hands.

"You most certainly can and will." Jarvis' voice was suddenly harsh. "There is no reason at all for you not to go. Indeed, there are many reasons why you can and must. That is all I'm going to say about the matter. Now, be off and get yourself prepared for this evening. And a word of advice: you and Lucy should be particularly friendly to Mr Rivers and Sophie. Your children will be grateful to you for ensuring they have easy and intimate access to Millington Hall."

George nodded. Jarvis had always been an indulgent father but when he did draw a line, his children knew better than to disobey. In the depths of his misery, George heard the tone of authority and submitted to it. A great weariness came over him and he struggled to his feet.

"Yes, I'll rest for a couple of hours, as you suggest."

"Good lad. Now remember what I said."

George nodded again and allowed himself to be hustled out of the room and out of the house before his mother and sisters could pounce on him.

Jarvis returned to the parlour, gave himself another large brandy and sat down with a sigh. If they could get through the next few days, then he reckoned they would be out of the woods.

Chapter Twenty

Millington en fete was an awe-inspiring sight: flaring torches guided the guests' carriages along the drive to the front door and glowing light poured from many windows in welcome contrast to the sparkling frosty night.

Mr and Mrs Latham, arriving with George and Lucy in the Harries' carriage, were somewhat overwhelmed by its splendour and fell silent.

Fortunately for George, the Latham self-absorption had been strongly in evidence during the journey, so that his unhappy withdrawn silence went unnoticed by his wife and her parents.

Unable to face wearing one of his more peacock outfits, George was soberly dressed in a black coat and biscuit knee breeches and consequently looked more the gentleman than was usual. Lucy made up for him in flamboyance, wearing a deep pink gown, trimmed a little too fussily and cut perhaps a little too low. Whilst George was very pale, she was flushed with excitement, her great brown eyes even larger than usual.

She does look beautiful, Sophie thought, as the sisters greeted each other. Up to that moment, Sophie had been more than pleased with her own appearance. Caroline's dress was a particularly lovely creamy yellow that gave warmth to Sophie's pale skin and with her hair elegantly dressed by Mathilda, she had felt a match for anyone. But as soon as she saw Lucy, she had to admit that she was, as usual, eclipsed. Then she saw the look in Benedict's eyes and the envy of Lucy's beauty vanished. She was much loved: that was all she needed. It was perhaps just as well for her peace of mind that she didn't see James Howard, carefully standing some way off, staring at the sisters with a stunned look on his face.

"You look as if you've been hit by a thunderbolt," said Robert, who, after greeting his family, had retreated as soon as politeness allowed.

"I think I have. I think I've been a complete and utter fool."

Robert followed his eyes. "You chose the wrong sister?"

James was startled. "Oh my God, how much do you know?"

"Did you really think that Lucy would be discreet?"

"We-ell, I hoped that self-preservation would make her so."

"If it wasn't my silly sister involved, I'd be highly amused to watch how you cope. She's predatory, is Lucy, so you're going to have quite an evening."

James groaned. "Thank you."

In the same conversational tone, Robert added: "And if you have any thoughts of laying siege to Sophie, forget them."

"Robert, on my honour, I would never do so."

Robert let it rest there. "George is looking a little washed out," he said.

"Yes, I wonder what's wrong."

"In a sulk over something, I suppose, stupid fellow."

"You don't think…"

"I doubt it. If he did know, you'd have heard from him, threats of pistols at dawn, that sort of thing. Just threats, mind you, no action."

"I don't know how safe it was for me to come back to this part of the world. A quick unnoticed retreat to Slepe would perhaps be the most sensible thing to do."

"Unusual for you to be the hunted, not the hunter?" Robert asked sardonically.

"Very. But why don't you come with me? You've finished your work here. You promised you'd help me, remember?"

"I'd be delighted to."

"Good. Now, I must go and greet your parents," James said but he was waylaid by Lucy, with George in tow.

"Major Howard, I thought you were going to ignore me," Lucy fluttered at him.

"Mrs Harries, it would be impossible to do that." James raised her hand to his lips and then quickly turned to George. "My dear Harries, your wife is lovelier than ever. You're a lucky fellow."

George looked blankly at him. "Oh, yes?" he said vaguely.

"Anything the matter, George?" asked Robert.

"Not feeling quite m'self," admitted George. "Friend of mine killed today, out hunting."

"Only that strange Freeman boy," said Lucy pettishly, "but George seems to think it was his fault. I'm sure I don't know why."

"My horse," said George miserably and the memory of Richard's broken body came flooding back.

"You shouldn't blame yourself. We all know accidents happen in hunting." Robert was surprised but rather touched by George's obvious distress. There was more feeling in George than he would have ever suspected.

"Still, it's always a shock, no doubt about it." James was also sympathetic but seized a way which, with luck, would get rid of Lucy until dinner was served. "Why doesn't Robert show you your sister's future home and all the work he's done?"

"Yes, do come and see." Robert took up the idea with equal enthusiasm and before Lucy realised what had happened, Major Howard had bowed and moved away, and Robert was shepherding them in quite the opposite direction. George was dimly grateful that he was being spared the ordeal of making polite conversation, but for Lucy, it was the start of an evening of constant frustration.

Robert managed to prolong the tour until dinner was announced, ignoring Lucy's open discontent. During dinner, she was seated on the same side of the table as James but some distance away, so she could neither hear him nor see him. The admiration of an elderly colonel and an even more elderly admiral on either side of her did not compensate for her loss. She consoled herself that when the dancing began, all would be different.

The Great Hall, despite Lady Rivers' forebodings, proved a magnificent backdrop to the ball. The huge fires, the blaze of candles, the richly embroidered tapestries, the strange exotic brassware, all combined to create an atmosphere of romantic grandeur.

"We should have made it a ball in medieval dress," said Sophie to Benedict, as they danced for the first time together in one of the country dances. "Our modern dress doesn't seem – what is the word I want – splendid? Grand? Ornate enough for this."

"Next time," promised Benedict, astonishing himself that he would actually want to go through the turmoil of having a ball again.

"On your word?"

"It shall be part of the marriage contract."

They smiled happily at each other and a number of mothers and daughters ground their teeth that a little nobody had managed to capture the most eligible bachelor to have come into the neighbourhood for years.

As a result of the hospitality, he and Benedict had enjoyed in the autumn, Robert was acquainted with many of the guests and after dinner, he used this as part of the campaign to keep Lucy occupied. To his delight, he was ably assisted by Caroline who had not needed the hint dropped by Lady Rivers the evening before. She was all too aware of Lucy's propensity for indiscretion.

When Lucy was safely dancing with the third very young man corralled for this purpose, Caroline said to Robert, "I think we deserve a medal for our efforts. Come, let's sit down for a moment. I've run myself dry of light civilities."

Only too happy to agree, he led her to a sofa tucked away beside one of Sophie's large Indian pots and they watched the pattern of dancers for a while in companionable silence.

"It's been a great success," said Caroline, "and I'm so pleased about Benedict and my dear Sophie. Don't they look so happy and so right together?"

"From some of the comments I've overheard, I don't think many of the fond Mamas would agree with you."

"Good," she said with great satisfaction and they both laughed.

The laughter faded as they looked at each other and in an uncertain voice, unlike her usual decisive tones, she said,

"I think we'd better be sociable again, otherwise Lucy will escape our net."

"Bother Lucy," he muttered but saw that they were too late: Lucy had tracked James down. She was smiling a little ominously as she went up to him where he and another man were flirting with a lovely fair girl, who in her way, rivalled Lucy in beauty. Displeased even further by this, Lucy put a possessive hand on James' arm and said, "I've been looking for you forever. Where have you been?"

James' heart sank. If he didn't deflect her swiftly, she would betray herself, and more importantly, him, completely.

"My dear Mrs Harries, I've been skulking in the background, terrified of the throng of admirers around you. I thought that if I dared venture one word to you, at least three would challenge me to a duel at dawn. And," he gave an exaggerated shiver, "much as I would want to defend your honour, it is very cold outside, and I don't like getting up early in the morning."

The other two laughed and Lucy was forced to appear good-natured and smiled a tight, humourless smile.

James swiftly continued: "So, having confessed that I'm a lily-livered coward, I must remember my manners and make introductions: Mrs George Harries, Miss Ramsey, and Lord Harper. Mrs Harries is Miss Latham's sister."

"Dashed nice girl. I sat next to her at dinner," said Lord Harper. "Wish her and Rivers happiness. Good for the rest of us; now he's spoken for, the ladies will be able to think about the rest of us, instead of dreaming of spending his fortune."

Lucy stiffened. She didn't appreciate being introduced as Sophie's sister. It was the first time she had been in

Sophie's shadow, and the awareness of how far already Sophie had advanced beyond her was a cold grip on her heart. More than ever, she must release herself from George and become mistress of Slepe. Then she would again be in her rightful place, superior in all ways to Sophie.

James felt her clasp on his right arm tighten and saw the appearance of a frown on her face and again, to divert an embarrassing outburst, he said, "As you've won Miss Ramsey's hand for the next dance, Rupert, it would seem that she has taken your advice. You'll regret it, Miss Ramsey, he's a hopelessly bad dancer, I warn you."

"I'm not. Come away, Miss Ramsey, and I won't step on your toes more than ten times, I promise you."

"And if you do, what will you forfeit?"

"My heart, dear lady, my heart." Lord Harper put his hand theatrically to his breast and still bantering, they joined the dancing.

"Well, Lucy," said James, unsmiling.

Lucy was supremely confident that as soon as she was near him, touching him, he would want her as fiercely as ever and she believed she could reproach him for his neglect.

"It's been so long. I've waited for you. Why didn't you come? Why didn't you write?"

"I couldn't, Lucy." James thought, *Oh God, what am I doing to do? If I tell her the affair is over, dead and gone, she'll have hysterics. If I don't, she'll cling to me like a leech for the rest of the evening, making us all too obvious.* He looked round, a harassed look on his face which changed to utter relief as Caroline and Robert approached. Lucy bit her lip to prevent herself screaming with frustration. Even worse, reinforcements in the shape of Lady Rivers and Benedict and Sophie came up at the rear.

"Isn't it a wonderful evening?" asked Caroline. "Everything is exactly right."

"Robert," said Benedict solemnly, "you'll be relieved to know that my mother has approved of the musicians. You've no idea, Mrs Harries, how concerned we were about them. It kept us awake with worry."

"I was concerned that you were not concerned," retorted Lady Rivers. "I'm only thankful that they are much better than I dared hope or than you deserved. Now, I must check that everything is prepared for supper. I don't know where the evening has gone."

She bustled off, the Lucy crisis, as she thought of it, headed off for the moment.

"Your mother is quite amazing, Benedict," said James, and ever the opportunist, seized the moment to ask what he had wanted to do all evening. "If supper will be soon, may I ask Miss Sophie to dance with me? I promise I'll restore her to you, so you can take her into supper."

With a slight pang, Benedict nodded his assent and turned to Lucy to ask her for the dance. With sulky acquiescence, Lucy allowed herself to be taken away.

"Poor Lucy," said Caroline, "it really would be the most entertaining ball I've ever been to, if I didn't feel a little sorry for her."

"I know," said Robert, "and supper will be the next hurdle."

"Where's her husband?"

"Sitting next to my mother. He's another person I feel a little sorry for tonight."

"I know it's the wrong adjective to use to describe a man, but he was really quite beautiful, that boy."

"George seems to have taken it badly. I hope he doesn't drown his sorrows too liberally. George is tiresome when he's drunk."

At that moment, his mother looked across at them and beckoned to Robert.

"Duty calls," said Caroline.

"Yes," Robert sighed. "And I shouldn't monopolise you anyway." But he made no move to go. Mrs Latham's beckoning becoming more agitated.

"Go on, do your duty. After supper you can continue to be dutiful as I insist that you ask me to waltz with you."

"I don't deserve such a reward," and he kissed her hand.

As he walked away, she thought, *I think I'm on the verge of making a fool of myself and I really don't care*. She smiled brilliantly at an elderly gentleman who approached her, claiming acquaintanceship with her grandmother.

As James led her to complete a set which included Lord Harper and Miss Ramsey, Sophie felt the odd sensation that she was now safe. She knew with absolute certainty that she was cured of her brief, violent infatuation. But there remained a residue of exasperated affection, similar to that which Caroline admitted she felt for him, which meant that whatever he did, she would not be able to refuse to help him. So far as she was concerned, they were back to being the friends they were when he stayed at the rectory and with this thought, she gave him a wide, sunny smile.

His heart missed a beat. Elegantly dressed, shining with happiness, she was quite beautiful. He must have been mad not to have recognised her potential immediately. Her smile faded and he realised he must have been frowning, and he pulled himself together.

"Forgive me, Miss Sophie. I suddenly had an unwelcome thought. But it's gone: a problem for tomorrow. This reminds me of your sister's engagement party." This reference to Lucy wasn't right and he hastily added, "Do you remember Miss Anne organising us in that complicated dance which only she knew? It was quite the most exhausting evening I've ever spent."

I'm sounding like a babbling fool, he thought in some panic. *What on earth has happened to me?* The music started and as they went through the movements of the dance, Sophie was also remembering that evening.

"It was very funny seeing you and Robert cowering before her."

"We didn't. I refuse to believe we cowered." A little better, almost back to control.

"I shouldn't mock you as I most certainly cowered before Mr Freeman."

"You had reason, I think. A ruthless man."

"Yes, but poor man, to lose his son. He had such ambitions for him, and I feel so sorry for Mrs Freeman. She idolised him."

"George is taking it to heart."

"Yes." A shadow passed over Sophie's face which made him curious.

"What is it?" he asked.

"Nothing. Just, oh just, what a waste."

"Yes, indeed. But at the risk of sounding callous, let's talk about something happier. I can't have you in tears while dancing with me. It would do my credit no good at all."

Lord Harper, hearing this statement, called out, "Since when have you had any credit anyway, James?"

"How many times have you stepped on Miss Ramsey's feet? Is your credit all used up?"

The dance continued in a light-hearted vein. In another set, Benedict and Lucy, with nothing to say to each other, covertly watched with jealous interest.

Supper passed without incident; James managed the considerable feat of sitting opposite Sophie so he could look at her face without doing so too obviously, and out of sight of Lucy so he could avoid her reproachful brown eyes. But he knew he could not avoid her forever, and as the first elderly guests began to drift away, he asked her for the last waltz of the evening. She had seen that Caroline Firth, Miss Ramsey, and Sophie had all been chosen before her and reproach had turned into anger. She accepted his hand for the dance with icy dignity, and he thought a gentle flirtation would be the only way to calm her.

"So, Lucy, at last we can waltz together again," he said softly and gave her his most winning smile.

"I really do not see why you found it so difficult," she answered sulkily. "You seem to have found asking Lady Firth, that other girl and even Sophie easy enough."

"Duty, my dear, I assure you."

Lucy sniffed.

"Come, let's not argue. Let's just enjoy being together again, even if it's only for a brief moment."

They danced in silence, but he felt her body relax under his arm and she followed his lead with graceful ease, and he remembered how much he had enjoyed making love to her and he was ruefully aware that he was perilously close to succumbing to temptation yet again.

Unwittingly, Lucy put paid to her last chance to ensnare James Howard by returning to her grievances.

"Tell me why you've neglected me all this evening? What have I done to deserve it? Why have you left me all these months without a word, after all you promised me?"

"Lucy, I promised you nothing."

She stared at him. "What do you mean? You said that you loved me. I believed you meant it forever. Why should I have thought otherwise?"

"My dear, it was an enchanting and enchanted few days, but it wasn't the real world. Think of it as a treasured memory, as I will, but that's all it can ever be."

"Why?" Lucy was close to tears. "I don't believe you. Why won't you take me away from here? You can't be so cruel as to leave me again." The tears began welling up in her eyes.

James was feeling more than a little harassed and said, "Look, come into this little room. It seems empty and we can talk this over without tears. Come, come."

He hurried her through the door and sat her down on a sofa. He closed the door and stood, uncertain what to do, looking down on her. She was now crying in earnest.

"You promised me," she said in irritating repetition. "I know you did. Maybe not in words, but in every other way. You were to keep me forever. I would leave George and marry you."

Exasperation made him brutal. "If every one of my married mistresses had expected me to pay for an act of divorce, Parliament wouldn't have time for any other business and I would be bankrupt. Wake up, Lucy, it was a pleasant dalliance, enjoyed by both of us but that was all. You're married to George and that is that."

Lucy had hysterics.

* * *

James and Lucy's disappearance into the antechamber had been observed by George. Mrs Latham had wearied of his glum presence and before supper, had left him to his own devices. She was overwhelmed with the excitement of talking to the Bishop's wife while Mr Latham talked to the Bishop. Sophie's alliance with Benedict Rivers was elevating them to a different social sphere altogether and Mrs Latham was ecstatic.

George, adrift and unhappy, had joined his wife at the supper table, but unable to eat anything, took solace in wine and continued to drink heavily for the rest of the evening.

The Lathams said fulsome and obsequious farewells to the Bishop and his wife and Mrs Latham realised that she was very tired, and she wanted to go home. Mr Latham willingly agreed, and Sophie was summoned to find Lucy and George so their carriage could be called.

Sophie looked around; she had seen James and Lucy waltzing together, but they seemed to have vanished. The sight of them dancing in perfect harmony had disturbed her and she had preferred not to watch them. But watching Caroline and Robert dance together was not much better. They were so obviously in a world of their own that it brought a lump to her throat. She tracked George down to a dark corner of the Hall, on his own, with a half empty bottle of claret in front of him.

"George, my parents think it's time for you to leave. Do you know where Lucy is?"

George looked at her with unfocused eyes. "Think she's over there. In that room," he slurred and pointed vaguely at the opposite side with his glass. "With Howard. Funny, that. Wonder what they're doing."

So did Sophie, with a sinking heart. "I expect Lucy has a headache. She hasn't seemed that bright this evening."

"Nor me. I don't feel that bright this evening. I want to go home. I'd better go and look for her."

"Don't worry, I'll find her." Sophie hastily crossed the floor. Taking a deep breath, she opened the door and saw Lucy on the sofa, drumming her heels and crying uncontrollably.

"Oh dear," she said and quickly closed the door. "Whatever have you done to her?" she asked of the hapless James. Without waiting for an answer, she looked around, grabbed her carefully arranged flowers from their vase and threw the water over Lucy's face. The sobs stopped abruptly and with some satisfaction, Sophie thrust the flowers back into the vase. She felt intense irritation with both James and Lucy. This ridiculous scene was spoiling what had been the most magical evening of her life and she thought it would be hard to forgive them.

Lucy struggled to sit up, gulping from the shock of the water which dropped down her face and dress.

"Have you a handkerchief?" Sophie asked James. He produced one wordlessly and Sophie proceeded to mop up the water from Lucy and gave James back a soggy handkerchief.

"Thank you," he said meekly.

Lucy sat on the sofa like a puppet and Sophie was a little alarmed that she had been too ruthless with her.

"I think it would be of great assistance if you would find my mother and explain that Lucy has a bad headache and arrange for her cloak to be brought."

James nodded and went obediently off to do her bidding. The sisters remained in silence, and he returned within a few minutes with the cloak but fortunately, no Mrs Latham. As Sophie had hoped, another person's illness was a strong deterrent to Mrs Latham getting involved.

"Come on, Lucy," she said briskly. "Here's your cloak. Wrap it round you. There. Now come on, it's time for you to go home."

James opened the door for them and Lucy, supported by Sophie, walked through without looking at him.

George, by this time, had decided it was incumbent upon him to find out what his wife and that fellow Howard were up to and making his unsteady way towards them.

"Hey," he said loudly, "what's going on?"

People turned to look.

"Oh no," muttered Sophie and then said clearly, "Lucy has been taken ill, as I thought, and wants to go home."

George nodded. "Yes, let's go home," he mumbled and clutching James' arm, staggered out in their wake.

Benedict joined Sophie and James in seeing the carriage off and as it disappeared, they both let out sighs of relief.

"I think I've missed some drama," said Benedict.

"County yourself lucky. I've just had one of the most harrowing experiences of my life. I was only saved by Miss Sophie's resourcefulness."

"I'm not sure how much was your own fault," said Sophie.

"For a change, in this instance, I think I was more sinned against than sinning."

"What happened?"

James described how Sophie had stopped Lucy's hysterics. He didn't explain what had led up to the hysterics and no-one felt the need to ask. But he did feel the need to justify himself to Sophie and as soon as he could, he drew her to one side and said quietly, "I think you know that I have perhaps not treated your sister as well as I should and it's something I regret. But I regret even more that you should have had to become involved, although I thank you from the bottom of my heart for your help."

Sophie was embarrassed. "Please say no more about it."

"As you wish." He took her hand and kissed it. "The next time I see you, you'll no doubt be Mrs Rivers, but for me, you'll always be Miss Sophie."

Overcome, she could only blush with confusion and to lighten the tone, he added, "Who dances jigs when she's excited," and had the bitter-sweet pleasure of hearing her laughter.

The last of the guests were dawdling over their farewells, reluctant to leave what was by universal acclaim the best ball anyone could remember. Robert and Caroline retreated to the library and sat on a window seat overlooking the river valley. Moonlight lay upon the bank opposite them dramatising the shadowy depths of the river. It was a silent, silver-black world far away from the warmth and colour and noise of the ball.

"In a few days, I'll be leaving for Slepe with James," he said.

"When will I see you again?" she asked, betraying herself.

He took her hand. "I have so little to offer you. Only my love and the belief that I could make you happy."

"I think you could," she said and raised her face for his kiss.

"I'm scared that it's moonlit madness," she whispered.

"Do you really think that?"

"No, but I have been foolish in the past."

"Who hasn't? Do you love me?"

"Yes."

"Then stop worrying." He kissed her again. "Will you come to Slepe soon?"

"Yes. After Christmas."

"You promise?"

"I promise."

"You're being foolish, you know."

"I know."

"Do you mind?"

"No."

"Then you do love me." He kissed her again and then reluctantly let her go.

"I hope you realise," he said, "that while other men no doubt have expressed their love for you in poetry and pretty language, my way will be with drawings and plans of the perfect house for us to live in."

"I think I'd like that much more."

"Some of the poetry was pretty terrible, was it?"

"Well, shall we say that I'm sure it was sincerely meant, but could have been better expressed."

"I remember my first effort," he said nostalgically. "I was so pleased with myself for thinking of rhyming moon with June."

"I've known that a few times, even when the lines were composed in October."

"I did find October difficult. September was easy with remember so usefully rhyming, but October was a problem."

"Now I see why designing the perfect house is much, much easier. And that you must have been a very susceptible young man."

"It was the uniform. It had a wonderful effect on young ladies' hearts."

"Are you trying to tell me you're a libertine?"

"On my honour, they were all very sickly-sweet romantic. Poetry of the moon on June variety and philandering just do not go together."

"How very true. I can vouch for that."

"I suppose we'd better join the others before suspicions are aroused."

"I suspect it may be too late. Sophie gave me a very knowing smile. But no announcement. Not yet."

"Cold feet?"

"No, no. Just a lovely feeling that it's us and us alone. No interference, kind or otherwise, from anyone else. I've been exposed to public view for too long."

"I understand. But tell me, your ladyship, how are you going to adjust to being plain Mrs Latham and not her Ladyship, Countess of Firth?"

"I'll relinquish that name with the utmost of joy and relief."

"Shall we let Sophie and Benedict have their day and then very quietly have ours?"

"Yes, oh yes."

He kissed her again and as he held her, he said, "I wish, oh how I wish, that I could hold you with two arms. Does it upset you?"

"No," she said and as they walked out of the library, she added: "At the risk of pandering to your vanity, even out of uniform and injured, there have been a fair number of young ladies here tonight susceptible to your charms. 'The romantic Mr Latham,' I've heard whispered."

"Then you must marry me as soon as possible to protect me from them."

"I'll do what I can. But Miss Anne Harries may be more difficult to repel."

"Anne? Whatever do you mean?"

"My dear, surely you realise the poor girl is eating her heart out for you?"

Robert shook his head, stunned.

"I don't believe it."

Sophie came up. "What don't you believe?"

Caroline answered. "That Miss Anne Harries has a tendresse for him."

"Oh yes, we've always known that," said Sophie.

"I didn't," said Robert.

Sophie and Caroline shook their heads at his obtuseness.

Chapter Twenty-One

The Harries' coach trundled its way back to Darkleigh, its occupants silent. Mr and Mrs Latham dozed, George slept, and Lucy sat lost in angry bitter thoughts. How dared he use her and discard her as it she was nothing but a common whore. How dared he. Somehow, she was going to have her revenge on James Howard. If at that moment she had the means and opportunity to murder him, preferably by a slow and agonising poison, she would do it. It would be the fate he deserved.

She roused herself enough to say a bare goodnight to her parents at the rectory. George remained fast asleep, and her temper was not improved by having to wake him when they reached their home.

"Oh, for Heaven's sake, George, come on. Wake up," she snapped, and he stumbled out of the coach fuddled with sleep and alcohol. The coachman helped him to the door and was dismissed with an impatient nod from Lucy. She pushed George through the door.

"We're home," he said with bleary surprise.

"Where else did you expect us to be?" she asked and called impatiently for her maid. The girl came down the stairs with a candle and in grumpy silence, helped Lucy to bed.

George had woken sufficiently to make the decision that he wanted a drink and poured himself a brandy. He drank it slowly, staring out at the moonlit garden. The last thing he could remember was seeing Lucy and that fellow Howard disappear into a room off the ballroom. Now he was back home in his dining parlour. What had happened in the meantime? They had obviously all come home in the carriage, but before that? What had Lucy and that fellow Howard been up to? Another glass of brandy helped him to resolve that it was something he had to investigate. If he concentrated on that, then the pain of the memory of his dear lost boy might for a while be kept in check.

As he climbed the stairs, he muttered with repetitive drunken solemnity that he must find out what Lucy and that fellow Howard were up to. With some effort, he managed to undress himself and put on his nightshirt. He looked down on his wife, lying in the bed with her eyes closed.

"What were you and that fellow Howard up to?" he asked.

"I don't know what you're talking about."

"Yes you do. In that room. What were you doing there?"

"I didn't feel well. I needed to get away from all the noise."

"Why with him? Why with that fellow?"

"Because I had been dancing with him. George, stop asking stupid questions. Just get into bed and go to sleep."

George climbed into the bed but grumbled on: "Don't understand it. Don't trust that fellow. What were you doing in that room? On your own with him. Don't seem right. If you were feeling ill, you should have asked your mother or Sophie for help, not that fellow."

Lucy clenched her teeth and remained silent.

"It seems to me," said George a few moment later, "that fellow took too much upon himself. Did you encourage him? Lucy, I'm asking, did you encourage him so you could go into a private room with him on your own?"

"Sophie was with us. We weren't on our own."

"Oh." George thought about this. Something seemed wrong. Then he remembered. "Ha, I remember. Sophie came and asked me where you were. So she wasn't with you all the time, was she?"

Driven by exasperation, Lucy sat up and glared at him. "No, she wasn't. But you need not worry. He didn't seduce me this time," and she clapped her hands to her mouth in fright.

George repeated, puzzled, "This time? What do you mean, this time?"

"Nothing. Nothing at all."

"Are you saying that there was a time when he did make love to you?"

"No, no, of course not. No, no not at all. I shouldn't have said it. I just wanted to make you a little jealous, that's all. I meant that if you continue to neglect me the way you have over the past few months, then I might be tempted. I was only teasing, George, truly. And I shouldn't have, I know, when you're upset about that boy's death. So, let's forget I said anything, all right?"

She patted his hand and came closer to him. Unused to such demonstrations of kindness from his wife, George was utterly disarmed and clung to her, seeking comfort. So relieved at her escape, Lucy responded and the two of them, having lost their loves that day, sought refuge in each other's arms.

* * *

Mrs Freeman kept vigil over her dead son's body. In the moonlight, his face took on an unearthly beauty and his mother, as motionless as he, sat hour upon hour looking at it. From the moment the men had brought in the broken body on the hurdle, she had refused to leave it, deaf and blind to anything or anyone else. Mr Freeman retreated to his study. An affecting performance of the grief-stricken father to an unseeing audience of one soon palled and he left his wife alone. For the first time in their married life, she was indifferent to his presence and Mr Freeman found that almost as upsetting as his son's death.

The moon travelled through the sky and as its light finally slid away from the boy's face, leaving it in shadowy darkness, Mrs Freeman gave a sudden harsh cry. He had gone. The only person who had mattered in her miserable life had left her forever. How was she to bear living any longer? She couldn't bear it; there was nothing left for her in this world. All she wanted to do was to be with her boy in his eternal rest. If by extinguishing her own life she could be reunited with him, why prolong her dreadful existence? It was the obvious answer: she would join him. A great peace came over her and with something approaching happiness, she searched in Richard's closet for some cord and smiled with pleasure when she found the long tie belt of his dressing gown. A beam arched over the room and now humming gently, she put a stool under it, stood on the stool and tied one end of the belt around the beam. Her heart beat fast and as she tied a slipknot in the other end of the belt, her hands were shaking, not with fear, but with a glorious feeling of excitement and joy. She put the loop round her neck, and she could hear him calling her to come, just as he had as a little boy, and in the misty distance, she could see him beckoning her. She stretched out her arms and kicked the stool out of her way as she ran towards him.

* * *

Three days later, in a bitter wind, Emma and Richard Freeman were buried in a corner of the north side of Knight's Darkleigh churchyard. The only mourner was Mr Freeman who had expressed the wish that the funeral was to be completely private.

Mr Latham took the service, his words accompanied by Mr Freeman's loud sobs which continued as the coffins were lowered into the ground and reached a crescendo as Mr Freeman threw a handful of earth on the plain unadorned coffins. The two men watched the grave-diggers filling in the grave. Mr Latham was dithering over whether or not to invite Mr Freeman back to the rectory. After some wrestling with his conscience, he reluctantly decided it would be an act of Christian charity to do so. He turned to Mr Freeman, but his words of invitation died on his lips. Instead of the grief-stricken features he was expecting to see, Mr Freeman's face showed contempt and annoyance. It was as if, Mr Latham thought, Mr Freeman was angered by the inconvenience to his comfort, occasioned by the sad deaths and the noisy exhibition of grief was a mere pretence. Mr Latham was shocked out of his usual lack of interest in his fellow men, so he just nodded to Mr Freeman and left him at the graveside.

Mr Freeman was indeed angry at the expense and inconvenience to which he had been put. He was little moved by their deaths; his wife and his son had merely been pawns on the chessboard of his life, to be pushed around as he had commanded, entirely at the mercy of his will. By dying, they had escaped.

As he went back to the Chantry, he thought of Polly who had also escaped from him, who had robbed him and was still alive. He retired to his study, and as Christmas came and went, uncelebrated by him, he brooded over his brandy at the iniquities to which he had been subjected. With the emptying of each bottle, the belief grew stronger that all his problems should be laid at the door of that ungrateful slut.

The brandy ran out. Money was also rapidly running out and he urgently needed a new source of income. He would sell his wife's wedding ring and her pearl broach, but apart from that, there was nothing left. The most valuable piece had been taken by the girl. He was going to have to track her down, find where she had disposed of the pendant, bring her to justice. Hanging was too good for her, and he regretted that drawing and quartering had fallen into disuse. With Richard and Emma dead, there was no substance to her allegations, and he could go after her with impunity. It would be the old story of a servant stealing from her master and running away.

Invigorated by these thoughts, he went first into Cirencester, but his enquiries proved fruitless. The only jeweller there denied vehemently any knowledge and Mr Freeman eventually accepted that he was telling the truth. Then if she didn't go into Cirencester, she must have gone the other way, to Gloucester. The next day, Mr Freeman went that way. He whiled away the journey by weighing the pros and cons of whether justice under the law should be meted out on her or his own personal form. The latter appealed most to him, but it would entail taking her by force back to the Chantry and that would be difficult for she would be as wary of him as a wild animal.

After a short search, he found the jeweller's shop, but the jeweller refused to return the pendant, saying that Mr Freeman must produce proof that it was his and that it had been stolen and a justice would have to decide the issue. Seeing the ugly look on Mr Freeman's face, the jeweller, usually a staunch upholder of the law, felt sympathy with the cheerful girl who had bargained with him.

Mr Freeman slammed the door of the shop behind him and with angry determination set about tracking down Polly. The thought that she might have moved on to Bristol, or farther afield, reduced him to a state of cold fury. He considered the position over lunch in one of Gloucester's many inns and reasoned that country-bred Polly, in a city for the first time, would be dazzled by it, think herself safe and would stay put. With money in her pocket – he ground his teeth at the thought of his money – she would find lodgings but having no idea of the value of money, would be duped and would fritter it all away and she would have to find work. The only work she knew was domestic labour, but having tasted some days of freedom, she would be loathe to go back to that. If his reading of Polly's character was correct, she would be attracted to one of the less savoury taverns where ale and her body would both be for sale.

Mr Freeman's conclusions were remarkably accurate. Polly was enjoying life enormously. The money had soon slipped through her fingers, and she had found work at a large inn on the dockside. She loved it: the endless hustle and bustle of people, the noise, the raucous good humour, the fights, even the city stench and, above all, the unceasing stream of men, a multitude of nationalities all in search of one thing and she was only too happy to oblige. Mr Freeman's degradations became a distant nightmare, almost forgotten.

The shock, therefore, of seeing him come into the tavern was considerable. She let out a squawk, dropped the tankard she was carrying and spilt its contents over a huge sailor who bellowed at her, grabbed her and shook her, cursing and swearing and making sufficient commotion for the crowded tavern to be quietened momentarily, as people turned to see what all the fuss was about. Thus, it was that Mr Freeman, thrusting people aside, was able to confront his errant servant.

The next few hours were spent in complete and utter bewilderment for Polly. The landlord was summoned; her room was searched, and the carpet bag and cloak were found.

"The mistress gave them to me," said Polly. "She'll tell 'ee that. You ask 'er."

"Your mistress is dead," said Mr Freeman harshly.

Polly gaped at him.

"As a result of your actions. You drove her to it."

"What do 'ee mean?"

"She hanged herself."

"No, oh no." Polly crouched in a corner, trapped.

The landlord and his wife looked grimly on, blocking the door.

"You blackmailed a kind, gentle woman and drove her to her death. You murdered her."

"I never. I never. She knew I'd never come back. She'd never see me again. Mr Richard was safe from me."

"My son is dead. He was killed in a hunting accident."

There were gasps of horror from the landlord and landlady. The connection between the son's death and the mother's suicide was not made by them or by Polly, who felt a great, black terror descend upon her. *A hanging matter*, she had said with relish to Mrs Freeman. And now it was she who was faced with that terrible prospect. A servant stealing from her master was a hanging matter. The landlord, who like most of her employers had a soft spot for Polly, might have supported her until he heard about her apparent involvement in Mrs Freeman's death and his wife, who had not viewed Polly with the same indulgence, wholeheartedly agreed that Polly should be brought before a justice of the peace.

Mr Freeman, taking the role of the stern but just master, regretfully bringing to justice the servant who had betrayed his trust, was impressive.

"It grieves me and I have wrestled long and hard with the need for Christian charity on the one side and the dictate of justice on the other. But I have concluded that an example must be made of her. If servants thought they could steal from their masters with impunity, what would happen to the moral fabric of society? We have a duty, do we not, to punish those who break the legal and moral law of this land?"

Mr Dawkins, the justice, quite overwhelmed by Mr Freeman's authoritative presence, nodded in agreement, scribbled his signature to the complaint laid before him and ordered his constable to take the sobbing Polly directly to Gloucester prison.

* * *

On his return from Gloucester, Mr Freeman called upon Jarvis Harries and, in sorrowful tones, described the apprehension of the wicked servant. Jarvis was angry and upset.

"Why couldn't you let the girl be? She can't harm either of us any longer. Why go after her? She would never have come back here."

Mr Freeman swelled in outrage. "You seem to be forgetting the girl stole from me. She is a common thief and a blackmailer. Do you really think she should be allowed to get away scot-free to inflict the same on some other innocent person who, out of the kindness of his heart, gives her employment? She deserves all that is coming to her."

"I don't know."

Jarvis felt wretched. He had known Polly from birth; he knew her faults, but she was part of the valley, his valley. He had the suspicion that Mr Freeman had been motivated by an unpleasant desire for revenge, something dark and ugly, not by a pure disinterested sense of justice. Whatever it was, he didn't like the situation, he couldn't do anything about it, and, above all, he wanted to get this man out of his house and out of the valley as soon as possible.

"Will you be leaving the Chantry?" he asked. Rumours of Mr Freeman's financial problems had reached his ears.

"Yes. It has such unhappy memories for me." Mr Freeman gave one of his deep sighs. "My beloved wife, my only son, they will be in my heart forever. But this place is not for me. Alas, the cost of moving, the heavy cost of distancing myself from the scene tragedy, is a concern, a source of anguish to me which in my present grieving state, is one I could do without." He blew his nose hard, gave another mournful sigh and, hand to forehead, drooped sadly.

Bowing to the inevitable, Jarvis said, "I can understand that to remain in Knight's Darkleigh would be impossible for you. In the circumstances, perhaps you would be prepared to accept a small gift to ease your burden." He went to the bureau and from a locked drawer, took out fifty pounds.

"You are too kind, my dear Harries," said Mr Freeman, much moved. "Your generosity overwhelms me."

With continued effusive thanks, he allowed himself to be escorted to the door. He gave an emotional speech of farewell to Jarvis from his horse and clattered off.

"Thank God for that," muttered Jarvis. Much as he begrudged giving Freeman that money, fifty guineas was well worth the price of getting rid of him.

Mr Freeman, who had hoped for one hundred guineas but had expected nothing as he no longer had any hold over Harries, decided fifty guineas was a very satisfactory outcome. Tomorrow he would make arrangements to move. He would pay his servants part of the wages they were owed, just sufficient for them to believe it was worth remaining in his service, but the other bills and the rent he would ignore. Tradesmen should consider the honour of supplying him with their goods was recompense enough. Vulgar concepts such as paying in cash should not come into the equation.

* * *

Jarvis rode over to Knight's Darkleigh the next afternoon to acquaint Mr Latham with Polly's plight. He arrived shortly after Sophie and Robert, Sophie returning home after a stay at Millington that had extended as long as her conscience would allow her, and Robert to say goodbye to his parents before going down to Slepe.

Caroline had returned to Cheltenham a couple of days after the ball, followed a week later by a reluctant James. He had been told by all that he had a duty to visit his grandmother and although he grumbled about it, he submitted to the general will. Living in the same house as an unattainable Sophie was harder than he could have imagined. She had no idea that the openly friendly affection with which she treated him drove him mad with desire. He wanted her to look at him in the way she looked at Benedict, to hold her hand in the way Benedict did and to kindle in her a passion that would surpass anything she would ever know. But it could not happen and removal to his grandmother's chilling presence would be an escape from an exquisite agony. Caroline and Robert's happiness was observed by all and kindly left unremarked. Robert wondered whether he could survive a whole month without seeing her. He was to join James in Cheltenham, and they were to go from there to Slepe. The prospect of seeing her again after a few weeks' absence made him delirious with joy.

Mr Harries' news of Polly struck dismay in all the Lathams. Mrs Latham had been genuinely saddened by Mrs Freeman's death and to hear that Polly had stolen from a stricken family truly shocked her.

"The wicked girl. To do that to a poor grieving woman."

"But, Mama," protested Sophie, "Polly is supposed to have stolen the cloak and bag and escaped the house hours before Richard died. And I don't believe she did steal them."

"The evidence all points to the fact that she did," said Mr Latham.

"But why did she do it?" asked Robert.

"I understand she wanted to get away," said Jarvis vaguely.

"There must have been more reason than that. I'd seen her not long before and she would have told me she was so unhappy that she had to run away." Sophie was almost in tears. "What is to happen to her?"

"It's a serious matter, a servant stealing from her master. But I doubt that she will hang," said Jarvis and added hastily as Sophie went quite white. "She will be transported more than likely. Start afresh in the colonies."

"If she survives the journey," said Robert. "Why did that man go after her? It was only an old cloak and a bag. Why did he bother?"

Jarvis felt it wiser to say nothing. Mr Latham suggested that Mr Freeman's strong moral sense might have impelled him to seek out the wrong doer.

"I don't believe he has any moral sense at all," said Robert angrily. "He is a sham and a humbug. I reckon it was to get away from him that drove Polly to run away."

"How can you say that?" cried Mrs Latham. "You have no reason to believe that he didn't treat her, and all his servants, properly."

"Well, I'm going to Gloucester to find out," said Robert. "There's more to this, that's for sure."

He strode out of the room and Sophie ran after him.

"Freeman will be leaving the Chantry soon, I understand," said Jarvis.

"It's as well. There's nothing for him here," replied Mr Latham.

* * *

By a mixture of charm and bribery, Robert managed to gain access to the women's wing of Gloucester gaol and was shown into a cold, stinking cell occupied by about twenty women all, like Polly, waiting for trial at the next Assizes. His appearance was greeted with loud screeches and jeers, a barrage of obscene language and filthy scrabbling hands. They were violently pushed aside by a wild-looking Polly.

"Get your stinkin' hands off him or Oi'll kill the lot of 'ee," she screamed and to his great relief, they backed off, retreating into the darkness of the cell and so all he could see were eyes staring at him. If he had thought Waterloo was hell on earth, then he was wrong. This was far, far worse.

"Why have 'ee come 'ere?" she asked suspiciously.

"I wanted to find out what happened. To see if I could help in any way."

"Too late for that. Oi'll be brought before the Judge in a fortnight, and Oi'll be sentenced to hang. Just for taking a rubbishy old cloak and bag. After what 'e did to me, 'e should be hanging, not Oi."

"What did he do to you, Polly?"

She hesitated. Two days in gaol had taught her to mistrust everyone; there was no charity, no kindness left in her world. For a moment, she hated him for coming as he brought memories of how pleasant life could be, and with the shadow of the hangman's noose over her, she could do without them. But the desire to tell someone her side of the story was overwhelming and it all poured out of her: her feud with Richard Freeman, the fear Mr Freeman instilled in his household, her discovery of Richard and George's affair, her rape by Mr Freeman, her need to get away and her persuading Mrs Freeman to help her.

Robert had some difficulty unravelling her jumbled narrative, but he had no doubt that she was mainly telling the truth. He was dismayed, though he realised not entirely surprised, at the revelation about George and Richard and aghast at the thought of the scandal there would be if the affair became known. He had a suspicion that Jarvis Harries knew more than he let on but, like himself, would never reveal his knowledge. He had some doubts that Mrs Freeman had willingly given the pendant to Polly, but Robert couldn't blame Polly for taking desperate measures.

"Why didn't you tell someone, my father or Mr Harries, of Mr Freeman's treatment of you?"

"Who would believe me? Oi knows what folks think of me."

"I, for one, would always believe you rather than that dreadful man. So would Sophie."

"You weren't in the valley. You was gorn to Millington. And how could Oi tell such a thing to Miss Sophie?"

"Oh Polly, what an awful mess."

"It is an' all. Oi thought at first of saying Oi was innocent but what's the use? Oi knows 'e can persuade people, and 'e'd win over a jury easy as anything. So, Oi's going to say Oi done it."

Robert could only admire her realism. "I don't know that it will help, but I'll ask my father to write a letter of recommendation for you."

"So Oi'll be transported instead of hanged. That 'ud be something."

"If anyone can survive and prosper in the colonies, it's you."

"Oi reckon Oi'll do fine." For the first time since Mr Freeman entered the tavern on the quay, Polly smiled.

The warder approached.

"I must go," said Robert. "Good luck, my dear Polly."

"Goodbye," whispered Polly. The door crashed behind him. "My dear Mr Robert."

Chapter Twenty-Two

One bright June morning, a young man, soberly dressed in clerical garb, rode up the drive to the rectory. His name, he said to Mr Latham, was the Reverent Thaddeus Drinkwater and he had been sent by Trinity College to investigate the dispute over the strip of Glebe land.

His visitor was entirely unwelcome to Mr Latham; nothing had been heard from the rector or the college since the previous summer and Mr Latham had become convinced that the dispute had quietly disappeared. But he should have known that the rector was terrier-like in his tenacity to keep on at a problem. Mr Drinkwater produced maps of varying degrees of antiquity and legibility and a bewildered Mr Latham finally said, "I don't know, I really don't know who is correct. Mr Edwards is convinced that there's a map which clearly shows the land as being Glebe, but I cannot be certain with any of these."

Mr Drinkwater was non-committal. "May I suggest we go to see the land and then discuss the matter further with Mr Harries?"

As they walked up the lane, Mr Drinkwater said, "I understand that one of your daughters is married to Mr Harries' son."

"Yes, indeed," said Mr Latham. "It makes this dispute between the Rector and Mr Harries particularly distressing for me."

"Yes." Mr Drinkwater was again neutral.

They reached the Millington turning and inspected the wood. Mr Drinkwater frowned slightly when he saw the fencing, but said nothing.

Six months before, Mr Latham would have been crushed by his visitor's lofty, judicious attitude, but in those six months, much had happened to bolster his self-confidence. First and foremost, Sophie's marriage to Benedict Rivers three months previously had resulted in a flow of gifts which made life at the rectory much more comfortable. Mr Latham had the warm feeling that much as his pride would, of course, be hurt at the suggestion that he became his son-in-law's pensioner, he had to accept that his health would soon make this a necessity. He would at last be liberated from the toil of having to earn his living.

Robert's marriage a month after his sister's to Caroline Firth had relieved Mr Latham of any lingering concern he might have harboured for his son's future. He was somewhat in awe of his daughter-in-law and secretly astonished that she should have wished to exchange being Lady Firth for plain Mrs Robert Latham.

And as for Lucy. Here Mr Latham allowed himself a sentimental smile. Lucy was expecting a child, due in September, and was blooming. George was the original, doting expectant father and only outdone in his anxious fussing by Jarvis Harries. There had been some weeks in the early part of the year when even Mr Latham had observed that Lucy was not her usual self, but her pregnancy explained that, and now she was luxuriating in being the centre of attention.

Mr Drinkwater broke into Mr Latham's musings. "May we proceed to see Mr Harries?"

"Yes, of course. This is all his land." Mr Latham struggled to make conversation as they continued along the road. "If one looks back to the woodland from this slight rise, you'll observe that it does seem likely that all the land this side of the Millington lane belongs to him and the Glebe extends the other side."

"It is a possibility," said Mr Drinkwater.

They walked on in silence. Mr Latham was pleased to note that Mr Drinkwater's boots were not suited to walking in rutted country lanes and there was no doubt that by the time Manor Farm came into view, they were pinching him.

Jarvis Harries gave them his usual hearty welcome to visitors and offered them refreshments. Mr Drinkwater sank back into his comfortable chair and sighed with relief.

"You young city men," said Jarvis, "you can't take our country air."

"Your country roads, perhaps," said Mr Drinkwater and accepted a tankard of homebrew. He rarely took alcohol, just an occasional glass of port, but he was tired and thirsty and assumed, wrongly, that Mr Harries' beer was not very strong.

Half an hour later, he felt relaxed and pleasantly light-headed. It was quite obvious from what Mr Harries said and from the maps which he produced, that the woodland must belong to him and not the rector. Such an affable, transparently honest old man, who had some difficulty in reading, could not possibly be the devious person depicted by the rector.

A large luncheon, more homebrew and the offer of a carriage back to the rectory, convinced Mr Drinkwater that his conclusion was the correct one.

As they were leaving, Jarvis said to Mr Latham, "Bannerman's nephew has written to me asking if I would be interested in buying the Chantry. He hasn't been able to find another tenant. Freeman left owing two quarters' rent and he just wants to be rid of it."

"I'm not surprised," said Mr Latham. "It's not a house I would feel comfortable living in."

"My wife says the same. Indeed, she goes as far as to say that it should be demolished, it has such unhappy connections."

"I wonder where Freeman is now, and what he's doing," mused Mr Latham.

"No doubt convincing some luckless unsuspecting people of the nobility of his moral crusade. The bogus hypocrite. The man is a menace," said Jarvis, vehemently. Robert had seen no reason why Mr Freeman's treatment of Polly should not be made known, indeed the reverse, and the valley had been shocked and distressed by the revelations. There had been some hand-wringing over the matter and a few uneasy consciences that Polly had felt unable to ask for help from anyone.

Mr Latham had, with reluctance, written a recommendation for her – Robert had been very forceful about it – but now, six months later, he felt a glow of righteous pride that he had assisted in saving Polly from the gallows.

"Polly would agree with you. I pray that she has survived the passage to Australia and is making a new life for herself out there."

Mr Drinkwater had been following this conversation with fuzzy difficulty but increasing worry. "This Mr Freeman you mention. Is he a very large striking-looking man, a widower who has recently tragically lost his wife and son?"

Jarvis nodded.

"But you speak of him with such disapproval. I can't understand that you can say such things about a man who battles so nobly against sin, despite his deep grief."

His listeners could hear Mr Freeman's voice gushing out these words and although two men could not be more dissimilar in character and attitude to life, both shuddered.

"Young man," said Jarvis. "Take my advice: avoid that man like the plague. Have no dealings with him. He'll take every penny you have and more."

"But he has a respectable fortune, he assures me. The money he's given is all for the great cause of bringing our Lord to the people. He has been a great comfort to my mother; she is a widow living in a small village in Kent and is often a little lonely. His visits are a source of spiritual solace to her."

"Oh dear," said Mr Latham inadequately.

They climbed into the carriage. Jarvis said, "Mr Latham is too much the Christian gentleman to say it but I'm a down-to-earth farmer, and I can. Get your mother out of that man's clutches before it's too late or you can say goodbye to your inheritance. So far as I'm concerned, he's a man who bullied his wife to death and treated his servant most terribly." He stood back and nodded to the coachman and watched them go.

Mr Drinkwater sat bolt upright, gnawing his underlip as he stared ahead. He remained so as they drew up in front of the rectory and Mr Latham had to give a little cough.

Mr Drinkwater asked in a strangled voice for his horse and then abruptly said, "I will give my recommendation about the land shortly. As to the other matter," he paused and gulped, "I must think what to do."

He sounded so much younger and less self-assured and even a little frightened. Mr Latham felt sorry for him as he watched him ride away. He was glad it was not he who was faced with the task of extricating an elderly lady from Mr Freeman's web.

Mr Latham turned, intending to go indoors. Bright sunlight glinting on one of the Chantry's windows drew his eye. It looked so peaceful, nestling in its hillside, glowing in the afternoon sun. It was a house suited to a sleeping princess waiting for her Prince Charming, not one in which violent, unhappy deeds had been perpetrated. It had been sullied. Mrs Harries was right: it should be demolished.

Surprised and embarrassed by his romantic notions, Mr Latham retreated into the dining parlour, sat down in his favourite chair and closed his eyes.

THE END